WICKED SIN

AINSLEY BOOTH

www.AINSLEYBOOTH.COM

Bad girls shouldn't have to beg to be punished. And once upon a time, Taylor Dashford Reid was very, very bad.

Detective Luke Vasquez knows better than to get tangled up with a complicated woman—no matter how tempting she might be. But Taylor is in his house now. Living with his rules. Sparring with him, hissing like a frightened kitten. Maybe the rules need to be broken, for both of their sakes.

This is the complete story of Taylor Dashford Reid and Luke Vasquez. The Forbidden Bodyguard series continues…

the **Frisky Beavers** series

co-written with Sadie Haller

Prime Minister

Dr. Bad Boy

Full Mountie

Mr. Hat Trick

Page of Swords

Bull of the Woods

the **Forbidden Bodyguards** series

Hate F*@k

Booty Call

Dirty Love

the **Billionaire Secrets** series

Personal Delivery

Personal Escort

Personal Disaster

the **Secrets and Lies** series

Stuck

Crave

Shame

DEDICATION

*For everyone who sees themselves in Taylor, past or present.
None of us get through life without making mistakes.*

[1]

LUKE

I LIKE CATCHING A NEW CASE. It means I'm going to close it.
Win. It gives me a goal, a target. Something to focus on.

Unless it's the week I'm supposed to go on vacation.

Captain Woods asks me to hang back after the morning
briefing—the first sign that my vacation isn't going to start as
planned.

She pulls me into her office and closes the door. The way
she takes off her suit jacket, rolls her neck, and grabs a Coke
from the mini fridge under her desk all contribute to the pile of
evidence that she's working up to telling me something has
come up.

And not a good case, either. Something messy, because she's
working up to it.

She wiggles the cola at me. "You want one?"

"I'm good."

She nods.

I like the captain. She has nearly twenty-five years on the
job, a lot of them when she was the only black woman in her

division. Sometimes she's a little too by-the-book, but that's true for everyone who gets promoted up.

Not me. I'm going to be promoted out. Transferred. Any day now, which is nothing to do with her and everything to do with my urge to get my hands dirty.

"Detective Vasquez," she begins, and I cock an eyebrow.

This is formal. I don't like formal. "Yes, ma'am?"

"How flexible are your vacation plans?"

Completely. I wasn't going to do much beyond hitting some clubs and blowing off some steam. Sleep in each day and go out for a late lunch. Take a long run on the beach, then rinse and repeat. Something tells me my plans are about to change. "Depends who's asking, ma'am."

"We've caught a case I think you might be interested in. The feds have requested our assistance."

"Requested or demanded?" I reach for the file. She doesn't hand it over right away.

"Semantics. The L.A. field office reported an anonymous tip, which they aren't taking seriously, except..." She trails off. That's not a good sign.

"The FBI is asking the LAPD to run down bad leads now?"

"Not the FBI." I take the file as she sighs. "Secret Service. They want to be hands-off for political reasons. Read the file. The thing is, the timing is funny. Charges were laid this morning in D.C. Her father's wearing an ankle monitor, her mother is cooperating and has handed over her passport."

"Her..." I snap my gaze to the label on the file.

Dashford Reid, Taylor.

Son of a— "The Blow Job Princess?"

"Detective."

"Come on, if *Time* magazine calls her that—"

"They didn't."

"I swear I saw it in a headline."

"Drudge Report, maybe. You need to upgrade to a better caliber of news media, Vasquez."

"Yes, ma'am." I don't argue. I don't read trash news, but sometimes the verbiage that starts there makes its way into the common lexicon. I know better.

But how often does an honest-to-god celebrity file land on my desk? Less often than you might think for Los Angeles. Now it's my turn to sigh.

Ms. Dashford Reid is famously—or infamously—known for recording herself giving the Vice President of the United States a sloppy, giggly happy ending, and then leaking that to the press. Years have passed, and the VP in question didn't run again.

The scandal will forever live on in Wikipedia entry references, I guess. And everyone's collective memory, because the Dashford Reids don't do shame. They don't hide.

Except now that I think about it, I didn't even know she lived on the west coast.

And the last I remember of her was the *last* scandal about her family when her sister Hailey was involved in the takedown of Gerome Lively.

Her father's arrest today made headlines, of course. I saw it while I had my coffee and flipped through the news sites.

But his daughter wasn't anywhere on the screen in the footage of the comings and goings from lawyers' offices and courthouses.

None of the Reid daughters were visible. Only the son, who stands to take over the family business if his father goes to jail.

When his father goes to jail. He surrendered to a special prosecutor charged with investigating Russian interference into our—everything, really. Elections, lobbying for industry, lobbying for foreign countries, shaping foreign policy. Shaping domestic policy. You name it, Washington D.C. has Russia smeared all over it.

And it's Morgan Reid's third time facing serious charges.

This time, the feds are going to make sure they stick. It doesn't matter what his top-notch crisis management firms do this time. The man isn't going to skate.

"So what's the so-called tip, exactly? Because I just passed my psych eval with flying colors. I'm as good as loaded into the undercover unit. I can't get tangled up with a long-term case. Might be better off handing it to—"

"This isn't that."

I laugh out loud because we both know there's no way to promise that. I open the file. Address. Workplace.

Workplace? The Blow Job Princess has a job? She doesn't need to work, surely.

I scan down the cover page. The next two pages are so heavily redacted they're illegible. Fucking Secret Service. The same name is scrawled at the bottom of each of the pages. Perry Newcomb, Financial Crimes Division. That makes me wonder if this is related to her father's criminal difficulties after all.

But the fourth page has enough of a communiqué that it becomes clear why they've punted this task to the LAPD.

Our princess was a tad hostile with federal agents.

Fantastic.

And according to an anonymous tip—probably a crank call, after her father's arrest—she had cocaine and meth in her car.

"Drugs? Do they think she's dealing?"

"That would seem to be the angle."

"She's loaded. Why'd she be dealing? One call to Daddy—"

"I get it. It doesn't smell right."

I flip back to the cover page, looking for something that twigged in my mind. Her job. She's working with a local non-profit for survivors of sexual violence, L.A.S.T. It took a minute for that to register, but it's an odd choice for someone who—

The captain chuckles at me, and I glance up. Past the nameplate on her desk—Captain Deandra Woods—to her knowing gaze.

"What?"

"You're struggling with this one. It's all over your face."

I frown. "She's a contradiction, that's all. Hard to make sense of her."

My boss gives me a serene look and nods. "Aren't we all, Vasquez?"

I walked right into that life lesson like a pro. "Yes, ma'am."

"You want to go undercover, you need to stop fitting people into boxes. That's not how life works. Sometimes people make choices for reasons we don't understand, but they always have a reason."

Yeah. And my task for the next few days—hopefully just the next few hours—is to figure out the right angle to not turn a nothing crank complaint into a big-fucking-deal investigation when the Blow Job Princess has proven she couldn't care less about destroying someone's reputation.

I'm going to have to make her trust me when she doesn't trust anyone in a uniform. Maybe anyone with a dick, for all I know.

"Go talk to her. With an open mind," the captain says, again reminding me not to pre-judge this situation. Whatever the fuck it is.

"You think this is a false report?"

"Almost certainly. Why report drugs to the Secret Service?"

I crack my jaw back and forth. Right. *Fuck.* This could get sticky at the highest levels.

"So, I need to do due diligence, but also make this go away if at all possible?"

"Something like that. I didn't ask any questions. I thought I'd leave that to you to figure out after you talk to her and get a sense of the situation."

"This is highly irregular."

Her brows pull together in a tight frown. "Sure is."

"I don't understand why the feds are okay with us messing in their sandbox."

"Gives them plausible deniability."

I groan. Right. "If this turns into a PR nightmare, we'll wear that, not them."

"Try not to turn it into a PR nightmare, then." She smiles. "Play nice with the woman."

"Of course." I wink. "And I'll get my vacation after this? Maybe a few extra days for the trouble?"

"Don't push your luck."

I smirk. "You can come dancing too, Captain."

She grins. "Get out of my office."

[2]

TAYLOR

"I should have known," my client says. Four soft, broken words.

First rule of peer counseling—it's not about me. Curiosity and comparison have no place in the kind of support we offer. We offer the kind of support survivors of sexual violence have trouble finding anywhere else.

But deep in the back of my mind, the comparison whirls anyway.

I know how you feel, I want to say. I don't. Of course, I don't. Just like nobody can truly know how *I* feel about how I was raised.

I was twenty-seven when I realized I'd been groomed by my mother to use sex and beauty to control men. That in the process, she'd let men use *me,* long before I could consent.

It took me another year—three hundred and sixty-five days —to do anything about that.

Another three to get to this side of the counseling table, here in this cozy, warm space in a security-monitored building on the other side of the continent from my family.

It took me way too long to figure out how to be good.

Deep down, I know I have nothing to be proud of.

So I push away the thoughts of myself—don't intrude now, don't ever intrude here, I'm trying to be fucking helpful—and lean in.

"We are the hardest on ourselves," I murmur to my peer counseling client. Easy to say. Not easy to do anything about.

"I just..." The woman sitting across from me sobs and wraps her arms tight around herself.

"You took a big step by coming here and talking to me." I scribble that on the pad of paper between us. The first point on a tangible list of successes I want her to look at over the next week until session number two. "What else are you proud of?"

"Boundaries," she mumbles.

Maintained healthy boundaries, I add to the list. "Great."

It takes twenty minutes to get two more things jotted down, but when she leaves, she's clutching the list tight in her hands, and I've done my job for another day.

I put my notes in her folder, and then lock that away in my filing cabinet.

Then I sit back down in my chair and close my eyes. I share this office with two other peer counselors, and one of them will be coming in shortly. But I have a few minutes to myself. I'm going to take them.

Deep breaths. In and out. Focus on the now. *That was a good day*. It was. There's something calming about coming in for a shift here. I turn my phone off when I arrive, and the outside world fades away.

Nothing but healing. Nothing but service.

It comes with a price. I'll be exhausted and need to have a nap when I get home. But later...maybe later I'll go dancing.

I need to cut loose.

I'm wound tight, tighter than usual. There's a faint, nervous tremor in my belly and my chest, and it won't go away. I don't believe in full moon stuff, but there's something in the air today, and it's not good.

Taking one last long, slow breath, I open my eyes and stand up. Time to go outside. Head home and figure out how to bring some of this calm with me.

Three days until my next shift.

It's not healthy to need this job to be mentally stable. Nope. But that's how it is, anyway.

I grab my bag, put on my sunglasses, and lock up. In the anteroom, one of our volunteers is staffing the front desk. She points to the video monitor we have that shows a live feed of the front door of the building.

"There's a guy loitering out front, FYI. He hasn't tried the front door or the intercom."

There are a few other agencies in this building, and people are allowed to wait in the parking lot. But our general practice is to keep each other, and our clients, appraised of people at the entrance. Just in case it's someone we know—and want to avoid.

I peer at the screen.

I don't recognize him. Tall, fit, with dark hair, long on top— enough that he could tie it back if he wanted to, but he clearly doesn't—and short on the sides. He's wearing jeans and heavy boots, and a leather jacket even though it's close to ninety degrees outside.

He looks like an extra from a show about a romanticized biker club. No, he's too good looking to be the extra. He looks like the star.

He looks like sex on legs.

He looks, most definitely, like danger.

But I stare danger in the face and give it the finger, so whatever, I don't care.

Shrugging, I pull my phone from my bag. "I'll steer clear of him, thanks."

She waves goodbye, and I head for the stairs. As I take them down to the lobby, my phone starts to vibrate with the incoming messages I've missed while it was turned off today. I slow down as I hit the ground floor, scanning the space beyond the locked entrance. I could check those messages, but that guy has wandered away from the entrance, so now's a good time to get outside and make sure the door locks behind me.

Digging out the key fob for my car, I shove through the door, catch it as I step out, and push it closed again in one fluid motion. If he's loitering to get inside without permission, it won't be because of me.

I beeline toward my car. When I'm thirty feet away, I tap the fob.

Nothing happens. Nothing from the car, anyway.

The guy—taller and bigger out here in the lot—appears to my right. "Ms. Reid?"

I keep going. Maybe he's a process server. Maybe he's paparazzi. Whoever he is, whatever he is, we're not doing this here. *Damn it, how did he find me?* I tap the key fob again, and the lights don't flash. Fucking hell.

"A moment of your time, please." He says it like it's not a request. And then he flashes a badge. "LAPD."

That pulls me up short.

The cops?

Inside my bag, my phone vibrates against my thigh.

I'm starting to think I should have checked those messages before I stepped outside. "I'm running late for something," I lie.

"I'm Detective Vasquez," he says, like I didn't just tell him I can't do this right now.

Or ever.

"No, thanks."

He laughs. "That's not a response to what I just said, princess."

I whip my frowning face around so I can glare at him. "Excuse me?"

He doesn't blink. "Excellent. Now that I have your attention—"

"How long have you been loitering here in the hopes of accosting me?"

"A while. I have some questions for you. If here isn't good, we can go down to the precinct."

It's been a while since I've been questioned by the police. Not long enough to forget all the rules about not exposing myself to any legal liability. "I'll call my attorney." I don't have a lawyer right now, but I can find one. My name is good enough to ensure someone would get a decent payday out of whatever bullshit this is.

He frowns. "Were you instructed to say that by your father?"

"I haven't spoken to my father in over a year." I definitely should have checked my messages. Cold dread slithers through my belly. "What's happened?"

One eyebrow jacks up. Shit. "You haven't heard."

I point to the building behind me. "I turn my phone off when I'm at work. I've been here all day."

"Your father was arrested today."

Again. The proper sentence there should be, *your father was arrested again today*. It's happened before, it will happen again.

I force an *I don't care* smile to my face. "That sounds like a personal problem for him. I don't have any contact with my parents."

Anymore. The proper sentence would be, *I don't have any contact with my parents anymore.* Qualifying words matter. They're the difference between the truth and something that falls short of honesty.

"Do you watch the news?"

"No." I give him my best cool, I-can't-be-bothered look. It's none of his business that watching the news is triggering for me, and I avoid it for my fragile mental health.

"Can we go somewhere to talk?" He points at the building. My office. "Look, I'm going to be straight with you. We got a tip that you're moving stuff out of your car."

"What!?" My mouth drops open. "No. That's ridiculous."

"Sure. Sure. If it is, this is easy enough to clear up. Would you just open your trunk for me?"

"You have no basis for a search. You said yourself that something happened today, with my father, and that's probably—"

"I can get a warrant, Ms. Reid. And I can wait here, in front of your office, until it arrives. Or you could quietly cooperate, and we can go our separate ways before anyone notices that you're being questioned by the police."

"That sounds like a threat, officer." I tap my key fob again. Still, nothing happens. Fuck.

"It's detective, actually."

Who the fuck cares? "I think my battery's dead," I mutter. "I must have left the lights on." I make another attempt to open my car. The fucking fob isn't working, and I want to throw it across the parking lot, but that won't help me get away from this situation.

"Ms. Reid—"

"Leave me alone, okay? I don't know anything. I don't want to know anything. I haven't done anything wrong, at least not lately, and—" I spin away from him, desperate to get to my car now. I break out into a run as he reaches for me, and I try the fob one more time as he spins me around.

Everything happens at once. A pop. A sharp, awful bang.

A heavy thud against my back, like someone just shoved me.

Heat.

Weird crackles.

And then nothing.

[3]

LUKE

Her fucking car just exploded.

Glass everywhere, bright fucking light.

Why the fuck are we not dead?

Nothing ever truly prepares you for a car bomb—what the fuck—but that was not supposed to fucking happen here. Today. With this case that was just supposed to be a pain in the ass hoax call confirmation.

We're still standing, so it wasn't a very good car bomb at least. My ears are ringing, and I see spots, but Taylor's gone completely white. She can't pass out on me here. Not if cars are exploding.

We don't have time for reactions. I grab her and turn, pulling and pushing to get her in front of me. Put myself between her and the parking lot. "Go," I order. "Run for the building."

"It's locked," she gasps. I see her lips moving and hear the words on a bit of a delay. Whatever that explosive was, it was loud enough to give my head a good ring. "My card—" She looks back toward the parking lot. Her bag is lying on the concrete, contents spilled everywhere. No, we're not going back for it.

"Corner." I point, and when she doesn't move, I shove her. As nicely as one can in a life or death situation. We need to get to cover.

She stumbles as she runs onto the grass, and I realize she's in heels. I'm willing to carry her if I God damn need to, but she picks up her feet and scrambles forward, faster now.

My hearing is coming back and beside me, Taylor is sucking in big, gulping breaths.

I pull my phone out as we round the corner of the building. I need backup right the fuck now.

"Nine-one-one, what's your emergency?"

I give the dispatcher my name and badge number, and report what I know. Explosive device detonated, address, no injuries but potentially an unsafe scene. "Advise the bomb squad the device may not have completely detonated. Live explosive potential. There was a blast, enough to feel a heavy pulse, but we weren't knocked down."

The dispatcher repeats the address to me, confirming it. "Two patrol cars are on the way, detective."

"Helicopter?"

"We'll patch you in so you can talk to the eyes in the sky."

I suck in a breath. Fuck.

"Are you visible from the road?"

"No. We took cover around the corner of the building." I look at Taylor. "How many people are inside?"

She blinks at me and shakes her head. "I don't know. A few, at least. We've got two volunteers in our office."

"Civilians need to be evacuated," I bark into the phone. I look at Taylor again. "Is there a back entrance?"

She nods, her face drained completely of color.

"Hey, stay with me," I say.

In my ear, the dispatcher catches that. "Still no injuries, detective?"

"Ms. Reid may need medical attention for shock."

"Ambulances are on their way." The beats of an emergency response. They're second nature to me now, and I sink into that.

Just another job.

Just another lucky break that means I live to see another day.

But Taylor doesn't have that advantage. And as I sit back on my heels, as I settle myself into the task of seeing the crime scene as a puzzle to be solved, she lets out a shuddering breath and topples sideways.

$$[\ 4\ ]$$

TAYLOR

"Whoa there," I hear. A low, warm voice right in my ear.

Hands on my shoulders haul me upright.

I just want to go to sleep.

"Keep talking, Taylor."

"Can't," I mumble.

"You know anyone who might want to kill you, princess?"

Kill me.

Cold sweat slicks my body as I start to shiver.

"You're okay. You're alive."

I guess so.

"Can you open your eyes for me?"

I blink slowly. It feels like sandpaper, dragging my eyelids up my eyeballs. My face feels puffy and tight.

All of me feels tight. It doesn't matter how big a gulp of air I try to take, it's not enough. My chest is constricted and my head feels like it's wrapped in a vise.

"Ms. Reid. Look at me." The cop—the detective—is squatting in front of me, holding me up against the wall.

"Shouldn't move an injured person," I whisper. Oh, good.

Words. Nice to be able to talk. Might pass out, but at least I can talk.

"You aren't injured. You're freaking out. Try to slow down your breathing."

"What?"

He moves around me, his hand sliding over my shoulder and into the middle of my back. I focus on that. His hand. Warm. Alive.

We're alive.

My car blew up. The tightness grows.

"Let it out. Exhale. More. Exhale. Slow it down."

I shrug off his touch. "I'm fine."

I'm not. But I can hear sirens now. Distant, but getting closer. Detective Vasquez mutters something that sounds like code, and I realize he's on the phone.

"I need you to walk," he says. Not code. I blink at him. "Up you get, princess."

Oh. Me. I stumble to my feet and he takes me by the arm, leading me to the back of the building. My building, which I brought a car bomb to, apparently.

I'm the worst employee ever.

Oh, God. Hysterical laughing burbles up inside me, and then it's sliding out in wild, choking sobs. Not laughter really at all. I stumble again, but then a cop car is there. A woman in a uniform runs toward us and takes my other arm. Detective Vasquez tells her something that I miss, and she lets go. He's got me, apparently.

He opens the back door and guides me to the seat.

A seat in the back of an ordinary LAPD cop car.

People like me usually get to turn ourselves in with high-priced lawyers at our sides.

Not that I've ever had to do that, but I'm aware of the process.

I don't care. My thighs are shaking.

The air conditioning feels good, and I close my eyes.

"I'll be right back," he says. I hear it dully through the roar in my ears.

I nod as tears slide down my face.

[5]

LUKE

It doesn't take long for the cavalry to arrive. Three cars, then two more. I task the next uniform I see to securing the perimeter, and then point at the third. "You." I flash him my badge, then gesture to the first car. "Watch her. Flag me if she moves. The second the ambulance gets here, have her checked out for shock."

Our chopper is circling overhead, and I press my phone to my ear again, eager to hear their radio feed. "*Negative. No suspicious movement on Eagle Rock. I'll circle back.*" My phone beeps. Call waiting. It's the captain. I switch lines and answer the call. "This is Vasquez."

"This escalated quickly," she says crisply in my ear. "Give me the quick report because you know the next call is going to be from the Secret Service for reasons neither of us properly understand."

"You've got as much information as I do. Unexpected car bomb in our definitely-not-a-real-suspect's vehicle. Detonated when Ms. Reid pressed her key fob to unlock the car. Uh..." I do the quick math in my head again. "Fifth push of the button. Something went wrong with the explosive, though. Maybe only partially detonated. Won't know until the bomb squad gets here. Ms. Reid is unharmed but distressed. She's secured in my car at the moment, and I'm doing a quick walkthrough before I hand off control of the scene and escort Ms. Reid to the hospital. Partly to have her looked at, and partly to get her into a secure location where I can question her without being obvious about it. She's not particularly cooperative."

"Did she deny the drug possession charge?"

"We didn't get that far into the conversation."

"Any chance she blew up the car herself to dispose of the evidence?"

I laugh out loud. "Stranger things have happened, but I don't think so. Plus if she did happen to have that pre-rigged, which would be wild, she did a shit job. The car isn't demolished. Once the bomb squad clears it, forensics will be able to confirm the presence of drugs."

She sighs in my ear. "All right. Keep me posted on what they say, and keep Ms. Reid occupied until you know one way or another. The feds are going to be alarmed. I wouldn't be surprised if the FBI is involved by the end of the day."

Bombs tend to get attention. Which was probably the point, and something the Secret Service seems to have shit the bed on anticipating. "I'm not handing over the investigation."

Another pause. "Let's discuss this further when you get to the station."

I'm not taking Taylor Reid anywhere near the Secret Service or the FBI until I know more about my crime scene here. "It'll be a while. You know how emergency rooms can be."

"Understood."

"I could be dancing right now, Captain."

"You and me both, Vasquez."

———

Once the bomb squad and forensics team arrive, my car is cleared to be moved from the parking lot. I pull it around to the back of the building where I find Taylor sitting in an ambulance, giving one-word answers to the veteran female paramedic looking her over.

She's still pale, and dark circles have formed under her eyes.

"Knock-knock," I say from the open door at the back.

They both turn and look at me.

"Detective Vasquez," I say to the paramedic.

Taylor rolls her eyes. "I haven't forgotten."

"I wasn't introducing myself to you," I point out.

That gets me a faint smile.

If her attitude has returned, that's a great sign.

"She's refusing transport to the hospital," the paramedic says. "But she should see a doctor. Sleeping tonight is going to be hard."

"Sleep is for the weak," Taylor mutters.

"I'll take her to the hospital," I say.

The *her* in question gives me a look of alarm. "You will not."

I give her the blandest look possible then follow it with a not-at-all-serious threat. "Then I'll arrest you."

That gets me a wide-eyed *what the hell's with the overreaction, dude* look from the paramedic.

I shrug. I think I have Ms. Reid's number, that's all.

Taylor narrows her eyes. "Maybe I'd rather take the ambulance."

"That's an option, for sure."

But she shrugs out of the blanket they'd wrapped around her and nods. "No, it's okay. You can take me. I don't need..." She waves her hand around the interior of the ambulance. "This is overkill."

The paramedic gives her a form to sign, and then she's free.

She stops when she steps into the sunshine, wincing. Then she does a double-take. "My bag."

"It's in my car. You dropped it when the explosive device went off."

She nods.

The bomb squad commander is waiting for us when we get to my vehicle.

"Ms. Reid." He introduces himself. "We're going to need to search your office and home. Your apartment building has already been evacuated, but the team there is waiting for my go-ahead to send our dog in."

Her eyes are as big as saucers. "Okay."

"Is there anything we should know about before we go in there? Anything that might be dangerous?"

"No." Her face pinches tight. "I have no idea why someone would do this to me. Do you think there's really another bomb at my apartment?"

"Let's hope not, ma'am."

After he takes his leave, and we're in the car, she lets out a rough, shaky breath. "He was nicer than you, by the way."

"Most people are."

"You threatened to arrest me."

"I did."

"That usually leads to a charge of some kind."

"You're familiar with the process."

She shrugs. "Growing up in my family, the threat of police showing up and taking everything away was just a given."

That's pretty fucked up. "How often did that happen?"

"Never, actually." Her voice is distant, and it occurs to me that a lawyer would have a field day with me questioning her in this condition.

But I don't think that's going to be an issue, because I don't think Taylor Reid has done anything wrong here. I'm quite sure forensics won't find any drugs in her car, and the heads-up from the Secret Service was supposed to be a big, splashy front page oops.

But they bunted the investigation to me, and what's another car fire in the life of the LAPD? That's how we're going to talk about it publicly. The LAPD doesn't make a big deal about minor vehicle mishaps.

But that means whoever is playing a game with Ms. Reid may—will—try again.

And as I predicted, my vacation plans are toast.

I don't like dancing that much anyway.

"It was an idle threat," I admit. "Designed to get a reaction out of you. You seem prickly."

"I am."

"That makes two of us, Ms. Reid. Maybe we can lean on that to understand each other."

Taylor snorts. "Sure. Fine. Okay. Understand this: I don't want to be dragged into whatever my father is doing." She looks at me. "Has done?"

I don't say anything. I can't.

She frowns. "But I won't protect him, either."

It's a good line. It may even be the truth. But someone planting an explosive device in her car says that she's involved, whether she wants to be or not. The question is, why? Why try to kill a woman who has distanced herself from her family, on the same day that family is indicted for a host of financial crimes?

The Secret Service may be able to provide more insight into that. There are probably sealed elements of the case that could be shared inter-departmentally now that we've got an attempted murder case on our hands. Or depending on how it plays out, a simple case of mischief. Officially.

"This must have been a mistake," she says softly. I glance across the car at her. Her face is pinched.

"Nobody has a motive to kill you?"

The corners of her mouth tug down. "The worst of what I've done is in the past." She gives me a sideways glance. "And pretty public knowledge."

"Your affair with the Vice President." I say it neutrally, but infidelity is a powerful motive—for all involved parties. "When was the last time you spoke to him?"

She doesn't question how I know about that.

Everyone knows about that.

"Years ago." Her jaw juts forward. "That's not—I'm not—"

"People harbor grudges for a long time."

She casts her eyes down and nods. "I guess."

"Any contact there at all? With him, or his wife?"

"No."

"Any apologies or amends?"

She hesitates. "No."

Was that beat a lie, or a regret? Did she want to make amends, or did she try and it didn't work? I can't push too hard here if I want to maintain her fragile willingness to talk to me. And my gut says this isn't about the affair she had.

"Anything happen at work? Maybe something out of the ordinary? A disgruntled client?"

She shakes her head. "No. I haven't been doing counseling there that long—I used to be a client myself. And so far, everyone has been really great."

"Any of your clients have angry exes?"

Her lips press tight.

"Ms. Reid, this might be a matter of life or death."

"Might be? My car blew up. I'm aware. Thanks. But my clients' personal lives are confidential and none of your business."

I can get a warrant that makes it my business, but I don't want to push her on that point. At least not yet.

Which brings us to the third potential reason why someone might target her today—the federal indictments against her father.

———

My badge helps to get us into a bed in Emergency pretty quickly. The doctor takes one look at me, then at the scowl on Taylor's face, and she points to the hall.

I tip my fingers to my temple in a mock salute and step outside to check my messages while they have a private chat about whether or not the big, bad detective was being mean to her.

The first message is from the bomb squad. Taylor's apartment is clean. They're doing a broader sweep before letting residents back in. I reply and advise them that I'll bring her around to pack a bag later. There's no chance I'm letting her stay there alone tonight.

I also have a brief update from Forensics. They were able to recover parts of the explosive, which is great news. It'll take weeks to put it back together, but it's a start. I fire that news off to the captain.

She replies immediately.

Woods: Do you want me to share that detail with the FBI? Their labs could process the pieces sooner.

I hesitate. Handing over any part of this investigation feels wrong. Is that my ego, or am I doing my due diligence? Integrity wins out, although it's a close call.

Vasquez: The sooner we get anything off it, the better.

Woods: On it.

Vasquez: We'll need a safe house or hotel budget for Ms. Reid, too. At least for tonight, preferably a couple of days. If the FBI wants to pony up for that...

Woods: I'll find a way to make that request too.

When I'm invited back inside, Taylor looks drawn and tired. She gives me a half-hearted attempt at a smile. "Doc didn't like my blood pressure. Says car bombs are bad for my health. Who could've guessed that?"

"Yeah."

"Do you have any more questions for me, detective?"

I shake my head. "Not right now."

"You haven't asked about my parents." Her eyes are sharp. Focused. She may be tired, but she won't be tricked here. She's on guard. "While you were outside, I checked my messages. And the news. Why were you asking about what happened years ago? Don't you think the attack on me is related to the arrest today?"

"Do you?"

"I'm not the cop. You tell me, *Detective.*"

A male nurse interrupts us, holding a small paper cup of water and a smaller cup with two pills in it. "Here you go,

Taylor. And I'll be back in a few with the prescription once the doctor signs off on it."

I don't miss the twitch of her jaw as she says thank you. Or the way she avoids my gaze as she downs the pills together in a single swallow, waving off the water as unnecessary.

The nurse takes her blood pressure again and then wordlessly disappears.

Silence stretches between us.

Finally, I exhale, loudly, and sit in the chair beside her hospital chair. "I think it's possible we're both being played here."

Her right eyebrow arches sky-high.

"I got your name this afternoon in a file. A request from the Secret Service, who for their own reasons, did not want to contact you directly."

"Because I would refuse to speak to them."

"I got that distinct impression, yes."

"Are we putting the Secret Service on the short list of assholes who might bomb my car?"

"No."

"It feels like you're missing a prime opportunity to nail a big suspect, then."

"Do you think the US government wants to kill you?"

She hesitates long enough for me to think she actually might, but then she sighs and shakes her head. "No. I just really don't like any of them. And frankly, I don't think I'm going to like you, either. No offense."

"None taken. But regardless of how I got here, and whether or not that was spurious, the fact is, someone targeted you with an explosive. That's a crime. I investigate crimes, so you're stuck with me. At least until I'm replaced by some of those people who you loathe."

Her eyes go wide. "What?"

"Your choice, of course. But it's just a matter of time before the FBI makes noise about taking over this case."

"Because they'll link it to my family's legal trouble?"

I shrug. It's as good a theory as any.

She closes her eyes. End of conversation.

I sit there and listen to the beeping from a monitor in the next room. The distant squawk of a dispatch radio, maybe at the nurses' station, and footsteps in the hall.

Hospitals are not my favorite place.

They're no dance club, that's for sure.

I look at my watch. It's just after four in the afternoon. God damn it, there's still so much more of today that could go fucking sideways.

Taylor has the right idea by closing her eyes and grabbing some rest.

[6]

TAYLOR

It doesn't take long for the pills they gave me to work. The tightness in my chest recedes and the dark, flashing images—of my car blowing up, of Detective Vasquez holding me up when I desperately wanted to just sleep, of sitting in the back of the ambulance as people fled my building—get a little less intense.

I can still see it all over and over again, like a silent film or a grotesque vacation slide show. But there's some distance, finally, and I can breathe.

It's something.

But that fragile peace doesn't last long. When I'm discharged with a prescription for sleeping pills clutched in my hand, we go straight to the hospital pharmacy to fill it—and my debit card doesn't work.

"Do you have the cash to cover it?" the clerk asks.

I roll my eyes. "No. Who carries cash anymore?"

Luke wordlessly pulls two twenties from his wallet and hands them over.

"Thanks," I mutter.

He doesn't say anything.

When we're sitting in his car, I try again. "I have cash at my apartment. I can repay you."

"That's where we're going. You need to pack a few things."

"I can't stay there?"

"Not right now."

I frown. "Can I go to a hotel?"

"Do you have money for that?" He says it without judgment, but fuck, I don't know if I do.

Why doesn't my bank card work?

I huff out a frustrated breath and close my eyes, sinking into the sweet dullness of the drugs still numbing my pain.

It takes half an hour to get to my apartment. We don't talk and that's just fine by me.

When we get there, a marked cop car is sitting out front, but otherwise, everything looks normal.

Nothing feels normal, though. I have had my world crash down around me before. And yet this is different. I didn't see this coming.

I'd thought I'd escaped the madness.

I was wrong.

I blink. My eyelashes feel wet. No, that won't do. I've cried enough today.

When we get upstairs, I don't know where to start. Panic rises again, and I try my best to channel it into a blithe indifference. It comes out as bitchy, I'm pretty sure. "How long are you going to hold me hostage?"

Vasquez shrugs. "That might be up to the Feds."

"You didn't explain why the LAPD is doing this."

"No. I didn't."

"Is that because you don't know?"

His eyes flash to my face. I grin. "Got it in one, didn't I, detective?"

"Pack your bags, princess. The clock is ticking."

"You could call me Ms. Reid."

"I could."

"Are you hoping I complain to the police superintendent and get you booted off this detail?"

His jaw twitches.

"What?"

"What do you mean, what?"

I point. "Your jaw twitched. Why?"

"No reason. Do you need help packing?"

"You're laughing at me."

"There's no such thing as a police superintendent in the LAPD. So I'd enjoy you trying to figure out who you should actually complain to about me when I'm just trying to keep you alive."

"So who should I actually complain to, then?"

Now he laughs out loud, not even trying to hide it. "No offense, Ms. Reid, but that's not how it works."

I'm pretty sure he's wrong on that score, but whatever. I'm not actually going to try to get him booted off this case. I don't know what to make of him, exactly, but as far as cops go, he's not bad.

He's got an attitude, anyway. I know how to deal with attitude.

"Well, cops aren't really my thing, so..."

Another twitch. "Rich people aren't mine. And yet here we are, so..."

This time I don't reply to the obvious goad. I just stare at the twitch. At his jaw. Dark skin stretched taut over muscle and sinew. Five o'clock shadow at precisely five o'clock.

Detective Vasquez is a handsome man.

I hate that I notice.

I hate that I'm conditioned to notice, that I can't help it, that deep down, there's a part of my twisted soul already working on a way to use that to my advantage.

Handsome men are easy marks, in a different way than wealthy men, and different again from men who have obvious soft spots.

Handsome men think they are God's gift to women, and they couldn't be more wrong. This blind spot is exploitable.

It was one of the first lessons my mother ever taught me.

And I don't want to think about that, so I drop my bag on my sofa and go to the hall closet where I keep my suitcases.

He clears his throat and shakes his head no when I reach for the biggest one.

"What?"

"An overnight bag will suffice."

"Are we going to be only gone overnight?"

He gives me a pained look. "The small suitcase, then. Something reasonable."

I don't even know what that word means, but okay, sure.

In my bedroom, I try to ignore him as he watches me pull out jeans, leggings, t-shirts, and a hoodie. Then I go to my dresser, and I don't need him watching me pack my thongs and bras, so I wiggle my fingers at him. "Shoo."

He doesn't go anywhere.

I shift gears, going into the bathroom instead to grab my makeup bag and toiletries. When I come back, I pull open my top drawer—universally known as the keeper of lace and things, is it not?—and give him a pointed a look. "Can I have some privacy, please?"

"I've seen lingerie before. I need to make sure you aren't packing anything electronic. No cell phone. Nothing trackable."

I hold up the velvet pouch I'd been looking for—and

wouldn't be going anywhere without. "Do you think someone's planted a bug in my vibrator?"

He holds out his hand. "Let me see it."

"What? No. Don't be a pervert." The accusation tumbled out before I could think of a better way to establish the boundary of no; he can't touch my sex toy. Oh well. I stand by it.

"Then you can't bring it with you."

"Nobody bugged it."

"Bet you didn't think anyone would have planted a bomb in your car, either."

All the sass drains out of me, and I hand it over. Instead of taking it, his fingers wrap around my fist. His gaze locks on my face.

"I'm sorry, that was out of line."

"You aren't wrong," I mutter. "Check it."

He squeezes my hand then takes the pouch. He doesn't have any smart-ass comments about the palm-sized clit sucker, so either he knows about the newest trend in sex toys, or he's decided discretion is the way to go here. Turning it over in his hand, he inspects the USB charging port and the soft, malleable tip.

Heat crawls up my neck, and I turn around, giving my attention to my shoes stacked in a custom shelf beside my dresser. "Do you want to check these over, too?" I ask crisply, holding up a pair of wedge heels.

It takes him a moment to reply. "Do you own any shoes that are easy to run in?"

And the smart-ass comments are back. Fine, let's do this. "Nope," I toss over my shoulder. "I don't break a sweat for anyone."

"Not even your little friend here?" He reaches around me and dangles the velvet pouch in front of my face. "It looks fine. You can pack it."

Snatching it from his hand, I shove it in my suitcase then pull my gym bag out from under my bed. Of course, I own shoes I can run in. This body doesn't just magically keep itself looking the way it does.

He doesn't say anything as I finish packing.

My last stop is the safe in my closet. My heart pounds as I grab cash. It's just a reflex, something I've seen my parents do many times when they are leaving an off-the-books this or that.

We never asked any questions. But children see everything, and internalize the weird, probably criminal tics their parents have.

Okay, maybe most people just learn to yell or be passive-aggressive.

I learned to stash cash, just in case.

And lo and behold, now just in case has happened...

Pulse thumping, I grab my passport.

Just in case.

[7]

LUKE

TAYLOR EMERGES from her closet different than when she went in. On guard.

In her hand is a roll of money and her passport. She doesn't try to hide it from me, which is good.

"This is the last of what I need," she says quietly.

I nod. "All right. Let's go. We need to go to the station next."

The wariness spikes. "Why?"

"Because that's where I solve crimes."

"If this is all an elaborate ruse to get me to confess to some crime, it's not going to work."

I ignore her jab. "My captain is working on getting you a safe house, but until then, you can rack out on the couch in our break room."

"The chances of me falling asleep in a police station are slim to none."

I know this isn't a great plan, that it's been a long fucking day for her, but I need to get on my computer. "I get that. I'm sorry about everything you've been through today, Ms. Reid. I truly am. But the sooner we figure out what the hell is going on and who might want to hurt you, the sooner you can get back to your life here."

Her face crumples. "I guess I can't go to work, either?"

I shake my head. "Afraid not."

"I need to call my boss."

"You can do that from the station."

She scowls. "You're serious about the no electronics thing, aren't you?"

"I am."

With a sigh, she closes up her suitcase and carries it into the living room. She looks at her purse, dumps it out, and sighs again. Then she picks up her wallet from the pile. A lip-gloss. And nothing else. "I'm good to go."

———

Captain Woods meets us by the elevators, accompanied by someone from Victim Services and warmly introduces them both to Taylor.

"Ms. Reid, I'm the commanding officer here, and I'd like to thank you for your patience. You've been through a lot today. Yumi here is going to sit with you while Detective Vasquez has a meeting with his team and writes his report. Then we'll get you off to a safe house for the night."

Taylor nods. Understanding, calm—at least on the outside. She doesn't give me a second glance as they head down the hall.

I watch her until she's out of sight.

"Everything okay, Detective?" the Captain asks.

I turn my attention to her, fully. "Yes, ma'am."

"Was she cooperative?"

"Relatively."

"Let's go to my office first so I can brief you on the discussion with the Feds. Then we'll go into the conference room, and you can pull together the facts as we know them right now."

"I'll meet you in your office. I need to ask Singh and McBride to pull her financials." I swing past the desks of my fellow detectives, who already got the heads up from Woods that we'd be pulling them into the investigation tonight.

"I thought you were off for two weeks?" Ram Singh asks when I stop in front of him. "I hear you caught a hot case instead."

Sarah McBride looks up from the stack of files she was reading. "Don't give him the idea that we can take this off his hands. We've got enough going on with the reservoir murders."

"Vacation has been postponed," I reassure her. "It's fine. I'll get back to that after you guys help me solve this case." I tell them about Taylor's bankcard not working. "Find out what you can and meet us in the conference room in ten."

Then I go and find my boss, who has yet another Coke in her hand. This time, I take the drink she offers me.

And this time, she doesn't beat around the bush. "So I gotta tell you, the Secret Service is being tight-lipped over this whole thing."

"They literally handed us a live bomb. I imagine they're covering their asses."

Captain Woods pulls a face. "Yeah."

"Is there more to the reluctance there?"

She shrugs. "It's a political hot potato. But the FBI doesn't have the same resistance. They would be willing to take over the investigation. I'm expecting a field agent to arrive any minute. This isn't a nuisance report any longer. You can go on vacation if you want."

Over my dead body. "I'll accept any help they want to offer, but I'm not giving this up without a fight. There's no evidence to connect it to any federal crime."

"Ms. Reid's family is under intense investigation."

"A family she doesn't have any contact with."

The captain raises an eyebrow. "Really?"

"She says she hasn't spoken to them in a year. Also, I think she trusts me. At least as far as she trusts anyone. So at least for the weekend—at least until we understand what we're dealing with here—I don't mind taking lead here."

"All right."

My phone vibrates. I pull it out. "Forensics report is in from the garage. There was no evidence of drugs in her car."

She points in the general direction of the conference room. "Let's go figure out what's next, then."

Waiting for us are McBride and Singh. They prefer to work on cases as a team.

I usually work on my own except for team meetings like this, where I present the facts of the case and figure out next steps. Right now, I can use all the help I get, because this file is nothing but holes right now.

"Did your work for you," Sarah says, before sticking her tongue out at me. She shoves a print out in my direction. "All her accounts were seized by the Feds, along with her parents."

"They didn't tell you that?" I turned to the captain.

Her lips pull tight into a thin line. "They did not."

More fuckery. So much for inter-departmental cooperation.

She waves her hand. "Let's get on with it, anyway.

I launch into a rundown of the day, starting and ending with the drug claims, now disproven. "So that report was a false flag, designed to draw attention to the vehicle or ensure that Ms. Reid opened it on demand."

Sarah frowns. "Do you think the bomb was intended to harm a police officer, then?"

If it were, that would change the motive. And the charges. "It's a possibility." Everything is a possibility.

Ram shakes his head. "The anonymous tip went through the Secret Service first, and there was no controlling who would investigate that. Maybe they didn't care who was included as collateral damage."

"Right. I'm working on the assumption that Ms. Reid was the target." I log in to the computer system, pull up some photos from our records, and send them to the smart board on the wall. Taylor's picture from her driver's license, the photos of the car taken today at the crime scene populate on the screen. "And whoever set the explosive was an amateur. It didn't go off properly, or I wouldn't be standing here right now."

Sarah taps her pen against her chin. "Which makes it personal. Can we work backward from motive?"

Money. Jealousy. Revenge. *An affair*. A broken heart. Professional interference or violations. Anger. Some combination of the above. "Her past is complicated, but I don't see a motive yet."

"Then it's time to interview her," Captain Woods says. "Formally. Take McBride with you."

"Hey, I've got files to read through," Sarah protests.

I hesitate a beat too long.

"Is that a problem, Vasquez?"

"No." I say it slowly. *Noooo*. It's not a problem. But it is something. "She's not completely cooperative. With good reason, I believe. She needs to be handled carefully."

"A few hours ago, you were calling her the Blow Job Princess. Suddenly you're her staunch protector?"

"You called her *what*?" Sarah glares at me.

I wince. "Bad choice of language. And I wouldn't say I'm protecting her. Just giving her the due consideration any witness deserves. You said it yourself, Captain. We're all more complicated than we look."

In unison, the captain and McBride roll their eyes at me.

Ram stands up and shakes his head. "I'm not taking your side on this one, man."

"I don't have a side," I protest. "It's all good. Happy to interview her like any other witness. Happy to have Sarah sit in on it and kick me in the shins whenever I say the wrong thing."

"Happy to let the FBI take over because clearly, they're keeping a lot from us?"

"Whoa," I say, my indignation half self-mocking, half real-as-hell. "That's too far, Captain."

"Then get cracking on this before they take it from you."

I reach across the table and grab the financial report. "Will do."

———

Taylor looks at Sarah with guarded suspicion as she follows me into the interview room. "When you said an interview, I assumed you just meant asking me some of those same questions again. Do I need an attorney?"

McBride has agreed to play bad cop. "That's up to you. You are not a suspect at this time."

"I shouldn't be a suspect at all," she says hotly.

Sarah shoots me an amused look. I spread my hands wide.

"That's exactly why we appreciate your assistance. We just want to get to the bottom of why this happened."

"Fine."

"This interview will be recorded," Sarah says crisply.

Taylor's voice chills noticeably, but her response is the same. "Fine."

"For the record, can you please identify yourself?"

"My name is Taylor Dashford Reid." She gives her address next, then sits back in her chair and crosses her arms over her chest.

"And what is your job?"

"I work part-time as a peer counselor with LAST."

"How long have you been doing that?"

"Three months."

"Your work before that?"

She looks at Sarah, who's been quiet this whole time. "I didn't have a job before that. I was working on myself, I guess."

"And does working on yourself pay well?" McBride asks.

"I have a trust fund. I don't need to work."

Sarah glances obviously at the folder on the table in front of me. Taylor follows the pointed look with her eyes then gives me a look that asks, *What is going on?*

It's not personal, Princess. I clear my throat. "When your father was arrested this afternoon in Washington, all of the family accounts were seized."

"Is that why my debit card didn't work at the pharmacy?" She does a good job of looking genuinely distressed. "Well, that's bullshit. That was my personal account. That has nothing to do with my parents."

"Take that up with the FBI."

My timing couldn't have been better. A knock sounds at the door, and McBride opens it. In steps a white guy in a suit. Generic federal agent. Older, in good shape. Obviously unhappy.

The captain is right behind him.

He flashes a badge at the room. "Ferdinand. FBI."

Behind him, Sarah stifles a giggle, and the captain gives her a warning look.

"Agent Ferdinand," I say smoothly. "Please join us. Perhaps you can provide some more clarity to Ms. Reid here about why her bank accounts have been frozen."

He pulls a warrant from his pocket and hands it to my

witness, who has turned into an ice princess for real. She takes it gingerly and glances at the page with disdain.

"Like I said. Bullshit. But do what you want. I'll just lean heavily on the hospitality of the LAPD if you're going to be a money-stealing monster."

"It's a temporary measure, Ms. Reid," Ferdinand says. "Your personal accounts will be reviewed first and released to as soon as possible. We appreciate your cooperation."

"I'm not cooperating with anyone," she says. "Just in case you were wondering."

"Hey, I thought we were getting along great," I deadpan. "We had that whole near-miss-on-death bonding experience earlier."

"And then you dragged me in here like I'm some kind of suspect in my own car bombing, so no, dude. We're not getting along great." She looks at the captain. "I'm ready for an attorney now, please."

"You haven't been charged with anything, Ms. Reid."

"Then, in that case, I'd like to leave. I can do that right?"

I stand up. There are too many people in the room. I need Taylor to sit her ass down, and I need everyone else to leave. "You're welcome to leave at any time. But I can't let you go far. The break room, if you want a cup of coffee. If you insist on leaving this building, I will follow you."

She stands up, too. "That sounds like a threat, Detective."

"More of a promise, Princess." I move around the table, closing out the rest of the crowded space. It's just her and me. "Where are you going to go? You really want to put your life on the line just to show me who's boss? I'm the boss. Don't forget it."

"You don't seem like the boss here," she says brightly.

"That's because I play well with others. But the good agent behind me? And my captain? They're going to step outside.

We're going to keep talking, you and me, because we've got a lot of ground to cover. So I can figure out who's got it out for you enough to blow your car up. Got it?"

She hesitates. And in that moment, my gamble proves itself worthwhile. As long as I keep the witness talking, what I said is true. My captain and the FBI agent are going to want to hear what she says, and they'll put up with any kind of unconventional interrogation technique on my part as long as I get the goods.

The door opens behind me.

And just like that, the air in the room gets a bit lighter. It's easier for Taylor to breathe.

Sarah closes the door, and then leans against. "I'm going to stay," she says dryly. "Y'all seem like you could use a chaperone."

I don't look over at her. My attention is all on Taylor. "Do we, Princess?" I murmur under my breath. "How about you? Can you play well with others?"

She glares at me. But she doesn't move.

I lower my voice even more. "Trust me, Taylor. Give me something to work with here."

Searching my face, she wavers. I can see it. And then, in a whisper, she says, "This is way beyond your pay grade, Detective."

My pulse jacks up. *Bring it on.* "Let me be the judge of that."

[8]

TAYLOR

I SHOULDN'T HAVE SAID that. I don't know why I did, but now that it's hanging in the air between us, my mind is spinning to cover it up.

Which means I can't just walk out.

Fucking fuck.

I step back from him and pull out my chair. For extra measure, I give the female cop an arch look. "Could I have some water?"

Her lips twitch in an almost-smile. "Sure."

Vasquez waits until she returns with a too-small cup for me before he begins. "As I was saying before we were interrupted, your accounts have been temporarily frozen by the FBI."

"That isn't exactly what you said," I point out. "He said that when he came in. Let's not forget that you're just as much in the dark about all of this as I am."

"Sure." He taps his fingers on the mysterious folder that promises we're not *exactly* in the same amount of confusion here.

Whatever.

I take a deep breath.

It's fine. I don't need the money. My sister Hailey has lived without our parents' money for years now. I can try it. I should try it. This is a good thing.

Sure. Maybe if I tell myself that enough times, I'll believe it eventually.

I've done a lot of soul searching over the last three years. Learned to deal with the consequences of my past decisions. Accept my failings and see them as a clear path for repentance and rehabilitation.

But I'm still *me*. I still like money, and pampering myself, and I definitely don't like to be weak. No money is a real problem.

"So, just to clarify." I look at the folder. "You can see all of my financial details in there?"

"Why?"

"I have two trust funds," I point out. "Just—"

Detective Vasquez looks at me like I'm an idiot. "Yes, both of your illegally grown trust funds are frozen."

"Allegedly illegal. And it was just a question. It'll be hard for me to get to the bottom of this if I don't have access to my usual funds."

"You aren't getting to the bottom of anything," he says, incredulity dripping off his words. "But that does bring us back to the very interesting question of what is beyond my pay grade."

"Probably a lot?" I say innocently. "I don't know how much you make exactly, but..."

"You meant something specific, Taylor."

"Did I? Oh man, it must have come and gone in this brain of mine. Trauma has a way of fucking you up big time. I'm sorry."

"It's fine. If it comes back to you, let me know." But his jaw flexes. That's a tell. He doesn't like it when I play dumb.

I'll have to do it more often.

"Let's go over some of what we talked about earlier today, just to get it down on the record."

"I told you I had no interest in protecting my father."

"Sure. You also said you grew up with the constant threat of your parents being arrested. Is that accurate?"

"It was more subtle than that, but yes. They had friends who went to jail, were investigated for securities fraud, that sort of thing. It would be a casual conversation at a dinner party—of course, you don't say anything when detained. Of course, you just ask for an attorney, they make that go away. Pass the salad, Karen. That sort of thing."

"And who is Karen?"

I burst out laughing, but it's short and hollow. "Uh, it's just a saying."

"All right."

"You're no fun when you're on the record."

"Is he fun off the record?" Detective McBride asks from the door.

"Not really." I try to think of a way to better describe what it was like to grow up with limitless money and non-stop stress.

At any point, it could have all disappeared like it finally did today. But since it didn't, we got to live the high life. Even when my father murdered a sex worker—yes, really—we kept on skating.

You'd think murder would be the worst crime possible, but it turns out hiding money from the Feds gets the real investigative powers going. Fucking hell.

And now I'm here, in a small, musty room with mirrored glass, trying to explain a life that is really inexplicable.

There are many times over the last three years that I've wondered if I made the right decision by not running further. Not hiding under a new identity. This is one of those times. I could be on a beach somewhere right now, where bank accounts can't be seized by the government.

You wouldn't like yourself very much if you'd done that.

True. But I'd probably be so drunk or high it wouldn't matter.

I lift my chin and stare my interrogator in the face. I have nothing to hide. "What else do you want to get recorded for posterity, Detective Vasquez?"

"We spoke briefly about your affair with a married man."

A married man. Ha. If only it were that simple. "Yes."

"You indicated you didn't believe that was connected to this incident."

"Correct."

"Are there any other affairs that we should know about?"

Shame slams into me, and I can feel my cheeks getting hot. "None recently."

"Infidelity is a prime motive for violent crimes, Ms. Reid."

"Once upon a time, a long time ago, I had fucked up relationships with a lot of people. That all ended years ago. Now the only fucked up relationship I have is with myself. Okay?"

"Sure." He grabs a blank pad of lined paper and a pen, and shoves them across the table at me. "Could you make a list of everyone who might hate you?"

"That's hardly a scientific measure." My palms go slick. Can I list them all? I'm not even sure I know all of their names.

"Let's call it a seven out of ten scale. Anyone who might have a higher than that level of outrage when your name comes up might be a suspect."

"No." I swallow hard. "I'm not doing that."

"Who are you protecting?"

"Nobody." I rub my hands on my pants. Jesus, this is hard. "It's a long list, maybe. But none of them are local. I've kept my head down, Detective. All of my enemies are on the east coast."

And in the past.

I'm not naive enough—or egotistical enough—to think I'm a totally different person, but I have changed. I'm happy now, as much as that is possible.

In order to get to this point, I had to reassess so much of my life. My relationship with my mother, first and foremost. And that spilled out beyond that to the rest of my family, my role in Washington society, how much I'd embraced my role as a socialite.

Everything.

I gave up social media, the limelight, and all contact with my family.

But this is a test on a whole other level.

How much am I willing to give up? How many secrets will I spill in order to protect myself?

Not as many as Detective Vasquez would like, probably.

I know what I need to do, and it breaks my heart. "You know what? I need to go home."

"We've been over this. You can't leave. It's not safe."

"Not to my apartment." I take a deep breath. "I need to go to D.C. I need to find out what my sister knows. I don't have enough information to answer your questions, Detective."

"I can't let you do that."

I don't know anything about jurisdictions. Maybe he can't *let me*. But I'm going anyway, one way or another. "Then get those other people back in here, and we can talk about how I'm free to do whatever I want to do, and you can get out of my way."

His jaw flexes.

Is that a sore point? I don't care. "Crossing state lines makes it a federal investigation, doesn't it, Detective? And the purview of the FBI?"

"Not necessarily." He looks at the mirrored glass.

I lean in. "I thought you said you were in charge? Are they going to tell you no? Who's making the decisions here?"

His head whips around.

Oh, yeah. I see him. I know him. He's just the same as every other man I've ever had to manage. I don't back down. "This is your case. Right? I think the answer to the question of who wants to kill me is in Washington. You can come with me if you want. Or do you need the big boys to take over?"

"Don't play me, Taylor." His eyes glitter. "If you want to put yourself on the line, you'll have to do it by my rules. I'm in charge."

"Of course." I swallow hard. "That's just the way I like it."

[9]

LUKE

WE GET on the last flight out that night. Taylor sleeps the whole way.

I mainline coffee and settle in for some serious reading. Apparently, I don't know enough about the Dashford Reid family.

By the time we land in Washington, dawn has broken, and I have more questions than answers—but the answers I do have disturb me.

Taylor's father is a long-time friend of Gerome Lively, a disgraced billionaire charged a few years ago with multiple sex trafficking charges by the FBI in Florida. After her sister Hailey was kidnapped by some of his associates, his other crimes came to light.

But the guy got off with a slap on the wrist, thanks to a federal prosecutor who now has a high-ranking position in the administration of President Victor Best—another life-long friend of the family's.

President Best and Amelia Dashford Reid, Taylor's mother, were once close.

Who the fuck knows, maybe they still are.

And I got all of that from a combination of police reports and Google searches.

What the fuck does Taylor know?

This is way beyond your pay grade.

And I thought she was just being a rich bitch.

When we land, I pick up a rental car and head to a discount hotel that doesn't blink when I ask to rent a room for the day and pay cash.

"What are we doing?" Taylor asks once we're alone.

"I need to check in with my team back in L.A., and it's three in the morning there. I'm going to sleep for a couple of hours, and I suggest you do the same. This might be the last rest either of us gets for the next twenty-four hours." I grab a pillow and blanket from the closet. "You can have the bed."

"Where are you—" Her mouth drops open when I shove the pillow against the door and wedge myself into place against it. "You've got to be kidding."

"Tell me you aren't a flight risk."

"I'm not," she protests hotly.

Too hotly.

I shrug. "Then I'm just being paranoid, and you'll have to deal. Night, Princess. Get some rest."

———

She's watching CNN when I wake up. Her father is on the screen, and her expression doesn't change at all as the newscaster drones on and on about the list of charges, the speculation that more will be coming, and perhaps some may even be leveled at her mother.

When the next story comes on, her only reaction is to sigh and toss the controller aside—at which point she realizes I'm awake and watching her.

"Feel better, Detective?"

She sounds bitter.

So not completely unaffected by the criminal disintegration of her family's financial security, then.

"Yeah. And you can call me Luke while we're here. Keep the whole cop thing on the quiet." I stand up and roll my shoulders, working out the kinks from sleeping on the floor. A quick glance at my watch tells me I got three hours of sleep. It's almost time to wake up McBride and Singh—if they got any sleep at all. "Are you hungry?"

"No." She grabs her bag and disappears without another word into the bathroom.

I send a text to McBride, who calls me instead of texting back. "What's up, you maverick?"

"I'm holed up in a shitty motel room with someone who has never seen this much polyester in her life. How do you think it's going? What do you have for me?"

"We pulled the surveillance cameras at her office building, and in the general vicinity. Put a couple of young guys on scrolling through that detail, but so far, nothing. Not sure if the guy got lucky or if he knew where the cameras were pointed— and where they weren't. Either way, no visual on anyone planting the bomb."

I frown. It would have been a lucky break if we'd found something that way, but a shame that we didn't. "Okay."

"We did find you on the footage, though, loitering outside the building for a while."

"I didn't want to go in and risk her heading out the back. Thought it would be better to wait for her to come out to her car."

"She knew you were there, according to the volunteer who manned the front desk. They give each other a heads up when they see anyone out there."

"Interesting." So she wasn't too worried about a strange man waiting for her. "Any reports of other strangers in recent days?"

"Uh…" There's a shuffle of papers in the background. "That's not in the interview notes. I can follow up on that." Then she swears under her breath. "Sorry, Vasquez. I gotta go. We've just heard of another body dumped in the reservoir."

"Shit." I scrub my hand over my face. "Good luck. Thanks for taking those reports while I was in the air."

Taylor re-emerges from the bathroom when I hang up the call. She's put on fresh makeup, and her hair doesn't look like it was jammed into an economy aircraft window well for five hours. Not that it really had before she went into the bathroom, either.

One thing my witness is unquestionably good at is making herself look like a socialite on the red carpet, even when she's wearing leggings and a couple of layered tank tops.

"What's the plan?" she asks crisply.

I stand up. "That's up to you. You wanted to talk to your sister."

"That's easier said than done." She flicks her hair over her shoulder. "My sister hates my guts."

"You left that bit of information out of your persuasive case to the FBI."

"It didn't seem relevant."

"To them, maybe. To me? Do I need to remind you of our agreement?"

"I know. You're in charge. And you are, but I know how to handle my family. I need to bring my sister something that proves I'm not going to double-cross her."

"And where are we going to get that?"

"Tabard Inn. Where all of Washington's worst snakes go to make deals and be seen."

"I have a problem with both making deals and being seen."

"Why am I not surprised?" She points to the door.

"I'm going to need more than an imperious demand."

That gets me a roll of her eyes. "Fine. My name is good there. I'll be able to find out the last time my mother was there, for example. If we're in luck, she might even be there today. And if she isn't, then our next stop will be the St. Regis."

"The thing you're going to bring your sister is your mother's social calendar?"

"My mother doesn't have a social calendar. She has a sociopath's calendar, and yes, it's worth quite a lot."

That is not entirely surprising after my reading on the red-eye flight here, but I'm still struck by the cool way she says it. Like mommy dearest being dirty is a foregone conclusion.

Outside, I plug the inn she mentioned into the rental's GPS. None of the routes it suggests are good. Forty minutes to go the six miles into downtown Washington. Traffic here makes L.A. look like heaven. So does the weather. It's only mid-morning and already it's hot and sticky.

I keep my thoughts on the east coast to myself, and head into the non-stop traffic snarl.

When we arrive at the inn, an unassuming grey brick row house on a street of similar buildings, she sweeps in like she owns the place. "Taylor Dashford Reid," she says to the clerk who greets her. "We're here for lunch. Is there a private room available?"

"Of course, Ms. Reid." The staff person disappears, returning in moments with a manager in tow.

"Ms. Reid," this man says. "Sorry to hear about all the fuss."

"Mmm, I know," she murmurs. "But, you know."

"Of course. Follow me, please."

I don't know what the hell they are talking about. That was an exchange about literally nothing. But we follow him, and we're shown to a private room as requested, so apparently, the fact that her family is imploding doesn't make a whiff of difference for her pull in this city she left years ago.

Fascinating.

Before the manager leaves us alone, Taylor wraps her hand around his forearm and leans in. I catch her words, even as she clearly means for him to think they are for his ear only. "Is Mikhail working today? Or any of my mother's favorites?"

"Ah." The manager looks visibly uncomfortable. "I am afraid your mother has not been here in some time. And all of her favorites have left our employ."

"My goodness. Well, all right then. What else has changed? Do you still have that delicious caper salad?"

Who the fuck is this person? The performance Taylor is putting on is worthy of a fucking Oscar, but it makes me uncomfortable for reasons I can't put my finger on.

The manager soaks it up, though. "We would make it for you even if we didn't."

And with that, he takes his leave.

"What was that all about?" I ask as she gestures to the table.

She dodges the question, or maybe she doesn't understand I'm talking about her personality transplant. "I'm not sure. My mother used to come here to scheme with shady characters. If she doesn't do that anymore, that's probably a good thing." She picks up her napkin, and then sets it down again. "Actually, I need to pee first."

"Be my guest."

She rolls her eyes. "Let me guess, you want to come with me?"

I give her a you-guessed-it-in-one smile and point to the door. "After you."

She leads the way back downstairs and into a back hallway where men's and women's washrooms are next to each other. I lean back against the wall. "I'll wait here."

"How very reasonable," she says, giving me a bright smile. "Won't be long."

I check my messages while she's in there. Nothing from Singh and McBride, but I don't expect to hear from them today, not if they've caught another murder.

Murder trumps car bombs.

There is an update from the captain. Forensics has handed over the bomb components to the FBI. Good.

I turn my phone off and look up. No sign of Taylor.

Checking my watch, I wonder just how long I should give her before I can justify knocking on the door.

I hear water running then it stops.

How long does it take to dry your hands?

I give her another thirty seconds then I push the door open.

There's a woman at the sink applying lipstick, but it's not Taylor. The stranger gasps as I stride in. Flashing my badge at her gets her to shut up.

"Taylor?" I call out.

"There's nobody else in here," the woman says. "Another woman left a minute ago, though." She points to the far end of the bank of sinks.

There's another exit.

Motherfucker.

A minute ago. I take off at top speed, pushing through the door. I'm in another hallway running down the length of the building.

And there are exits at both ends. I roll the dice and bet on the back door, but when I step into the bright heat of the rear courtyard, it's empty.

The little witch ditched me.

[10]

TAYLOR

I probably don't have a lot of time. It won't take long for Detective Vasquez to realize I'm gone and lean on the resources of the D.C. police to find me.

I wasn't lying to Luke, exactly. My mother does—did—frequent Tabard Inn, and I wanted to find out when she'd been there last.

But that's not the real reason I picked this corner of D.C.

The Horus Group offices aren't far from here, and I need to confront Cole and his team. Let them know I won't be scared into covering up for my parents.

And if need be, I will threaten him with outing this despicable attack to his precious wife.

My sister.

Ms. Goody Two-Shoes herself.

Hailey won't like it if I use her name like that, but her husband may have tried to kill me by blowing up my car, so she can deal.

The St. Regis would have been even closer to their offices, but going there is a last resort. And there was less of a chance that I could find an employee who would recognize me enough to put on that little performance for the good detective.

One day, I will forget how to be a manipulative bitch.

Today is thankfully not that day.

I run full-tilt past the church behind Tabard Inn, dash across the street, and then cut down an alleyway between two buildings. But the lot across the way is blocked, fenced in for construction, so I'm forced to turn and walk down the sidewalk on M Street.

Sucking in a calming breath, I slow down and turn right—and slam right into a hard, unyielding chest, attached to a body that was definitely not there a second ago.

I gasp and look up.

Detective Vasquez.

Fuck.

"Hey, Luke," I say glibly. "That was fast."

"What the fuck?" He gets right in my face and shoves me back, into the shadows of the laneway and up against the wall. "Are you insane?"

The jury is really out on that point still. "I need to do something by myself. I wasn't going to ditch you forever."

"And how were you going to find me again?"

"You would find me. Like...you just did." Too fast. Damn it. "What did you do, completely violate my privacy and listen to me pee? Chase after me the second I was done?"

"No, you little brat. I gave you an inch of space, and you fled like a double-crosser."

"That doesn't explain how you found me."

"No," he ground out. "It doesn't. If you're keeping secrets, so am I. And no more of that *hey, Luke* bullshit. You can go back to calling me Detective like the mutant criminal you really are."

"That's rude."

"Yeah. I'm rude. Get the fuck used to it."

His grip on my shoulder is hard. Unyielding. I push against it, but he doesn't move. I'm pinned against the wall. Against my will, my body starts to react.

No.

But I can't help it. There's a twisted part of me that likes this. I've already noticed how good-looking he is. How nice he smells. And my asshole meter is strong.

Detective Vasquez is rude. Harsh. Domineering.

But he's not cruel.

That's key. I know, because I've been pinned against a wall by many a cruel man, and it doesn't feel anything like this.

More than a few of my fantasies involve being held against a wall by a man like Detective Vasquez. A good man. Rude, crude, harsh—and good.

Not now, Taylor.

Not ever.

But his face is right there. His full mouth, those perfect lips pushed up in an arrogant sneer. Why do arrogant sneers, fuelled by righteous indignation, have to be my undoing?

And again, that little voice in the back of my mind whispers that we could turn him. He's a good-looking man. We know how to play men.

We could play him and get laid in the process.

What's the harm?

"You could get yourself killed, Taylor." Luke drags me back into the very unsexy life-or-death conversation.

"I didn't."

"That's not the point." His grip tightens, and the hard press of his fingers against my upper arm is more effective than a caress on my breast or between my legs.

Heat rushes through me.

"We agreed this would be by my rules," he spits out angrily. "And then you tried to run. That's not going to work."

"Clearly." I don't bother to hide the edge in my voice. Let him think I'm a petulant brat. It's better than him knowing the truth. "I'll try harder next time."

"There will not be a next time."

"Or else?"

"Don't test me."

"Sorry, that's just how I roll."

"Fuck, Taylor. Do you have a death wish?"

"I don't know." Three little whispered words.

His eyes go wide.

Fuck.

The next thing I hear is his hand smacking the wall beside my head, and he brings his face—that mouth—right up against mine. "You're hiding too much from me," he snarls. "Too fucking much. I'm done playing in the dark, you hear me? Tell me what the hell is going on. Tell me why you're here. Why did we have to come to Washington?"

"I told you." I take as much of a breath as I can manage. There's an ugly lump in my throat. "I needed to talk to my sister and find out what she knows. She's not wrapped up in anything. I promise."

"This isn't where your sister lives."

"It's where her husband works."

"Who's her husband?"

"His name is Cole Parker. He's a crisis management expert."

"Jesus Christ, Taylor." He lets go of me and paces backward. His face is still twisted in anger. "That's what this is about? You tricked me to follow you just so you could start to cover everything up?"

"What? No!"

"I've read your father's file. Cole Parker is all over his earlier investigations. That guy is a pro at making things disappear. But you are wrong if you think that will keep you safe. Someone wants you to do this. They want you running scared. You get that? We played right into their hands. Maybe he planted that device. Did you ever think of that?"

"Why do you think I'm here?" I jut my chin at him. "I'm not stupid. That occurred to me the second you sat me down in that interrogation room. Who would want me to be scared? Cole, a thousand percent. That's. Why. I'm. Here."

[11]

LUKE

SHE SERIOUSLY PLANNED to walk into the lion's den herself. "And then what was your plan? Confront someone who wanted to kill you? Assume that a former Navy SEAL would just go, oops, my bad, so sorry?"

"If it was Cole, he didn't want to kill me." She looks me straight in the eye. None of the affected personality before.

I believe her, or at least, I believe that she believes herself. "That's a dangerous gamble."

"Wouldn't be the first, won't be the last. I know what I'm doing, Detective Vasquez." She trips over my name.

Hey, Luke.

The breathy, lippy response is still rocketing around in my brain. Like, oh, you caught me, ha-ha.

I'm playing with fire here. I can feel it, even if I can't see it. "The problem is, I don't know what you're doing. That needs to stop."

Slowly, she nods. "Okay. You can come with me."

Like there was any other option. "And what's the plan? The real plan this time. Not some cover story that allows you to abandon me, the person who is going to fucking keep you alive."

"We're going to The Horus Group. They're a crisis management firm that has worked for my family before. They're ruthless. Ex-cops, ex-special forces. You'll get along great with them."

"You don't like them."

She smiles, and it's sad. "I don't like anyone in this town. It's not personal."

I think it is completely personal, and when we're done with this ridiculous exploratory mission, I'm going to poke her hard in that wound and see what slides out. "And we're going to straight up ask them what they want with you?"

"Pretty much."

It's not the worst plan. "I'd like to give the D.C. police a heads up that I'm doing this. Questioning people out of jurisdiction and all that."

She screws up her face and nods.

I keep her pinned against the wall while I place a call to the contact Captain Woods gave me yesterday—just in case.

"Detective Kendra Browning," the woman answers.

"Detective, my name is Luke Vasquez, LAPD." I give her my badge number. "I'm in D.C. for the day, strictly on background, and something has come up where I'm going to be introducing myself as a cop and asking some questions. I wanted to let you know first."

There's a pause as she looks me up. "Okay, Detective. Shoot."

I give her the brief rundown of the car bomb yesterday, and the complicating factor of the Dashford Reid family connections. "So I'm going to a crisis management firm on K Street, and if you want to come with me, I'll understand. No intent to ruffle any feathers here."

This time the pause is longer. "The Horus Group?"

"Yeah. You know them? Anything I should be aware of?"

She laughs. "You can do this one alone, Detective. Full disclosure: my ex-husband is one of the principals there. Don't expect to get anything from them. But if you have any questions after, feel free to reach out again."

"Will do." I disconnect the call and give Taylor a hard look. "One of the Horus Group guys was married to a local cop?"

She shrugs. "I don't keep a spreadsheet on who's fucked who, Detective."

Yeah, I've noticed. "Let's start keeping track of these things, princess. Now, take me into the lion's den."

———

When Taylor announces herself at the locked entrance to the crisis management firm, we're immediately buzzed in.

The elevator indicates that the offices take up two floors. We get off at the first one.

There's a large man waiting in the middle of reception. I'm six foot three, and he looks like he's about the same, but he easily has twenty pounds of muscles on me, and I can hold my own at the gym. More than.

This guy is a tank.

"Taylor," he says, his voice full of barely contained fury.

She doesn't seem bothered in the least. "Cole. I missed your wedding."

"You weren't invited."

I step between them and hold out my hand. "Detective Luke Vasquez. We're here on official business, if you don't mind me breaking up this family reunion."

He does his best to crush my fingers. I give back as good as I get. He grunts and lets go then leads us into a conference room.

"You armed?" he asks me once we're alone.

"No." I look him over. I can't see a holster. "Are you?"

"No."

Great. This is going great so far. "Mr. Parker, yesterday afternoon Ms. Reid's car was destroyed by a car bomb."

"Here?" He turns his intense stare to his sister-in-law. "Are you back?"

I answer him. "No. I'm an LAPD detective. The explosive was set at her place of employment in Northeast L.A.. I was sent there to follow up on a bogus claim of Ms. Reid dealing drugs out of the back of her car. We've determined that was a false report, which raises the question of who would want to smear her reputation?"

"And you're looking at me? On the other side of the country?"

"You have considerable resources. You've done worse to detract from scandal, to derail investigations into significant crimes."

"I don't do shit like that anymore. As for the resources, most of the people Taylor here has pissed off over the years have a more significant reach than I might."

"How many of them have demolitions experts on staff?"

"Lots." He's not fazed by my questions. "We didn't do this."

"Do you have any associates in California right now?"

There's a long pause before he answers. "No," he says finally.

"That took you a while to consider."

"I was weighing the pros and cons of being helpful in another way."

"And what did you settle on?"

"Still unsure." He rubs his stubble-covered jaw. "What's your deal, Taylor? Bringing a cop here to accuse me of something?"

"I didn't bring him," she says smoothly. "He followed me. Trust me, I didn't want to air this out in front of him."

I spread my hands wide. "Hey, I'm right here. And I'm not the enemy."

Cole's eyebrows hit the roof. "You don't know much about her family, do you?"

"I know enough about her to know she's not fond of her family."

"Really?" He smirks. "That's new."

"And I understand you work for them."

"Worked. Past tense. Taylor's out of the loop on that score."

"And now it's my turn to say, *hey, I'm right here.*" Taylor snaps her fingers. "It's not *new* that I want nothing to do with my parents. I left D.C. three years ago because I knew I needed to be somewhere else. I've stayed away, and now something has happened that I am genuinely in the dark about, because I stayed away. So give me some credit, Cole. I came here knowing you would be adversarial. Knowing you wouldn't trust me. But I needed to look you in the eye and ask you if you tried to send me a nasty message yesterday on behalf of...who ever. Or even just yourself, because you can be that evil."

He glares at her. "It wasn't me. You think Hailey would let me live if I did that to you?"

"She hates me."

"She hates you because she loves you, and you hurt her. Repeatedly. But she wouldn't ever want to see you harmed. If there's anyone in your family who is that twisted, we both know it's your mother. Have you asked mommy dearest where she was yesterday?"

Mommy dearest. I had the same fleeting thought on the plane overnight, and discarded it. Now my gut twists hard.

It wouldn't be the first time I'd seen a parent hurt a child, but it's never easy to go down that line of investigation. Nobody wants to come to that conclusion. Especially not Taylor. She's gone white.

"That's offside, Cole."

"Is it? You know all sorts of sordid details about PRISM. Maybe she wants to keep you quiet, given that the Feds have shut down your trust funds."

"How did Hailey even notice? She doesn't touch hers."

"She didn't notice. She doesn't care. You should take a page from her book."

I need them to back up a step to *all sorts of sordid details about PRISM*, as in, what the fuck is PRISM, and just exactly how sordid are we talking?

But now we're on the topic of Hailey, apparently, and that's more important to both of them.

"How can I take a page from her book when she won't talk to me?"

"Suddenly you care about that? If you showed up here just to lean on your sister when—"

Another man appears in the doorway. He has a sleeping toddler strapped to his chest, which makes me do a double-take.

"Whoa, guys, keep it down." He points to the snoozing body attached to him. "Nap time."

"Wilson?" Now Taylor's doing a double-take, too. "Is that...yours?"

"Yeah. What the hell are you doing back here? I thought we agreed California was healthier for you in every way."

"We did." She turns to me. "Luke, this is Wilson Carter, the resident hacker, and the only member of the Horus Group who I actually like."

"Luke Vasquez, LAPD." I shake his hand. He doesn't try to murder my knuckles, so I like him more than Cole already.

"Interesting. When did Taylor start dating a cop?"

"This isn't a social call. I'm here because someone planted a bomb in Ms. Reid's car yesterday and nearly killed us both."

His sharp features break into a pleased expression. "And you think Cole did it? That's fun."

"Not fun," his colleague growls. "A pain in the ass."

"Yeah. Exactly. Fun." The bundle on his chest squirms and lets out a frustrated cry. "Well, fun for me, anyway. Come on, little bug. Let's get you some milk."

He leaves, and Taylor looks at Cole. "Wilson has a baby?"

"You've missed a lot."

"No kidding. I didn't even know that he had sex."

Cole gives her a disapproving look.

She just shrugs. "Okay, well, I'm going to leave the two of you to talk about...whatever, and I'm going to follow that adorable baby."

Cole's look gets worse.

"What? I like children."

"For brunch, with a nice chianti."

She growls and turns on her heel.

I pull out my phone and double-check that the GPS tracker I stuck on her is still working. It is. Good. I don't think she's going to run again, but just in case, I'll find her.

"So," I say, turning to the ex-commando turned Washington fixer. "I take it you didn't try to kill her."

"No."

"Scare her?"

"No."

"And PRISM is what?"

"PRISM is the **P**roject **R**esponsible for **I**nternational **S**ecurity **M**easures. An extra-governmental organization with unlimited funds and shadowy purpose."

And we've taken a left turn into some James Bond shit. "You're shitting me."

"I wish I was. Amelia Dashford Reid is a major principal

player in it, and they've invested heavily in America First. They got Victor Best elected president."

"He's a Democrat," I say dumbly. Though I know as well as anyone else that means nothing. He's also a billionaire who cares more about money than what's right or wrong. I voted for his Republican opponent, but she didn't have a chance in hell of winning California anyway.

Cole shrugs. "Everything has changed."

I'm aware of the political upheaval in this country.

I wasn't aware until this moment that it had anything to do with Taylor Dashford Reid, resident of Glendale, California for the last three years.

"So what does Taylor know that makes her a liability to her mother?"

"That's for her to tell you. Or not. To be honest, Detective, I'd assume that she'll pick not. The secrets she knows could get her killed if she's not careful."

No. That's not fucking acceptable. "I don't like anything about this."

"That makes two of us."

"You don't seem like you'd be heartbroken if anything happened to her."

"We have a history. Taylor does what Taylor needs to do for her own reasons, but she's trampled on her family in the past."

"You don't trust her."

He laughs. "That's an understatement."

I pull a card from my wallet. "Well, I do trust her. She's the victim of a violent crime, and I'm going to get to the bottom of it and arrest whoever is responsible. I won't hesitate to charge anyone who stands in the way of justice, either."

"Good luck with that."

"I don't need luck, thanks. I'll do my job." I hand over the card. "If you think of anything that maybe slipped your mind today, anything you think I should know, don't hesitate to get in touch."

I follow the sounds of a cooing baby and the corresponding laughing woman around the corner, where I find Taylor in a hacker's paradise. A dark office, lined with computer screens.

And the one thing that doesn't fit: a sweet, fat little toddler who shrieks and pulls her dad's hair.

"While I was in social hiding, Wilson went and met himself a beautiful woman and made a beautiful baby," Taylor says, beaming at me. "It's almost enough to make me believe in true love."

"Liar," Wilson says affectionately.

My Alice-through-the-looking-glass dysphoria is getting stronger by the second. "What is going on?"

Taylor makes a face, but then looks appropriately chastened —an act, no doubt. "Just catching up."

"We can get down to work, for sure." Wilson grabbed a puffy cracker from a package on his desk and gave it to the little girl. "What exactly do you guys want to know?"

Nope, we can't do this. I glance at the bank of screens. *A hacker.* "Nothing. None of this is legal, and all of it will be fruit of the poisoned tree if you tell me literally anything, so we're going to get going now."

Wilson shrugs. "Your choice man. But that's no fun."

"Pointing out that he's no fun will have zero effect," Taylor says pertly. "Or I'd have tried it sooner."

"Funny," I mutter, trying not to look at the dialog box open on the screen behind her. What could I ask him to look up? "Can we please leave?"

"Not yet." She hesitates. "I do want to ask Wilson a favor, though, so maybe you should step outside."

"No favors, Princess. Information by the book, without persuasion, or not at all."

"A personal request, not related to the thing that...happened."

I hesitate, but it's not my place to tell her she can't have a conversation with a friend. Even a hacker friend.

Nodding, I step into the hall and check my messages for what feels like the fiftieth time in the last twenty-four hours.

I need a shower and a break from my phone, but both of those things are probably on the far side of a flight back to the west coast.

Nothing new from L.A., so I start to make some free form notes on what I've learned so far. *More complicated than it all looks* is the punch line. An incestuous world where people are horrible to each other and get away with it because of power and privilege.

Not that different from Hollywood.

Just colder in the winter and more humid in the summer.

"I'm ready," Taylor announces.

I turn around and take her in. She looks tired. "What's next?"

Her mouth pinches in, uncomfortably. This is a new side to her. "We should go see my mother, I suppose."

"Sounds good." It doesn't. It sounds bad. I need to make a decision, fast, about how I can leave Taylor alone and do this next round of investigating on my own.

But it proves a moot point.

When we get back to the car, I put a call in to Kendra Browning, and she tells me as a matter of fact, Amelia Dashford Reid lawyered up earlier today. They were working on an immunity deal with the FBI, and there wouldn't be any questioning her without her attorneys for any reason—not unless I went through the proper channels.

When I hang up, we sit in the quiet of the car interior for a moment.

"So, hypothetically speaking," I finally start. "If your mother wanted to scare you into keeping her secrets, how would she arrange for a bomb to be planted in your car?"

Taylor doesn't say anything.

Of course she doesn't. I'm a monster who just suggested her mother is a monster. An extra-monster. It appears the monster-status was already known.

"Does she have associates?"

"She must." A whisper.

"It might be time to make that list of other people who would have a reason to hurt you," I say quietly. "Because right now..."

"She's the most obvious suspect. I get that." She takes a deep breath. "What I told you yesterday about not wanting to cover for my father? It goes doubly for my mother. There's no love lost there."

"Are you scared?"

"I don't know how to answer that. I grew up in chaos. I grew up scared. I don't know what it would be like to not be terrified that my life is going to crumble, any second, and probably by my own doing."

"This was not your own doing."

"No?" She turns and looks out the window. "Everything is connected, Detective. I got off relatively easy when I left here three years ago. Did my damage and ran."

"Tell me about that damage."

She makes a face. "Can we go and get some lunch first? I mean, it's going to take a while to walk you through it all."

I laugh. "Sure. How does takeout sound?"

"Probably revolting. Unless you don't mind salad, because I know a place."

That's more like it. I put the car in gear and steer into traffic once again.

———

She gives me directions to spot in Georgetown, where I run in and get her a custom order she rhymes off from memory. I get myself a chicken Caesar salad. Then we drive to a gravel parking lot along the Potomac, which spills out into a wide green space overlooking a boat dock.

"This is nice," I say.

"Nice enough to distract you from wanting to know all the..."

"Sordid details? Sadly, no."

"Damn." She picks at her salad. Then she takes a deep breath. "I came here once on a date."

I wait. She could be killing time, but I don't think so.

"That's what he called it. That's what my mother called it. I was sixteen, and he was a senator. We came here and went for a walk, which sounds perfectly normal—" She cuts herself off.

Because no, it really doesn't. My neck is getting hot already, and she's barely begun.

"*Seemed* more normal to me. I liked him more than the others."

The others. Lunch was a mistake. But Taylor keeps picking away at her salad, hunting for the blueberries.

"He was the first one I got dirt on, though. The others...they were warm-ups. A test, to see just how pliable I could be."

"How young were you when..."

"Fourteen. My mother caught me with a boy. I don't know what that conversation should have gone like, but it didn't resemble anything like I'd seen on TV or read in a book. It was... I knew it was weird. She seemed proud of me. She said—and I'll never forget this—'I wasn't sure if you'd be like me. But I'm glad you are. It'll take you far.' And I still don't know what she meant by that, because it hasn't."

"Cole told me that she's involved in high-level politics."

"Is that how he put it?" Her lips twist into an ugly, sad frown. "She inherited a seat at the most powerful table in the world. Well, inherited isn't quite the right word, because her father is still alive. But he groomed her for it, and I think she would have groomed me for it, too, if I hadn't fucked everything up."

The Blow Job Princess.

"What did you do?"

"You know." She laughs, sharp and hollow. A familiar sound already, after barely a day. "Everyone knows. You asked me about it so politely, like I'd accidentally slept with a powerful man, and oops, did his wife maybe resents me for that. There was no accident there. And if she does, so be it, because it was my out and I took it."

It's shockingly callous and painfully real at the same time. "That was..."

"My cruel and desperate attempt to destroy my future reputation. Yes."

I stare out at the river, then down to my salad, and finally back at her. The weird day has gotten weirder. "Well," I finally say. "It seems to have worked."

She makes a rueful face. "Yeah."

"I'm not really sure how I take this back to the captain as motive for attempted murder."

"I remember the first time I told my therapist in Los Angeles about all of this. She'd seen it play out on television and still couldn't believe it. So... I don't expect anyone to be held accountable for the car bomb if it was my mother."

"Or your grandfather?"

"He's not..." She drifts off, then stabs a big forkful of salad and eats it. "My grandfather is an alcoholic. No excuse for his behavior, but he's pretty incapable of making grand plans. Or any plan other than getting to mid-afternoon. I think he and my mother are locked in a mutually-assured destruction routine that's more depraved than I ever want to say out loud."

I'm starting to put the picture together. "Did he ever abuse you?"

"No. He was never interested in me like that. Her? Yes. They still have an inappropriate relationship. But I wasn't his type. Thank God for that. So I was just farmed out to his friends and business acquaintances."

My phone vibrates, interrupting us. Then it goes again, and she waves her fork at my hip. "Answer it if it's important. Have we dealt with enough heavy stuff for now?"

More than enough, and probably not nearly enough at the same time. I pull it out and chuckle as I read the screen. "Huh. It's your sister."

She jerks her head back in surprise. "Hailey?"

"No." I turn the screen around she can read it. "Your family moves fast."

I watch as she reads the messages. Both of them.

Alison: OMG, this is Taylor's sister Ali! Her phone isn't on, and Cole gave me this number. Can you please tell her to call me ASAP?

Alison: Also whoever you are, you better take good care of her or I will find you.

Her eyes go wide.

I clear my throat. "Just to be clear, is she threatening a police officer?"

Taylor shakes her head, and then hesitates. "Only in the most literal sense."

"That's the worst sense." I grin.

Taylor smiles too, and that's nice to see. "She's harmless."

"I don't think that's true for any of you. Do you want me to send her a message back?"

"Can you tell her to fly here and rescue me from your evil clutches?"

"No."

"Then, in that case, send her a picture of me, so she knows I'm really fine."

I take her photo, then text it back.

Luke: Message received. Taylor is fine.

"I wouldn't say I'm fine." She's reading it over my shoulder, which I should discourage—but she can't see my other messages. But she just unloaded a lot of personal stuff, and after wanting to see Hailey and being rebuffed, this is a small comfort.

"In the literal sense?"

She giggles softly. "Fine. But Ali will know that's not my language."

That's just too bad. I change the subject. "Where does she live?"

"San Francisco. It's nice to be on the same coast—and away from our family."

"She's younger?"

"The youngest, yeah. She's married, too. And way smarter than me."

"You're smart."

She stands up and packs away the last of her salad. "Shut up."

I follow her, dumping my container in a garbage bin on the way. "Take the compliment, Reid."

She twists around, shooting me a weird look over her shoulder. "I'm sorry, I'm only programmed to accept compliments on my tits and ass."

The latter is right in front of me, and it's not appropriate for me to notice in the least. "I'm not going there."

She stops, turns, and puts her hands on her hips. "You don't like my tits?"

"Stop goading me just because you can't take a real compliment."

One corner of her mouth twists up. "Damn it, Detective Vasquez, why are you not more easily manipulated?"

"Years of training."

But I'm not the only one who's had years of training, and only a couple of years of de-programming. I can't be too rough with her.

Taylor Dashford Reid is a fucking survivor, but she's been through hell.

"Come on, Princess. Let's see if we can get on an earlier flight back to the west coast, and find you a safe place to stay for the next few days."

[12]

TAYLOR

LUKE'S PHONE goes off just as we arrive at the airport. He ignores it until he's returned the rental car, although it keeps vibrating.

I'm hoping it's more snarkiness from my little sister, but the way his face goes tight, his whole body tensing, I know it's not.

My stomach drops.

He curls his hand around my upper arm and propels me toward the terminal. "Let's go."

"What's wrong?"

"I'll tell you on the other side of security."

"What?" Panic rises in my chest, fast and furious. "Luke?"

"You're okay. Breathe." He's moving fast now, cutting across a lane of traffic. We dart past the minivan unloading passengers, then through the sliding doors and into the terminal. "There's the airline counter, come on."

He ignores the regular line and takes the empty queue for people who have rewards cards. That's the queue I would usually take, except that none of my cards currently work.

At the desk, he flashes his badge and slides his credit card across the counter. "Your next two tickets to L.A."

"I'll need ID from both of you," the clerk drones, like this is no big deal.

Maybe it's not. I dig out my wallet and hand over my driver's license.

Luke isn't even looking around, but he's aware. He's listening, he's thinking. As soon as she prints the tickets, he grabs my hand and drags me to security, flashing his badge again to get around the line.

I take off my shoes. While Luke is ducked down, doing the same, I surreptitiously check the pager Wilson gave me that I stashed in my bag when Luke went to get salads. No message there. Whatever has happened, he doesn't know about it.

Was it a mistake to trust him? Every fiber of my being tells me he wouldn't do anything, and yet...

Maybe I should get rid of the pager.

On the other hand, it may be the only heads up I get if everything goes sideways.

Resolutely, I zip up my bag and put it on the conveyor belt. Then I walk through the metal detector.

On the other side, I turn and watch Luke follow. His face is still tight.

"What's going on?" I demand once we've collected our belongings.

He leads me to a private corner then looks me right in the eye. "There was a threat. A letter. It was pinned to the front door of the safe house the FBI had picked out for you."

The bottom of my stomach falls out, and I want to collapse. I can feel my insides twisting like I might puke, but I press my hands against my chest, my mouth, willing myself to keep it together.

No.

"What kind of threat?"

He doesn't waver. Doesn't look away. "*If you don't come*

back to the fold, things will only get worse. I don't want to hurt you, Taylor, but this has to stop. Do you know what means?"

My brain screams. It's primal and silent and awful. No, I have no idea what that means. But I have my fears, and they're worse than I ever could have imagined.

Everything I did was for nothing.

Squeezing my eyes shut, I count to ten. Then twenty when my pulse doesn't come back down.

"Taylor," Luke murmurs. "It's okay. We're safe. We're going to get on a plane and get back to L.A. in one piece. I promise. And at the other end, we're going to have a police escort."

What good is a police escort when the enemy is invisible and two steps ahead of you, though?

[13]

LUKE

As she did on the way to Washington, Taylor sleeps on the flight back.

Not me.

I spend the next five hours watching in horror, via text message, as the FBI takes over a case they don't fucking deserve because they've clearly fucked this up since it was their fucking safe house that got leaked.

Woods: They have given me their assurances she will be safe.

Luke: I need to go on record stating that I don't believe that to be true.

Woods: I hear that. Get her back, and we'll figure it out.

I'm not sure what there is to figure out. I'm not handing her over to the Feds. Not after all I saw today in D.C.

Her tense relationship with Cole Parker.

Her middle sister's refusal to see her.

The accusation that she knows all sorts of things about her mother, and the way she reacted when Parker said that.

I'll need to debrief that carefully to the FBI, though, because they'll have the resources to question everyone involved, including Amelia Dashford Reid.

They can question her about it while she's trying to flip on the financial crimes charges.

They can take the case.

But they can't take my witness.

———

When we land, Agent Ferdinand is waiting at the gate. With a flash of his badge, we're taken out a back exit to a car waiting on the tarmac. Another generic sedan is right behind it.

Armed to the max, but almost certainly without a plan.

"I'd like a chance to debrief with your team before you whisk her off to parts unknown." I give him a tight smile. "Compare notes, so you've got a complete picture of what's going on."

"We can do that as we drive," Ferdinand says. He shows me a copy of the note left at the safe house. "We've shared this with your team already."

It's not an agreement, and my internal warning flags go way up.

I don't need to look at Taylor to know that she's on guard, too.

"Is it time I speak to my attorney?" She's staring past the car, at an airplane taxiing. She sounds bored. "This is all a bit...I'm not sure I understand what's going on. Definitely time for legal counsel. Don't you agree, Agent Ferdinand?" She turns her gaze to him and flicks her eyelids.

I didn't even know that was a thing that could be done, but I just saw it happen.

Imperious to the max.

Obnoxious to the max, too.

It works, though.

He sighs and opens the door for her. "To the station we go, then."

I go around to the other side and get in behind the driver. Ferdinand takes the front passenger seat and off we go with the other car trailing behind us.

I give the captain a heads up that we're coming in, but I don't go into any details. I don't tell her that Taylor is demanding to see a lawyer who I'm pretty sure doesn't exist. I don't need a paper trail on what might go down. It needs to be spontaneous.

Taylor doesn't look at me, doesn't acknowledge anyone in the car for the agonizing drive from the airport to the northeast part of the city. Maybe she's on the same page.

Maybe she'll turn that imperious, obnoxious gaze on me next.

Who the fuck knows.

As she says, all of this is definitely beyond my pay grade. But I don't care. I'm going to get to the bottom of this.

We pull into the underground garage and exit the car, the FBI agents flanking Taylor as she stalks ahead of me. Her purse is slung over her shoulder, but her suitcase has been abandoned in the car behind us.

That's not ideal.

Suddenly she stops and turns. "Can someone please bring my bag?" She looks somewhere above the head of Ferdinand, not giving him any space to say no. "I need to freshen up."

In the next moment, Ram Singh appears at the stairwell,

holding the door open, and Ms. Reid keeps going as if she knows this station like the back of her hand.

One of the federal agents goes back and collects her suitcase, and I breathe a little easier.

I'm impressed with Taylor right now. She's on the brink of being taken into what will amount to protective custody, and she's pushing hard against it. Being raised in chaos and privilege may have some advantages in times of crisis with law enforcement—a fact I can appreciate when I am not the law enforcement in question.

Captain Woods is waiting upstairs.

"Captain," Taylor says. "If we could speak a moment about calling my attorney..."

The captain pauses a split second, then she nods. "Right. Come with me. Gentlemen, the conference room is yours. I'll take that suitcase, thank you. Detective Vasquez, I'll leave it to you to give them a complete briefing."

The directive is clear. Whatever Taylor and I are playing at, I can't let it get in the way of the investigation.

A fine line to walk.

This would almost be more fun than going dancing if it didn't feel painfully out of control.

As soon as Luke and the FBI agents disappear, I sag. Just a little.

Captain Woods gives me a reassuring smile. "It's going to okay."

"Is it? Apparently, someone wants me dead."

"We're not going to let that happen." She leads me into her office. "You should know that Detective Vasquez was protesting the FBI's involvement all the way across the continent."

"Oh." That explains his insistence that we come here and not wherever they planned to take me.

"He didn't give you a plan to demand a lawyer?"

"Uh, no. That was all me. Ad-libbing."

"*Do* you want to call your attorney?"

"No." I sag even further. I'm tired. "I want to get some sleep that isn't squeezed into an economy seat on a plane that smells like feet."

The captain laughs gently. "Our hospitality is not up to your usual standards?"

"No offense, Captain, but I don't think Detective Vasquez could even imagine my standards."

She doesn't reply to that. "Would you like a drink?"

"Do you have sparkling water?"

"I have Coke and Diet Coke."

"Then no thank you."

She gives me a patient smile. "All right. So...what do you want now?"

"A do-over on life."

"That's not how this works, unfortunately."

"Do I need to go with the FBI?"

She opens her soda can and leans back in her chair. "No..." she finally says, drawing the word out. *Nooooooo.* Which I'm hoping means, it would be better if I did, but there may be a narrow legal loophole that allows me to give the FBI the finger. "But we have limited resources."

"I have cash. I can disappear."

"I definitely can't let you do that."

One of the other detectives, the white woman, appears in the doorway. The captain turns her attention there. "Yes, McBride?"

"Sorry to interrupt, Captain. You wanted to see this." She hands over a folder and gives me a warm smile. "You're back."

I sigh. "Yep."

The captain looks back and forth between us. "McBride, can you loiter near the briefing Vasquez is giving, and when he finishes, let him know I've taken Ms. Reid out to get some food. Be clear about that. That Ms. Reid and I have gone out for tacos."

My eyes go wide. I must look like a panicked cartoon character because Captain Woods winks at me.

"Don't worry. You're not going anywhere. You're going to stay right here, in my office, where you are safe. I'm going to get some food, and when the FBI cavalry arrives on my tail, I'll inform them they were mistaken in what they heard because, of course, I would never take a witness out for tacos. That would be ridiculous."

"Ridiculous," I repeat in a confused whisper.

"Very," she says with more confidence than I feel.

"And then what?"

"Ms. Reid, you are not a suspect here, and the LAPD has limited resources. What you and Detective Vasquez decide to do next, while I am getting tacos, is entirely up to you both. He's on vacation for the next two weeks. If at any point you would like the FBI to protect you, that option is available to you, I'm sure. But I understand you are a young woman with considerable resources of your own, and my detective seems to have his own reasons for backing you up in your concern with how the federal agents have handled this case so far. Best of luck."

We both stand up. "Thank you," I say, my heart pounding. "Thank you so much."

"Don't thank me, Ms. Reid. Thank Luke. He's got your back here." She pats me on the shoulder then gestures for me to have a seat. "This may take a while. Will you be okay if I turn out the lights?"

I nod and sink back into my chair.

She locks up some of her files then flips a switch, giving me one last smile as the room falls dark, and she pulls the door closed.

With a deep breath, I settle in to play the waiting game.

I'm just finishing up when McBride slides into the back of the conference room. "Sarah McBride," I say, introducing to her to the room. "One of our detectives."

"Don't let me interrupt," she says. "But if you want a taco order, the captain and Ms. Reid are heading out to grab some food."

"They're doing *what*?" Ferdinand leaps to his feet.

My eyebrows hit the roof.

"I think Ms. Reid said something about needing fresh air." Sarah gives him an innocent look of alarm. "You could probably text her if you want some, too."

"Is she crazy?" He whirls on me. "What if Taylor runs for it?"

Then I'll track her down if she's still got my GPS tracker on her bag.

But my captain is the opposite of crazy. I spread my hands wide. "You got me. That doesn't sound like the captain, though. If Ms. Reid has walked, it's on her. Not the LAPD."

Ferdinand scowls at McBride. "When did they leave?"

"Just a few minutes ago." She points to the door. "Why?"

The Feds all head out the door as one monolithic group of suits and frustrated scowls.

Ferdinand stops in front of me and shakes his head. "You guys need to work with us here if you want us to catch this guy."

"Of course," I say smoothly. "You'll give me a call when your lab is ready to walk me through the evidence? I'm going on vacation, but I'm not leaving the city. I'll come in any time."

"Good." He scowls again. "We'll be in touch."

I wait until they're out of sight, then pull out my phone.

I do a double-take and laugh under my breath when I see where the GPS tracking app lights up Taylor's location. Ducking out into the unit space, I double-check to make sure the Feds have left.

First I go to the locker where I left my Glock before we went to D.C. It feels good to put on my shoulder holster again.

Then I crack open the door to the captain's dark office.

"Hey," I say quietly.

Taylor doesn't open her eyes. "This was your plan, right?"

"Sort of. I think the captain ran with it."

"Hmm." She cracks one eyelid open and looks over at me. "So now what?"

"We get the hell out of here."

She doesn't move.

"Taylor, time might be of the essence since you aren't really getting tacos with my boss. Window of opportunity here. Let's seize it."

She has a white-knuckle grip on her bag. "You understand this is the stuff that dark thrillers are written about? Scruffy cop stalks you, sets a bomb, writes a threatening note, says he needs to protect you, and takes you off to parts unknown where he will chop your body into a thousand pieces and feed you to his pet swordfish."

"Hey, whoa, I am *not* scruffy."

"You're not denying the pet swordfish, Detective Vasquez."

I grin. I can't help it. She's funny when she's staring danger in the face. "I want to keep you safe. I promise I'm not going to chop you into pieces. And I think I like it better when you call me Luke. So what do you say? Want to do something reckless with me?"

"Will it keep me alive?"

"That's the plan."

"Then I'm in."

———

"What just happened?" Taylor doesn't ask the question until we're up in the canyons, almost at my house.

For years, I lived closer to San Bernardino, where a lot of cops live. Out in the suburbs, away from where we work.

But two years ago I grabbed a sweet opportunity to move back into the city. A two-bedroom foreclosure that had stood empty for a couple of years, and needed a shit ton of TLC.

Fixing it up replaced going to the gym, and now it's a decent home.

It's also pretty off the grid because my official address is still the place I own out in the suburbs. That I rent out.

This one, I bought through a numbered corporation, which at the time gave me a chuckle, because who the fuck am I to play with shit like that?

Turns out my real estate lawyer was smart, and now I know this is a safe place to bring Taylor. At least for the night. At least to let her get some sleep.

I'm not kidding myself into thinking the Feds won't ever check me out, but right now, they're hunting for Taylor elsewhere.

Rodeo Drive, hopefully.

"My boss just bought you a night of sleep without federal agents watching you, that's what."

"Just one night?"

I turn onto my street and tap the remote button for my garage to open. "Let's play that by ear. If you're going to stay here, you're going to have to follow my rules. For real this time. No more running away. No more diva acts."

"If I say okay, are you going to believe me?"

That gets a half-smile. "I don't know. Try me."

She doesn't say anything. I park then go around to the trunk to grab her suitcase. She's still sitting in the front seat like she might just go to sleep there.

"Hey, Princess. Out of the car. You can deliberate on whether or not you want to trust me inside."

She gets out and rolls her eyes for effect.

I'd like to spank the brat right out of her.

It's a sudden, brutal thought. Unbidden and unwelcome. My throat goes tight as I picture what it might be like to bring her smart mouth to a breathy, happy pause. Make her focus her remarkable energy elsewhere.

Oh, Princess. If only we'd met under different circumstances.

I shove that thought away and let us into the house through the interior garage door then punch in my security code into the keypad on the wall.

Maybe I don't shove the thought far enough down, though, because when I catch her looking askance at my living room—my house, that I renovated with my bare fucking hands—the nickname rolls off my tongue again, and this time, it's deliberate. "How do you like your new digs, Princess?"

"Stop calling me that. You want me to call you Luke, you can call me Taylor. Or Ms. Reid, I like that."

"Deal. Now stop sneering at my house."

She whips around, her mouth dropping open. "Yours?"

"Yes, my house. Where did you think I was taking you?"

"I...don't know." She sighs. "My brain stopped working like ten hours ago."

"Well, nobody knows I live here. So it's pretty damn secure."

She worries her lip between her teeth. "I'm sorry. Your house is lovely."

That's better. And if things were different, I would reward her for being polite.

Things are not different.

She wanders around my living room. "You believed me that the federal government wasn't to be trusted?"

"I was on the fence before the threatening note. As soon as I got word of that, I knew you weren't safe unless nobody knew where you were. Too many potential leaks. Too many conflicting priorities. Too many cases, period. You're my only case right now, Taylor."

"Aww, I feel so special." She takes a deep breath and lightens her tone. "This place is nice. And clean."

"High praise from someone who thinks I'm scruffy."

"It was more of an evocative image than an accurate description." She hesitates a beat. "Of course you aren't scruffy."

I was trying to lighten the mood, but given the circumstances, maybe that's impossible. "This isn't a dark thriller, Taylor."

"I hope not."

"Whoever it is, and whatever they want to achieve, they will be caught. As much as I don't trust the leak on the FBI team—or whoever the leak is—I do trust the system. The process."

"The FBI doesn't always get their man," she says darkly. "Sometimes people get away with awful things."

I can't tell her she's wrong. She's not.

She's lived it.

"That can be tomorrow's big question, okay? How about I show you your room so you can get some sleep."

She nods, and I lead her up the stairs. The guest room is at the back of the house, overlooking the pool. It's bachelor basic. The bed doesn't even have a headboard, because I've never had a guest stay here until now.

"Here you go. Nobody's slept on this bed in a couple of years. It used to be mine, and when I moved here, I got a new bed, so...you're lucky I've got it. I don't entertain a lot."

"You don't say." She looks around the spartan space then drops her bag on the bed. I move in after her and set her suitcase against the wall.

When I turn around again, she's holding the pill bottle she got from the hospital. Staring at it. Rolling it back and forth in her palm.

"Those the sleeping pills they prescribed?"

"Yeah."

"You don't have to take them. You slept pretty well without them on the plane."

Her head jerks up. "Yeah. I know."

"You've been through a lot in the last two days."

A weak laugh. Then a hard, jerking nod. "Yeah."

"On the other hand, sleep is good, and if they'll help..."

She takes a deep, ragged breath. "Sleep is where the mess in my brain can roam freely, though."

I frown. "Do you have nightmares?"

A hesitation, then another nod. This one is nervous and little. "Yeah."

"That's okay. I'm here, just down the hall. I promise I won't ever be gone while you're asleep. And those may help."

"Or they might trap me in the nightmare, and I won't be able to wake up," she whispers.

Fuck. "That sounds terrifying."

"Yeah." She breathes in and exhales slowly. "The only way to know is to try them."

But she doesn't move.

"Come here," I say, reaching for her.

"What?" Her eyes go wide.

Jesus, has this woman never been hugged before? I hold my arms open. "It's called a hug, Taylor. It's a common way for one human being to comfort another. They feel good."

"I—" She stutters to a stop. "Oh."

"If you don't want one, that's—"

"Sorry," she mutters softly. "I'm a bit of a mess."

I drop my arms. "No, I'm the one who should be sorry. Nevermind me. Can I get you a glass of water for those pills? If you decide to take them."

"Sure."

I jog back downstairs and run the tap, hoping the sound of the water will drown out my groan of stupidity.

A hug? What the fuck was I thinking?

I'm not.

I need to realize I'm tired, too.

After filling a glass for her, I double-check the locks, the security system, and the camera feeds that go to my phone.

We're all locked up tight for the night.

And when I get upstairs, Taylor is stretched out on top of her blanket, fast asleep.

I set the glass on the bedside table, turn out her light, and leave the door ajar before going to my own room.

I DON'T HAVE A NIGHTMARE. I do have a panicky freakout for a second when I wake up, and I don't know where I am—and when I do remember. It's all very awful for a gross second before relief slides in. Limited, cautious relief.

I don't know what's going to happen next.

I don't know who to trust. But I passed out in Luke's house and he didn't hurt me, so that's something.

First order of business is having a shower. I feel disgusting.

I tiptoe out onto the landing. Downstairs, I hear Luke moving around in the kitchen. His house is small; he can probably hear me, too.

"Morning," I call down.

He appears at the bottom of the stairs. He's wearing jeans and a t-shirt. Bare feet. And a concerned expression. "Hey. How'd you sleep?"

No idea. So I don't answer. "Can I take a shower?"

"Sure. There are fresh towels in there."

I go back to the room I slept in and unzip my suitcase. Toiletries, new clothes. Maybe I can burn the ones I've worn for the last thirty-six hours.

Gross.

I stomp into the bathroom. So much for sleep being all that I needed to feel steady on my feet again. I'm angry, I realize. And then, with a start, other feelings pile in hard.

Grief has so many layers.

Tears are sliding down my face as I turn on the water. The part of my brain that is always a judgmental bitch notices how nice the bathroom is. Luke's house is tiny, and his guest room has the decor of a prison cell, but this room is completely modern. And he didn't buy most of these fixtures at a discount home store, either.

Count all the fancy shit, my brain screams. I try to guess at the cost of the mosaic tile, the marble floor, the European toilet. But I don't get to the tub before the tears take over, blinding me, and I sink to my knees, letting my sorrow become one with the steamy spray.

It takes ages for the silent sobs to abate. It occurs to me that Luke might worry and might come up and check on me. But I can't bring myself to stand, to pretend I'm fine.

I'm not.

He doesn't bother me though, and finally, the well of sadness runs dry. That's the thing about sadness. If you sit with it long enough—or lie in a steamy shower with it—eventually it morphs into something manageable. Smaller, tighter, put-in-your-pocket-able.

If you fight against it, that's when the sadness gets ugly. Too big, too scary to get on with your day.

It's okay to be sad. It's a mantra I tell peer counseling clients all the time. A lesson that took me a long time to learn.

My problem is that I'm not a nice sad person.

I'm not a nice person at all. I'm prickly and picky and generally high-maintenance.

Everyone is different. None of us are better or worse than others. Another mantra I tell people.

But this one isn't a lesson I've been able to internalize. I am definitely worse than others, and that's just my burden to bear.

I take my time once I'm out of the shower. Each step of putting myself back together is a piece of self-care. Moisturizing my face, braiding my hair, putting on clean clothes.

By the time I get downstairs, I feel nearly human.

Luke is on his phone, but he gestures at the kitchen, where I find coffee. *Yes.*

"Can I make you some breakfast?" he asks when he joins me a minute later.

"I'm not hungry."

"Okay." He sets his phone on the counter. "I just got an update from the captain. She got read the riot act last night, but stood her ground that the best place for you to be right now is somewhere *nobody* knows."

"So you're nobody?"

"Close enough." He taps his fingers on the counter. "The deal here is that both of us are going to keep our comings and goings to a minimum. Nobody knows I own this place, but I can't guarantee I won't be followed back from the station."

"Are you going to work?"

"Not today. But the FBI lab is almost done with our forensic evidence, and I'm going to want to be there when they get walked through what the techs have found."

"They'll allow that?"

"Sure. They don't like that we lost you, but that risk is on us, and we need to have a permanently functional working relationship between local and federal law enforcement. Right now there are at least three quiet investigations of LAPD wrongdoing by the FBI, and probably one going back the other way."

My mouth falls open. "No way."

"Way. Doesn't mean they won't be watching me like a hawk, though. They're not going to trust me any further than they can throw me."

I don't know why I'm shocked. Nothing should shock me now. But I really thought the dysfunctional world I grew up in was the worst, exceptionally terrible, and I'd gotten away from it.

Turns out, no so much.

"Maybe I should actually go somewhere on my own. So you don't need to lie to them."

"Get that thought out of your head."

"But you said—"

"I will find you."

"Like you did in Washington?"

"Yes, like—" He cuts himself off.

Tension lights up the space between us. "Wait. How *did* you—"

He moves in, lightning fast. Blocking me from moving, even though he isn't touching me. One of his hands presses against the cabinet beside my head, the other arm is out wide. A human barricade.

"Luke?"

"I did what I needed to do to keep you safe."

"You put a tracker on me. Where is it?"

"Your wallet."

"You fucking asshole."

"You ran away at the first fucking opportunity."

"And I was fine."

"Only because the asshole who wants you dead didn't know that you'd left the fucking state."

"But why didn't they?" My pulse is racing. "The FBI knew we were going to D.C."

Luke's eyes narrow.

"I'm not an idiot," I tell him. I'm so fired up right now. Jesus, how did they all miss that fact? "You should ask him that. And get off my fucking back until you have more information."

"You're a brat. You know that?"

"Excuse me?" I push against his chest, and he takes a step back. Now there's plenty of space between us again, and I fill with all my pent up feelings. "My life has completely exploded. Literally! In front of you! And I don't really care if you don't like me, *Detective Vasquez*. I'm doing the best I fucking can with the crappy cards that I have been dealt."

"I didn't say I don't like you, *Taylor*. I said you're a brat."

"And let me guess, you think I need a spanking? Go fuck yourself, Detective. You want me to get on my knees and give you an appreciative blowjob? Never going to happen. Never. Not in a million—"

"Stop it," he growls. "I don't want sexual favors from you."

"No? That would be a first." I step into his personal space. Now it's my turn to crowd him. "You know my past. You know what I'm capable of. You telling me you haven't thought about it?"

His jaw flexes, and he spreads his arms wide. "Bring it on, princess. Unload."

"I'm good," I whisper. "Glad to get all of our secrets aired like this. *Stalker*."

He laughs. "That's a good one. You're the queen of secrets, aren't you?"

"You don't have any right to my secrets," I hiss.

And then I hear myself. I'm hissing at him, picking a fight for no good reason.

With a gasp, I step back.

Luke follows, reaching for me. His hands curve around my biceps, then slide down my arms, until he's holding my hands. "Come here. It's okay."

"What? Are you going to try to hug me again? I'm so broken and angry I can't even be hugged."

"Enough," he says, his voice cracking now in anger. "Stop. That's enough."

"Is it?" I shake my head. "I don't know where the line is, Detective. Sorry. But I guess you're right about me. I guess I'm just—"

He lets go of my hand and hauls me close, one arm wrapping around me, the other hand clapping over my mouth.

Literally stopping the verbal assault that I cannot put a lid on my self.

So I lick him. I slide my tongue between his fingers, slicking his hand, and being as crude and lewd as I once was.

[17]

LUKE

SHE GOT under my skin with the spanking comment. That hit a little too close to home. But right now I don't want to paddle Taylor. Not at all.

I want to show her some basic human kindness. And I don't want her to say anything awful about herself.

God *damn* she's making it difficult to be nice her.

She glowers at me, her eyes bright and spiteful, as I refuse to move my hand.

But I see what she's doing. Taylor is testing all of my boundaries. Testing to make sure I'll still be on her side, no matter what. No matter how rude she is and no matter what buttons she tries to push.

Slowly, without breaking eye contact, I shift my hand from covering her mouth to cupping her face. "You done?"

"You did not just cover my mouth like that," she spits out.

Clearly not done.

I lean in, pushing my forehead against hers. "Taylor, Taylor, Tay—"

Her mouth collides with mine, shutting me up with a kiss

that knocks me back a step. I'm holding on to her, so she follows, and we slam into the wall behind me.

She. Just. Fucking. *Kissed*. Me.

I stare down at her face. Bright eyes, wide wet mouth. Shock is written all over her expression. I know the fucking feeling.

"Taylor," I whisper again, but this time my voice is rough and unsteady. She pushes up again until her lips are against mine.

Soft.

Wet.

I demand the next kiss, and it's so fucking wrong and so fucking good at the same time.

She tastes *right*. Like her mouth is supposed to be this soft, this responsive, this perfectly matched for mine. Everything else fades into a fuzzy blur. We're nothing but lips and tongues and hot, breathless pants as we jockey back and forth for more, deeper, harder.

"Luke," she whispers.

Hey, Luke.

Fuck.

"We can't do this." A lie. A fucking weak string of noises that mean nothing, because she's already on me again.

When we wrench apart, she stares at me.

I stare right back. The taste of her is still on my tongue.

And the walls go up. She glares at me. "What the hell was that?"

I hear the rudeness. But I also still hear the way she said my name. *Luke.*

Danger, danger.

I shake my head. "Nothing."

She touches her mouth. Her glorious, fuck-me-I'm-so-dead mouth. "You kissed me."

She kissed me first. But she's free to do that, and I am *not*. I stick with clarifying that it was a two-way kiss. "You kissed me back."

Pacing into the living room, she shakes her head. "This cannot happen."

I follow. "That's supposed to be my line. Obviously, it was a mistake." I scrub my hand over my face, a useless action which does nothing to reach the weird and inappropriate feelings swirling inside me right now. "I need to call the captain back. Talk to her about getting a map of who knew what, and when."

"What?"

"Your point about the FBI knowing you were in D.C.. That's a good one. We need to follow up on that."

"Oh." She goes still for a moment then nods. "Right. Yes. Do that."

"We're not done with—"

She laughs. "The mistake? Yeah, no, we're done with that."

"The conversation." I give her a tight, controlled smile. "We're going to be stuck together for a few days, though. Let's pace ourselves."

"Sure. Whatever you want."

———

I use a burner phone app to call the Captain from yet another encrypted number.

"Hello again," she says after I introduce myself. "How's vacation going?"

I leave out the fight—and the kiss it lead to. "We need to consider the angle that whoever left the note at the safe house expected Taylor to be there, or arrive there soon. As in, they didn't know she was in Washington."

"Unless the point was to spoil the safe house," Woods says,

musing it over. "But I hear what you're saying. The leak maybe wasn't internal to the FBI."

"Who else was looped in? The Secret Service?"

"Yeah, I believe they got a heads up on the safe house. But Ferdinand and I kept your travel plans tight."

"Well, that narrows down our list of leak suspects, doesn't it?"

"It sure does."

"Ferdinand should be relieved that the loose lips aren't on his own team."

"I'll be sure to point that out."

"Thanks. You'll let me know if they bump up the forensics report?"

"You got it." She ends the call. And I go hunting for my houseguest.

I need to spend the next thirty-six hours entertaining her in a more appropriate way than throwing my tongue down her throat.

I find her curled up in the window seat that overlooks the backyard—such as it is. There's a covered deck and a small pool.

"Can I go swimming?"

"I don't think I have a suit that would fit you," I joke. But that only brings up the image of her skinny-dipping.

"I brought one," she said. "Packed it when I thought I might be able to stay at the Wilshire while this was being sorted out."

"I'm sorry that this isn't the Wilshire." I take a deep breath. "How about when it's dark? I don't want to be too paranoid, but it's harder to be seen from overhead that way."

She nods, staring out the window. "After the last two days— and the rest of my life behind it—I don't think there's such a thing as too paranoid."

I sit down on the chair nearest her. Close enough to talk, but not so close that I'm crowding her. "About before..."

She pauses a beat before turning a brilliant, but cold smile on me. "That was wrong of me."

"It's been a long couple of days. It's normal to develop intense connections—"

"I use people for sex." She stares me down like she wants me to argue. "I manipulate men like other people breathe. Don't make this something that it's not."

Well, all right then. "Deal."

She looks back out the window for a moment, then sighs and turns back to the small living room. "Can I watch TV?"

"Knock yourself out."

I go to the kitchen and double-check what I have in terms of food on hand. I've got enough to get us through the day, but I'll need to do a grocery run soon.

I use people for sex.

Don't we all? Obviously, not the way she means it, but that's what dating is.

I manipulate men like other people breathe.

That one is harder to normalize. She probably does. Looking back over the last forty hours, I could probably pick out moments when she manipulated me.

Hey, Luke.

Heat crawls up the back of my neck.

But the kiss wasn't that. For one thing, she was out of control when she did it. For another, it didn't advance any kind of cause. It wasn't good misdirection; it wasn't getting me off course of an investigation.

She has no reason to truly want to manipulate me.

Which brings me to the thought that she just can't help it. That she was sexualized from an early age, and was manipulated herself through her teens. She learned a lot of harsh rules about life as she moved into adulthood.

Nobody has ever shown her any other way to be.

Police work isn't social work. That's a rule drilled into us all the time. But I don't think I'm trying to fix Taylor.

I wasn't lying to her when I said I like her. In a weird way, across our very different worlds, Taylor feels like someone I could be friends with. One of those rare personality matches where we just click.

And then I had to go and fuck it up by kissing her.

I'm not doing either of us any favors by pretending our relationship is a normal cop-protecting-a-witness dynamic. That went off the rails somewhere and we're not going to go back. But we can't move forward unless I try something else.

I can't expect her to be honest with me if I'm not honest with her.

I pour myself a cup of coffee and go back into the living room. The TV is on, but she's not watching it. She's flipping through a magazine.

Sitting down on the far end of the couch, I wait her out. She takes a while, but finally she sighs and puts down the magazine. "Yes?"

"I thought we could talk."

"No thanks."

"Not about the kiss. I thought we could get to know each other better."

"You know me as well as anyone." She says it flippantly, but I wonder if it's true. Which isn't to say that I know her—I don't. But maybe nobody does.

"Then I need to play catch up on the sharing. Remember how I told you that you're my only case?"

"Sure, I guess."

"You might be my last case as a detective. At least for a while. I've put in a transfer request to an undercover unit."

That gets a flash of interest. "Dangerous."

"It can be."

"Why do you want to transfer?"

Because it's dangerous. "I'm ready for the next challenge."

"Bullshit." Her eyes are bright now. Curious.

"That's the polite version of the answer, I guess. It's not a lie."

"But it's not the whole truth. You want to share, Detective, you gotta share for real. Because it's hard to compete with my mom pimped me out to her billionaire friends when I was a ripe little Lolita." She purses her lips. "Have you ever shot anyone?"

"Yes."

"Tell me about that."

"No."

"You're no fun."

And now we're back to bratty. Fantastic. Instead of rising to the bait, I relax back in my chair and drink my coffee.

It doesn't take long for her to shift uncomfortably.

I smile.

"Stop it."

"Stop what?"

"That's a classic trick, creating silence so I'll fill it."

"It's not a trick. You didn't seem to like my efforts to make conversation."

She looks down at her own mug, sitting on the coffee table.

"Do you want more coffee?"

She shakes her head. "I'm fine."

"Let me know when you're ready to eat something. I'm a decent cook."

"Stop!" The word tears out of her, a bark, and then she slaps her hand over her mouth—in exactly the same way I did just a little while ago.

I slowly raise my free hand, palm out. "Hey. It's okay."

"It's just...all too much."

"Sure. I get that."

"I'm not hungry."

"No problem."

"You don't need to be nice to me. I won't tell anyone we kissed, okay? It's fine. It's stupid and forgettable and really, very fine."

I resist the scowl that wants to pull my brows together. Stupid and fine, sure, I get that. But there was nothing forgettable about that kiss. And whoa, is she way off base about why I'm being kind. "You don't have anything to worry about like that from me. I'm not going to pressure you to keep my secrets."

"Then you would be the first."

"That's shitty."

"Yeah." She looks me over. "How about you? Broken man, haunted past?"

Unhealthy relationship with thrills and chills and commitment to anything—a job, a woman, even family. "I've got my issues."

"Come on, Detective. I gave you my issues in a perverted little box with a bow on it. Tell me more than that."

I crack my jaw to the side. *Click.* "My dad died when I was young. He was a Marine. Training accident. Bad luck."

"I'm sorry." She says it immediately, and everything softens. And then she doesn't say anything else. She doesn't try to make it better, doesn't stumble over trying to make sense of the thing that is insensible.

"Yeah," I say gruffly. "So there. That's another secret you've got of mine."

"Were you an only child?"

I bark a laugh. "God, no. Middle of five kids. My youngest sister was born after my dad died. All girls, except for me. And they all lost their shit on me when I joined the Corps."

"You followed in your dad's footsteps?"

I nod. "He wanted to be a cop, too. That was his life dream."

"Undercover?"

"No, not that. That's...my dad was a family man. Everything was for my mom, us kids. She tells us that all the time."

"Hard to lose a spouse like that."

"Brutal. She never re-married."

"So it was a house full of women growing up?"

I smile softly. "Yeah. I love them, of course, but I've been a solitary man since moving out. Still recovering from all the love, maybe."

"I have three siblings, but our family didn't really feel like a *big family* like other people described. I've never had to share a bathroom with anyone. Maybe I was missing out."

"You're sharing a bathroom with me," I point out.

"First time for everything." She opens her mouth again to say something else then snaps it shut.

"What?"

"Nothing."

"Taylor."

"You've busted my slumming it cherry, okay?" The corner of her mouth twitches up in a reluctant smile. "That's what I was thinking. And given...our accidental thing, I thought maybe it was best not shared with the class. But you dragged it out of me, so there you go."

My neck heats up.

It's a weird feeling, one that's hard to place at first.

When she flicks her hair over her shoulder, though, I recognize what this sensation is—she makes me feel like I'm in high school. Which is fucked. I'm the one in the position of power here.

Maybe she really is a pro at tying men up in knots.

Maybe I want her to get under my skin, because even as I think about it, I can't shut down the visceral reaction she tugs out of me.

I change the subject again. "You're a good listener, you know that?"

"Literally my job, Detective, but thanks."

The heat crawls higher, from my neck to my cheeks. "Right. Sorry."

She shrugs. "It's fine. I'm a bit of an enigma, and I'm fine with that."

But she can't hide the tiny twitch at the corner of her eye. *Liar, liar, pants on fire.* She wouldn't have corrected me if she didn't care. Taylor cares more than she'll ever let on about the one-eighty she's done with her life.

That's fine.

She keeps showing me who she is, and soon enough, that's going to lead me to the heart of why someone might want to hurt her. Eventually, I'll figure it all out, with or without her help.

She thought she could drag me to Washington and I'd end up thinking it was a fool's errand. Instead, we made whoever is stalking her—and I'm now convinced that's probably what we're dealing with—come out of the woodwork again. Hastily.

Now it's just a matter of time before the puzzle pieces slide together.

———

The joke about busting her cherry sticks in my subconscious, though, and I wake up in the middle of the night, disoriented and turned-on.

Flashes of a disrupted dream rocket through my mind as I lay in the dark, staring up at the ceiling. Taylor pretending to be an innocent young woman.

Hey, Luke.

Breathy. Curvy. Naked.

Biting her thumb and licking her lips.

Me holding her down, spreading her legs.

With a groan, I roll over. My cock presses hard against the mattress.

Go away.

But it's not that easy.

As the filthy dream fades into the ether, the memory of the kiss replaces it in my mind. And a different conversation than the one we had launches bright and dirty, a feverish radio play in my head.

We can't do this.

I won't tell anyone. I need you. Please, Luke...

With a violent start, I jump out of bed. My heart is pounding. I can't entertain those kinds of ideas. It's unprofessional. It's dangerous.

It's far too enticing.

Get some water, and get over yourself.

When I ease my bedroom door open, I'm surprised to see that Taylor's light is on, a skinny slice of yellow shining out from under her closed door.

And then I hear a quiet vibration.

Her toy. That little palm-sized sex toy.

My cock strains, hard and heavy.

I step back, closing my door with me on the right side of it. The private side of it.

Fuck.

Fucking no, fucking yes. Fuck fuck fuck. I close my eyes and groan again, swallowing the pained sound because she can't know that I'm awake.

I can't be awake right now.

Quiet as a mouse, I climb back into bed.

Then I shove my sweatpants down my hips, jack my cock three times, squeezing at the head each time. It doesn't take anything else. I can see her perched on my lap, holding that toy between her legs.

It doesn't count if our parts don't touch, Luke.

And I'm lost. I come all over my hand, a sticky spray of warm fluid. My weakness in corporeal form.

I can't sleep. And I can't come, either, which means I'm horny and grumpy and stuck in a too-quiet house, where I can't watch porn.

This must be hell.

I close my eyes and let the image I've been avoiding slide more freely from the back catalog of my dirty girl fantasies.

Detective Vasquez.

Luke.

No, better if he's the detective. Pressing me against the brick wall in the alley in D.C. Demanding to know what I'm hiding in my shirt. Rough hands molesting me as he searches, coming up empty, and punishing me anyway.

My pulse jacks up as the image spirals. Now we're here in this house. He's in a cop uniform, though. All buttoned up and official. I'm naked. Wet, splayed out. Showing him my pink pussy, my tight asshole, my eager wet mouth. All the holes I want him to violate.

His jaw flexes as I writhe around, his arms tightly crossed, and then, just when I think he won't touch me, he drops to his knees and latches his mouth on my bare mound, his tongue ruthlessly working my clit until I climax hard.

I come for real at the same time as I do in my fantasy. It's shaky and good and bad at the same time because now my sheets—his sheets—smell like sex and I have to face him in the morning.

But I got to come.

And now I'll be able to sleep.

One thing at a time.

———

I don't wake up again until nearly noon. A jolt of panic spikes through me because I think that I'm late for work, but of course, I don't have a job to go to right now.

Some asshole blew up my car in the parking lot of what should be a place of healing. So someone else is meeting my peer counseling clients, apologizing for the disruption in service, and gently assuring them that it's safe to talk to a new face.

Everything we share here is confidential.

I was once that client.

And until I met Luke, I hadn't shared anything outside of those walls. Then he showed up at the right-wrong time, and suddenly my secrets didn't protect me in the way I thought they had.

Now he's wringing them from me one by one, getting under my skin, and I don't know what to do about that. Touching myself to the most perverted version of him I can muster is probably not the best option. But it felt damn good, and I'm seriously tempted to do it again before I get out of bed.

A knock interrupts that plan.

"Are you up?"

He doesn't open it, just asks me through the closed door. Perverted Fantasy Detective Vasquez wouldn't be so polite.

"Yep," I call out. "Be right there."

When I get downstairs, he's wearing his shoulder holster, and his leather jacket is draped over the chair.

"Are we going somewhere?" I ask.

He doesn't answer my question. "You need to eat something."

Yesterday was a day of not really eating. As much as I want to be prickly about this again, my stomach is finally ready for a light something. "Fine. Where are we going? Do they have salad?"

"I'll get you a salad on my way back," he says, deftly ignoring the part where I clearly want to go with him and get out of this house. "I need to head to the station. So I'm going to leave you alone for a few hours."

"Alone? That sounds like a terrible plan."

"If I had a better one, I'd grab it with both hands. I can't trust anyone, Taylor. *You* can't trust anyone."

"That's usually my line. And I don't."

"Good." He looks at me, his gaze searching my face for God knows what. Then he nods and steps back. "So let's go over the six different ways I'm going to make sure you don't go anywhere."

"What?" That's not why I think it's a terrible idea. "I don't need an electronic babysitter."

"We've been over this. You clearly do because you've made a run for it once already."

"That was before the death threat!"

"But *after* the bomb. So whether you like it or not—"

"I don't."

"Noted. You're still being monitored. I will know if you

leave. I will know where you go if you do. I will track you down and bring you back here for your own safety."

"Rude. But at least now you're being creepy out in the open." And then another thought occurs to me, one that is possibly disturbing but also thrilling with just a side of disturbing. "Are there cameras in my bedroom?"

His jaw flexes. I think I must have Stockholm Syndrome because I'm coming to love that twitchy muscle.

"No. And none in the bathroom. I'm not looking to invade your privacy."

"As long as I stay put."

"Yeah. That's the boundary, and I'm fine with it on an ethical level." One corner of his mouth pulls up in a rueful smile. "Cameras are down here and outside."

Secretly, I'm fine with it too. I was panicked there for a second at the thought of truly being alone.

He hands over an ancient looking flip phone. "I'm monitoring this, too, but I won't leave you without a means to call 911 should something happen. Nothing will, though. But just in case."

"Can I text my sister?"

"No."

"Can *you* text her and let her know you're still holding me hostage?"

"No. And not because that wouldn't be fun." He gives me a pained look. "Fine. Look. I need to tell you something, but it doesn't change the fact that you cannot come with me. Your sisters are here. In L.A. They're stirring up trouble at headquarters, threatening to go public with the fact you're a missing person."

No. Oh, no. I told Wilson they couldn't get involved. But then I realize what Luke had said. "My sisters?"

"Yeah. Being missing is not a crime, though, so they're not getting far yet. But—"

"Both of them?"

"Yes."

My heart leaps. Sisters? Plural?

And then it shatters because of course; Hailey is only here if she's worried I'm dead. She's a good person. That doesn't mean she likes me.

"They've set up a command center at a hotel. I'm going to swing by and see if I can lower the temperature."

"You should take proof of life."

"You're not a hostage, Taylor."

"You know what I mean. Any chance you have a Polaroid camera?"

His eyes flash. "You want me to take a photo of you with today's headline and show it to your sisters in an effort to *calm them down?*"

"Okay, that wouldn't work." I click my fingers, trying to think of something, anything— "Wait, I've got it. Give me some paper and a pen. I'll write a note for my sisters. They'll know it's from me."

"You'll need to show it to me first."

"Absolutely, Detective Control-o."

He huffs a quiet laugh, then finds me a notepad.

I scribble the words I know only Hailey and Ali will understand, then hand it over. His face is funny as he reads it. He was probably expecting it to be dirty. It's not.

Remember when I said I would run away and join the circus? Yeah, me neither. So I didn't do that. I

did what I always said I would do if Gomez and Morticia lost their minds.

"Gomez and Morticia?"

"Our parents. Once upon a time, I thought they were very much in love. Maybe they were. They're not anymore, and I haven't called them that in twenty years. But my sisters will absolutely know that it's me, referring to them."

He frowns as he looks down at the paper again. "When you were a little kid, you had a plan for what might happen if your parents lost their minds?"

"Yeah, well. I didn't know that it wasn't normal to have emergency contingency plans at eight. Live and learn."

His mouth falls open then he closes it again. "Got it."

I give him a grim look. "I'm sorry in advance if my family gives you a hard time—but the note should help."

He laughs. "Just a part of the job."

Right. Where I'm a witness, he's a cop, and this is all entirely professional.

No masturbating.

No kissing.

The smile on his face falls away, his expression growing serious, and I have no doubt he's thinking the same thing. That kiss yesterday.

If only he knew what I did last night.

I touch my fingers to my lips. Luke's gaze follows and settles in there, hot and searching. Does he want the kiss to disappear from both of our memories? Or would he do it again if everything were different?

But he clears his throat and looks away, not revealing anything about how he feels. *Because he doesn't feel anything other than confusion and annoyance that I kissed him. He thinks that I used him for sex and I don't understand boundaries.*

I am a hot mess, and right now I'm his mess, and he has a job to do. Which means handling my hot mess of a family.

There is no reason in the world he should want to kiss me again.

I need to get over myself.

"Go," I say, putting on an air of indifference. "I'll be fine."

He frowns. "I won't be long."

"I'll be *fine*. It'll be nice to have some breathing room after a few days of forced captivity." He narrows his eyes at me, and I laugh lightly. "That was a joke, Vasquez."

"Jokes are funny, *Reid*."

That makes me smile for real. "Triple lock the doors, barricade me in my willing prison cell. I'm going to watch *House Hunters International* and judge people for their bad taste."

After he leaves, I make toast and coffee and watch a few episodes of reality TV. The house is too quiet, though, and my pulse is racing.

I try to do some cognitive behavior therapy self-talk, which helps enough to keep the panic at bay. I give myself options for self-care. Tea, a shower, or reading a book.

The shower wins out, although it's fast and not very relaxing because I decide to leave the door open so I can still hear the rest of the house. The silence is both terrifying and reassuring.

After I'm scrubbed clean, I sprawl out on my bed. Naked. Damp. Scared and, I realize to my surprise, horny again.

Fucking brains. They're wild things, giving us all sorts of intense coping strategies for getting through life.

I squeeze my eyes shut and slide my fingers against my pussy. Just a rub at first, pressure to grind against.

This time I don't fight the fantasy. I need to come, and I need it to happen fast. Imaginary Luke holds me down, his fingers thrusting inside me as he whispers lurid, dirty promises in my ear. Dark, twisted promises I wish someone would keep in real life, but I'm not that lucky.

With a sharp, gasping cry, I come on my hand. His hand. His words, my words. My fantasy in his house.

Flopping my arms wide, I let my breath recover. I stare at the ceiling and wonder where I could have made other choices —anything else—to avoid having ended up here.

When I get up, slowly, and get dressed, I notice the pager Wilson gave me in the bottom of my bag. It has a message.

Your sisters are in L.A. kicking up a shitstorm about your missing person case. Don't worry. Cole is going to keep them contained.

As soon as I read it, it disappears. Wilson told me the pager would send him a data packet back, letting him know I'd received the message.

Well, at least I know the pager works. How the rest of that is going to go...who the fuck knows.

[19]

LUKE

THE FIRST STOP I make is the W Hotel, where the Dashford Reid sisters and their protective John Cena-look-a-like husbands see me in a suite on the top floor.

I'm not going to stay long, so I don't sit down after Cole Parker introduces me to the others. His wife Hailey. Curvy, pretty, and very quiet. Looks at me with undisguised suspicion. Her younger sister Alison, who looks more like Taylor, but with a frank innocence that hits me right in the chest. *That's what Taylor might look like if she hadn't bore the brunt of the fucked-up family life.*

But they all have to know. Don't they?

And finally Scott Mayfair, Alison's husband. Much older, and vaguely familiar looking in that way that a lot of military guys are. Even if we've never met, I can spot a fellow service member at a hundred yards.

Interesting that all of the Dashford Reid sisters gravitated toward men of a certain type—nothing like their father. Military men, bodyguards. Fixers. Wealthy to be sure, but full of danger.

Danger that's on your side isn't really danger, though. It's protection.

And in an instant, I see that all of the Reid sisters are painfully aware of their need for protection—and to protect each other.

Even though Taylor hurt Hailey a long time ago, wounds that haven't healed, the middle sister is here, hating me for not protecting her sister enough.

"Thank you for seeing me. I understand you've been in contact with the Missing Persons Unit. And you get how it is. I can't say anything that would jeopardize the investigation." Or anything that might get picked up by microphones if the room is hot.

Cole reads my mind. "We've swept the space, and we've got signal disrupters in place. This is a safe space."

"Maybe it is. Maybe it isn't. But I don't know you people." I look at Hailey and Alison. "I know your sister. I know she wouldn't want you to worry."

"Someone wants to kill her," Hailey finally speaks. There's nothing soft about her voice. It's full of steel. Regal. "If she's harmed in any way, we'll make sure the LAPD and the FBI are all dragged for that. If you can't keep her safe—"

I can. I am.

"Could we speak privately?" I look at Alison. "Both of you. Just for a moment."

Cole and Scott don't move from their guard dog positions near their wives. Not until Hailey stands and nods. "Yes, all right."

When we're alone, I hand over the note.

Hailey starts to cry. "When did she write this?"

"After she left the police station." Technically, that's true.

"And she's safe right now?"

"Yes."

"They told us they didn't know where she was."

"Nobody does. *That* is keeping her safe, Ms. Reid. She's

very worried about leaks inside law enforcement that go to the highest levels of the government."

Hailey's eyes snap to my face. Searching. "And do you believe her?"

"Yes." I don't hesitate here. This is crucial. "I absolutely believe her. I know she's in danger. I know she's a survivor, and she knows things, and there are people who would hurt her for that knowledge."

"Our parents?" This question is from Ali. Her voice cracks, and I don't miss that Hailey takes her younger sister's hand and squeezes.

"Anyone in a position of extreme power and privilege has a lot to lose if that position is threatened." A lot of words to say, yes, maybe your fucking parents.

"Gerome Lively?" Hailey asks. Her voice doesn't crack and she doesn't need anyone to hold her hand. "The FBI won't look at him. The civil case ground to a halt when Victor Best was elected president. If you have any power to look into him, you should do that. My husband can provide you with any information you might need."

"Your husband's information isn't helpful to me, Ms. Reid."

"Mrs. Parker," she corrects me.

"I'm sorry."

"I'm not." She flicks her gaze to the far side of the room, and her husband appears from behind a door.

Protection. Fear.

For all their privilege, these women didn't know safety until they left their family—and still, threats bark at their door.

"Thank you for the tip," I tell her. "I'll see myself out."

———

My next stop is the station, where the captain has organized a teleconference with the forensics team in Quantico. I arrive early to give myself time to check in with my team before Ferdinand arrives. I'll stay well after he leaves, too, to make sure I'm not followed before I go home.

The first thing I do is run a more detailed report on Gerome Lively and make a few calls on the down low. A contact I trust in Miami, and another call to Kendra Browning in D.C.

She picks up on the first ring. "Detective Vasquez. I understand everything has gone sideways out there."

"Sometimes shit has to fall apart before it can get pieced back together properly."

"Is this an unofficial call? I heard the Feds have taken over the case."

"Something like that." I tell her about my conversation with Hailey Parker. "This guy seems above the law. That doesn't scare me, but I don't want to run into the same problems others have with getting blocked as the case moves through the system. Cop to cop, should I ask the Horus Group for their dossier on him?"

She hesitates. A long silence, followed by a frustrated sigh. "They're good guys. But their means are dubious at best."

"I got that impression."

"If you aren't sure you're going to be able to take a case forward, it's almost better to leave them alone to do their thing. Trust me on this—Cole Parker isn't going to let that guy go without justice being done. He's holding back for his wife's sake. She wants it to go down in a legal way. But he's watching. He's got Lively on a digital leash, for sure."

I don't like that. Vigilante justice isn't justice, because it's not available to everyone.

But I *get* it.

"Patience isn't the same as inaction," she says in my ear. "But it can feel too damn similar sometimes."

Don't I know it. I'm restless and ready for the case to break open. "Thanks."

"I'll put my ear to the ground here and let you know if anything comes up."

After I hang up, I rock back in my chair, thinking about how I want to document this new lead. It takes me a while to write up a short report on my brief interview with the Reid sisters. Then I carry it to Captain Woods' office myself.

She looks up from her computer when I knock on the door. "Vasquez, how's vacation going?"

"Turns out I don't like taking days off," I say, handing over the report. "Thanks for the heads up on the Reid sisters' arrival. I went to see them. Turned over a bit of a boulder there. Hailey Parker says we should look at Gerome Lively."

Her eyebrows hit the roof. "This isn't our case anymore."

"Then let's make a new case."

"You can't simply start investigating private citizens who've had their day in court already." She holds up her hand when I start to hotly protest. "I'm not telling you he's not worthy of investigating. I'll have your back here. But I thought you wanted to transfer to undercover? Are you sure you want to start something that could take months or even years to come to a close?"

That pulls me up short.

She gives me a grim frown. "Think before you leap, Vasquez."

Fuck.

Pulling open her drawer, she puts the report away. "After this video call with Quantico, I want you to take your vacation time. For real. Go home. Be bored. And think about what you really want to do for your next move. Maybe you don't need to get tangled up in a case here, when you've been itching to move on to a whole new challenge for the last year." Her knowing, experienced gaze searches my face. "Unless all of this has shifted your thinking."

Something has shifted. A seismic crack has formed beneath my feet, but God damned if I know what's going to happen next.

"I'll take some time," I finally say. Gruff. Humble.

She hears it, too. Her eyes light up with clear amusement. "Any chance you'll have company for that thinking time?"

The captain knows I know where Taylor is. She doesn't know that Taylor is at my house. "No comment."

"I like her," she says.

I hear footsteps behind me, and twist around to find Ram and Sarah approaching. Saved by the crowd. "Are you guys going to sit in on the conference call?"

"Wouldn't miss a chance to see how the big boys do things," McBride cracks.

"I'm bringing popcorn," Singh adds.

I roll my eyes. "Maybe I shouldn't transfer. Fewer chances of gold-level comedic relief on undercover details."

"You shouldn't transfer because we solve your cases for you and make you look good," Sarah says. "The real reason we're sitting in is because we've caught a break. There was a note left at the very first reservoir murder. And I think—"

Ram clears his throat.

"*Singh and I* think it may be from the same person who left the threatening note for Taylor Reid." She hands over a photocopied piece of paper.

My blood turns cold as I look down at it.

That does look like the same handwriting. "You've sent it to Quantico?"

"Our guys have uploaded the scan to their servers, yep."

"Jesus." I turn back to the captain, who already has my report pulled back out of her desk. I take it from her and hand it to McBride. "Then you might want to pull all flight records for Gerome Lively, and see if his travel to and from California line up with your murder dates."

"The billionaire?" Sarah scans the notes of my brief conversation with Hailey and Alison. "Shit, Vasquez. What have you gotten us into here?"

"A case that could make your career."

I don't want it. And as soon as that thought flashes through my mind, I know it's true. I'm too close to Taylor. I don't know what's going to happen next, but I can't be on the case. Not officially. But before I walk away, I'm going to make sure they know just exactly how complicated this could get.

"He's dirty, and well-connected. He got a sweetheart of a deal from the US attorney in Miami, who is now the Under Secretary for Agriculture for Natural Resources, not a portfolio he has any experience in—curious. Lively's relationship with the president goes back decades. And even though he was caught red-handed for kidnapping, somehow he managed to skate. The civil suit stalled out. The whole situation stinks. He will think he's above the law."

Singh whistles, a low, dark sound. "Maybe he is."

Anger curdles in my gut.

Captain Woods stands up, her eyes flashing. "Not if he's killed women in Los Angeles. We'll nail his ass to the fucking wall. I don't care if the president is his best fucking friend." Her gaze locks on my face for a moment then snaps to Singh and McBride. "Let's keep that element to ourselves for now. We're not handing this part of the case over to the FBI, and they've bungled the Lively file before. Got it?"

"Got it, boss."

She exhales roughly. "Let's go see what the lab rats have done with our evidence."

The elevator dings as we cross the squad room. Agent Ferdinand steps into the hallway, and he's not alone. There's another generic looking white guy with him, this one with white-blond hair.

"Newcomb," he says, holding out his hand to introduce himself. "Secret Service."

The same one who punted us the bad tip in the first place. I shake his hand as I size him up. "Vasquez."

His hand tightens around mine. "The one who went to Washington."

I give him a neutral, but rueful smile. "Yeah, that was a bit of a waste of time."

"Shame to hear that Ms. Reid went on the run. She didn't need to do that."

Captain Woods interrupts. "We were all disappointed in how that went down, and remain hopeful that she'll contact us—and her family, too. Shall we go into the briefing now?"

I'm disappointed that Ram doesn't actually have popcorn, but we don't need it because the Forensics lead agent on the other side of the country has some bombshell news for us once we're all seated and the video conference has begun.

They start with a round of introductions, then an overview of what analysis they've completed so far, and what is still outstanding. But it doesn't take them long to get to the meat of the news. "Long story short, the device was *not* a high explosive. It was designed to look like a bomb and scare someone good, but since they chose to set it off when she wasn't near the car..." She trails off when Ferdinand waves his hand at the camera on our end.

"Yes, Agent Ferdinand?"

"Can you clarify that? They chose to set it off when she wasn't near the car?"

"That's right. We have verified that the explosive was detonated by a cell phone signal, not the key fob trigger as initially hypothesized."

Shit. I share an alarmed look with McBride, and I can feel the captain looking at Ram in the same way.

My brain starts spinning, putting that afternoon together in a different way now. Did the stalker want her to think she'd detonated it? Was he watching her remotely? We fanned out pretty quickly. The bird in the sky didn't see anything. We'll have to go over the video footage again, but I don't think we missed anything there. *He wasn't right fucking there, watching her, was he?*

Or was it just a fluke that she'd been so desperate to get away from me that she happened to jab the key fob at the same moment the bomb detonated?

On the screen, the lab specialists go through the evidence.

The electric detonator, the container of the device stuffed with black powder, but less then they'd normally expect, and a lot of glitter tissue paper.

"Glitter tissue paper?" Again the question is from Ferdinand.

The agent on the screen nods. "I'm going to switch cameras so you can see it. It's fascinating."

Normally I'm all for the morbid curiosity of the Forensics crews, but not tonight. The burn in my gut gets worse as the screen flickers and changes to an overhead shot of an evidence table.

Taped-together tissue paper scraps litter one half of it like a bizarre ticker-tape parade had rained down on the lab counter. Pink, shiny glitter and torn scraps of gauzy white. The bizarre puzzle that needed to be solved.

She shows us the detonator next then Newcomb has some questions for her that I tune out because Sarah pokes me and shows me a scribbled note on her pad of paper. ***Glitter tissue*** *paper???? A PRESENT. A GIFT.* Then she pauses before adding, *STALKER.*

I nod. I'd already started thinking along that line, and this reinforces it. That kind of touch might be an accidental tell on the part of the perp. Presents, gifts—they're personal. It would change it from a crime for hire to something with a more sinister agenda.

Revenge?

Whoever did this didn't want to kill Taylor.

And if they've killed other women...

Sarah taps her pen against my fist, clenched at my side. Then she starts writing again.

We've got this. You can go to her.

I jerk my gaze up to find hers. She gives me a tight, small smile, then quietly rips off the top sheet of paper and pushes it into my hand

Go to her.

I'm on vacation, after all. I don't need to stay for this.

I need to trust my team and give them some distance before I do something that could endanger everything because I'm too close to the target.

Before I can talk myself out of being selfish, I get up and leave the conference room. I'm running by the time I hit the garage, the note shoved deep in my pocket.

I can't go straight home. But I will lose any tail they have waiting for me, and then, eventually, I will make my way back to Taylor tonight.

And I won't leave her again until they catch this fucker, whoever he is.

LUKE ISN'T BACK by the time it gets dark. I turn off most of the lights, leave him a note on the kitchen table, although I'm sure his observation net will catch that I'm going into the backyard. Then I put on my bathing suit and open the back door, stepping into the warm evening air.

It's nice to be outside after being cooped up all day, even if the space around the pool is completely fenced in and private enough that it might as well be a part of the house. If I had to sit and wait alone, for even a second more, I would have gone crazy. Swimming is just active enough that it may give my brain something to focus on instead of panic and worry.

What's taking him so long?

I sink into the water, up to my neck, and undo the strings of my bikini. That gives me a little rush, a dopamine hit that soothes my nerves.

When I first moved out here, I went through a long dark period. It wasn't until a therapist gently pointed out that I had been using sex to manage my brain chemistry—and deal with the trauma of my life—that I realized that by depriving myself of that completely was a mistake.

But I couldn't just jump onto Tinder. What would my profile look like? *Check out my highlight reel, widely available in all corners of the internet, starring me and the guy who used to be number two in line to run the country?*

And I didn't even want to have sex with men. Or women, although I did consider that as a seriously good idea for a while.

No. I needed to learn how to have sex with myself, first. How to flirt with myself, tease myself, make myself happy on my own terms.

So this is like a little date with myself. A little thrill, a little gimme of happiness in the middle of terrifying darkness.

Sadly, terror isn't new to me. I'm a pro at coping.

I roll onto my back and float like that, blinking up at the stars.

When the living room light blinks on, casting a yellow glow across part of the yard, I know Luke is home. But before I can swim to the edge and grab my bikini top, the back door opens, and he steps outside.

"Hey." His voice sounds rough. Tired.

"Welcome back."

"All was quiet?"

"Very." *Too quiet.*

He nods. For a moment, he looks like he's going to launch into saying something then he stops. He tips his head to the side. "Can I join you?"

I laugh. "You'll have to pass me my bikini top first." Lifting my arm out of the water, I point at the scrap of white fabric at his feet.

"Taylor, are you skinny dipping?"

"Not exactly. I just took my top off."

"Ah."

"Are you disappointed?"

"Not at all." He reaches down and snags my top then tosses it carefully so that it lands right in front of me. "I'll, uh—"

I rise up out of the water, droplets sliding over my body, sluicing between my breasts and over the tight curve of my waist. "It's fine."

As he watches, his face in the shadows, I put my top on, adjusting the triangles to cover my breasts.

Another dopamine rush. This one is decidedly less healthy. *Don't use other people for sex, Taylor.* Right. Well, it's been a long couple of days. Hard to be perfect.

I shrug off the pang of guilt and put on a flippant mask instead. "I don't get embarrassed, Luke." It's a lie. He's already gotten under my skin more than once. But it'll take more than his eyes on my skin. That, I'm numb to.

His gaze rakes over me. Hot. Investigative.

The bikini hides little. And maybe because I'm wearing it— a familiar mask—I have no problem hiding everything else. How scared I was while he was gone, for example.

None of his business.

"Go get your suit on," I say, sinking back into the water. "I'll wait here. Unless you want to skinny dip. That would be fine by me."

He laughs, low and warm. "I'll be right back."

It takes him less than two minutes to change, and when he steps outside again he's wearing swim trunks.

Luke Vasquez without a shirt on is a beautiful, make-me-weak-in-the-knees sight.

I blame the fact I haven't had sex with another living, breathing human being in three years for my reaction. And our kiss. Also, probably, his parents, for having the audacity to give him genes that gave him a body that wouldn't quit.

Hard.

He's so hard. Big and broad across the shoulders, bulky and

round and strong there, but then tight all the way down, tight and sculpted and—

It's a mistake to spend any time with him in a pool when I'm basically a born-again virgin.

I should grab one of the towels he's just dumped on the bench by the door and skedaddle inside before I do something stupid like climb him like a greedy little kitten scampers up a tree.

Of course, I don't. I tread water and watch him, more tigress than kitten, as he paces to the deep end and dives in.

It's a clean dive. Long and strong, and he swims all the way past me underwater and doesn't surface until he reaches the other end.

And he's even hotter with his hair all wet and slicked back.

Fuck me.

Yes, please, fuck me.

He won't. Damn him. But a girl can't help but want what her parched little body wants.

It's time I fully admit just how thirsty I am for the good detective.

But when he looks at me, now with his face well lit by the light from the living room, I see his face is tight with tension. Maybe now isn't the best time to indulge in my fantasies. I swallow down that hunger and reach for the right thing to ask.

"How did it go with my sisters?" I don't really want to know. It can't have gone well. Tension and conflict and all things Reid. "Was Ali upset?"

"She's okay. It went as well as an awkward conversation can go. They read your note and knew it was in your handwriting, so that was a great idea." He adds a thin smile at the end.

"Good."

He doesn't expand, and I don't know what to ask next. So I keep treading water, letting him sit in the silence like he made me yesterday. But he doesn't fall for it, and I eventually swim away. He watches me do a couple of laps, then joins me, swimming in the opposite direction, so we cross paths in the middle of the pool each time. Slow. Back and forth.

What happened today that he doesn't want to talk about?

Finally, my muscles start to tire. I do two more laps to push myself then slowly climb out of the pool.

I hope he's watching.

If we're not going to talk, maybe we can burn some inappropriate tension instead.

Behind me, I can hear him climbing out of the pool as well.

I grab a towel.

"I need to apologize for leaving you alone today. For so long. I ended up going shopping after I went to the station, and then I went for a long drive out to Big Bear Lake to make sure I wasn't being followed. And to clear my head. It's—"

"You don't need to apologize. I know you've thought all of this through."

"It's just that I realized today just how important security is to you. Meeting your sisters today showed me that in stark relief," he says from behind me.

I keep my head bowed low and keep drying off.

"Taylor, I know you need—"

"I don't need anything," I say, turning around. I wrap the towel around my body, tight under my arms, tucked in between my breasts. Suddenly I do care that I'm wearing next to nothing. Suddenly I feel very much like I can't hide anything from Luke. Because how the hell did he see that? I didn't show him anything.

And that makes me livid.

"You can't help me with that," I say, my words clipped. "And I don't need you playing armchair psychologist. You know what I've been through. You know I can't sleep in my own bed or go to my job, both of which are safe spaces for me. This?" I wave at his house. "This is your safe space. I'm a guest here. I'm on edge here. That's fine. I'll deal. But don't pretend this is going to get better if we talk about our feelings and my crappy childhood. It's not going to get better until we figure out who wants me dead."

"Maybe nobody does. Maybe that was a warning shot."

"What?"

"We got a briefing from the FBI Forensics Lab today. It was eye-opening."

I try to pull my towel tighter around me. "What are you talking about?"

He swipes his own towel across his face and sighs. "I should have said something right away." But he got distracted by my tits. Story of my fucking life.

I distracted him with my tits.

I scowl. "Get to the point now."

"Your key fob wasn't the trigger for the bomb."

"Yes, it was. I kept pushing it." Hysteria boils inside me. "You saw me, Luke. It didn't work, and then I turned and pointed it at the car, and pushed it, and—"

The edges of my vision go black, then white, as I see it all over again.

[21]

LUKE

I CATCH her as she sways sideways, and sweep her into my arms. The sob she lets out is heartbreaking, and she wraps her arms tight around my neck.

Taking her inside, I toss my towel on the couch and sink onto it before I draw in a rough, frustrated breath.

She's so brittle, so angry, it's easy to forget that she's fragile, too.

Fragile and hurt. Fragile *because* she's hurt.

And the last thing she wants is for me to coddle her.

I should have told her everything, and now I can't because she—

No.

I can.

"Taylor," I quietly murmur. "There's more."

She goes still in my arms. And then she pulls herself together, pushes herself off my lap, and sits next to me. A tight ball of brave fear. "What?"

"First of all, I'm now officially on vacation. I've handed over the case to Detectives McBride and Singh. I'm no longer investigating what happened to you."

"Why?" Her eyes are big. Bigger than they've ever been before, and maybe that's because she seems little for the first time since we met.

Too little, too scared.

She deserves the truth, but God damn it, I don't want to scare her further. "Because I'm too close to you."

Her nose twitches. That's it. A slight nostril flare and nothing else.

Well, fuck.

Her chin lifts. "What else is there?"

So we're moving past the feelings. Fine. For the best, really. "The bomb was detonated by a cell phone signal. It also was rigged to look like a high explosive, but not likely to kill someone."

"Someone wanted it to look worse than it really was?"

"Yes."

"Why?"

"Probably to scare you. Maybe to lure you into a trap. They may not have known who I was, why I was talking to you. They didn't expect a cop to be there. McBride is working on a stalker theory."

Her face goes pale.

I press on. "And your sister suggested I look into Gerome Lively."

"No." She shakes her head, hard and fast. "No, it's not him."

"He hurt your sister. Your family has a history with him."

"*I* have a history with him," she says. "And he's not interested in me. Trust me."

I do. I'll leave that for now.

I take a deep breath. "The Secret Service is involved again, too."

She rolls her eyes. "Fine. Whatever."

"There's a big task force on this. They'll get whoever it is."

"Okay."

"And—"

"Luke?" She reaches out and presses her fingers against my mouth. "That's enough. Okay? Unless there's something else I need to know right now."

I shake my head, my throat tight.

That's it.

She leans in. "You're officially on vacation? No longer working this case?"

I nod.

Slowly, she climbs into my lap. "Is this okay?"

Laughing, a wounded, desperate sound, I tug her hard against me and bite her bottom lip. Fuck yes, this is okay.

She licks her way into my mouth. This kiss is desperate. Hungry. Like she needs to bury that panic beneath a pile of rubble of her choosing. A controlled blast of lust rather than the uncontrollable pain.

Even though this is okay, officially, I know it's not really. I should take things slow. Be careful with her, and maintain some boundaries. But she wants this. And I can't hurt her. She's been hurt by everyone in her life. Over and over again.

I won't do that.

So I groan and pull her deeper onto my lap. I kiss her, because she wants it, and damn the consequences. And for all our chemistry from the first kiss, I never would have guessed Taylor liked this much aggression. Every time I squeeze or bite or push against her, she responds immediately. Little groans and squirms and pants that get my deepest, darkest fantasies going out of control. Heat spools low in my belly. It's been too long, and the memory of hearing her shift in her bed, a door between us, spikes my desire into the stratosphere.

I want to see her use that fucking toy. I want to pin her to the bed and bite her all over as she gets herself off. I want to roll her over my lap and spank her until her ass is glowing red and her pussy is so wet she's sliding around in her fucking juices.

Her hands skate down my sides, sending shivers up my spine. "Luke," she breathes. "Yes, fuck, Luke."

I squeeze her ass tighter and grind her against my erection. Need twists inside me. Closer, hotter. I thrust my hips up, desperate to find that contact again, but she's shifting around, just out of reach.

"That's better," she breathes as her lips break apart from mine. "You feel so good."

Fuck. Yeah. She's hot and wet, slick against me, and—

She took off her bikini. That barely there scrap of nothing had been there one second, and now was gone.

She was fucking naked, grinding against my cock, which she has pulled out of my trunks. And I can see how I absolutely green-lit all of this. But we absolutely cannot under any circumstances fuck, no matter how slick and hot she feels. I don't have a condom anywhere in this house. And then there's the small matter—fuck—of the power imbalance.

Boundaries.

Slow down.

Easier said than done when she's naked and feels like the best thing ever in my arms.

"Touch me," she whispers. "Please."

Please. Good lord, I can't say no to that.

Reaching between us, I push my hand past my straining cock and touch her for the first time. She's got a sweet, fat little pussy. Plump lips, slick and wet in the middle, and my fingers find her entrance like we've done this a dozen times before.

She rocks her hips, inviting the first thrust, and my brain short circuits.

"Get yourself off, Taylor." Fuck, I want to bury myself inside her. Instead, I settle for the sweet clutch of her pussy around my fingers. "Rub that clit. Show me how you come. I want to feel it."

Instead, she wraps her hands around my cock, and we slowly start to hand fuck each other. She's tight and hot around my hand, silky and soft. I can't tear my eyes away from the spread of her cunt around my fingers, her grip sure and steady on my cock just in the foreground.

It's the sexiest thing I've ever seen in my life.

And the sexiest thing I've ever heard is the little gasping inhales she makes as she rides up and down in my lap. Slow. My girl likes it slow. And deep. But hard. Rough. She grinds down when my hand bottoms out against her slick flesh, pulling more of me into her body. And she shakes as she lifts herself up, all needy and horny and perfect and so close already, I can see it.

Her neck flushes pink, her mouth swells, her nipples get puffy, just the tips going hard.

Her fucking nipples. I pull her close so I can get my mouth on them, suck her against my tongue, and she loses her hold on my dick.

"Ah, Luke, oh..." Yes. Fucking *yes*. Those are the words I want to hear. My name on her tongue, a breathy exhale as she shudders and shakes for me.

"Touch yourself," I growl against her flesh. "Taylor. Come on my fucking hand, baby. I'm going to fill you up with another finger, stretch you until it burns, and you're coming to come so hard."

With a whimper, she slides her hand between us again and rubs herself, her fingers bumping against mine.

We work together as she climbs the last cliff, as she gets tighter and hotter until she finally reaches the pinnacle. A fresh slickness coats us both, my good little girl coming like a rocket in my lap.

And I squeeze her pussy one last time, gently now. The time

for pain is over. "Beautiful," I whisper against her hair before I ease out of her, bringing my fingers to my mouth.

My cock throbs as I suck the taste of her off my fingers. Fuck.

She turns her head and sticks out her tongue.

Double fucking fuck. I feed her the last drop of herself, and then she turns to share it with me.

Our tongues slide slowly back and forth, and my mind dissolves into nothing but need.

To hold her.

To do that again.

To fuck her and fill her up and taste her and keep her safe.

Which means, for now, that has to be the end of what we just did.

When she wobbles up and off me, reaching for my cock, I cover her hand. Stilling her. "I'm good."

"Come here, don't be an orgasm martyr." She gives me a loose, wanton smile that turns me inside out.

I don't want to be any kind of martyr when it comes to her, and yet here I am, pulling up my swim trunks.

Her smile falls away as realization dawns in her eyes. "What?"

"That's enough."

"Oh." She grabs at the towel I'm sitting on, and I get up, letting her cover herself up. "Okay, well, thanks for the orgasm."

It's too bright, too sharp.

"Taylor—"

"It's fine."

"It *is* fine. It really is. We went too far, but that's okay."

"We didn't go *too far*. Well, maybe you think we did, but I asked you if it was okay. I *asked you*, Luke. Fuck, this was a mistake." She's shaking now. "Oh, God."

"Taylor, breathe."

She's crying now. I'm a fucking asshole, and I've yanked the rug out from under her, which I didn't mean to do. And God fucking damn it, my brain is still scrambled, and I can't think straight.

"Don't tell me to breathe," she mutters.

"I—"

"Damn it, Luke, you don't get to pretend that you didn't want this."

"Want? Yes, I fucking want this." I grab her hand and press it against my covered-again cock, still thick and heavy for her. "Don't doubt that I want you. It's just complicated."

"How is it complicated?"

How *isn't* it complicated?

But she asked if it was okay. I said yes.

Fuck.

"Never mind." She shakes her head, jumping up. Still naked, barely covered in a towel, bikini abandoned on the floor.

She's gorgeous and angry, and I don't know where this went sideways, but I've ruined what could have been a really good moment of escape for us both. And I don't know what to say. I'm sorry sounds empty. It *would* be empty because I'm not sorry I pumped the brakes.

But now I've rejected her like everyone else, caused her the same pain as everyone else.

Just another asshole who has hurt her.

THE NEXT MORNING, I wake up to the quiet click of my bedroom door.

A hot cup of coffee is sitting on the bedside table.

Stealth caffeine deliveries would be cute if someone wasn't trying to avoid me.

Taylor the Slut strikes again. Nothing like alienating someone who was just trying to help me.

There's nothing wrong with liking sex. With wanting sex, needing sex, having sex. I know this. I've worked on internalizing this truth for three years. And yet the first time I actually have sex, I fucked it up by being too much. Too needy, too dirty, too fast.

Too easy.

God, I would have fucked him right there, on his couch, without a condom. I would have let him come inside me like a fucking idiot, just to have the feel of his hands and mouth and body hard up against mine.

Even now, the thought of his cock, big and hard and rubbing right up against my clit, makes me wet. I wish I'd gotten my mouth on it. I wish he'd pushed me to my knees and made me gag on it.

Hot tears prick at the corners of my eyes.

Of course, it wasn't going to go well. I come with a bag of issues and feelings and prickly needs I haven't properly explained because instead of finding a normal, healthy sex partner, I had to try to and seduce a fucking cop tasked with protecting me.

Daddy issues will get you every fucking time.

I need to be a grown-up about this, go downstairs, and address this in a reasonable, mature fashion. The first time our chemistry got the better of us, he had to push me to talk about it. Not this time. I grab my cup and head straight downstairs, bedhead and all.

I find him standing at the back door, looking out the window and talking on the phone. I slow to a stop in the hallway, realizing I'm eavesdropping.

I don't turn around, though.

If he doesn't want me to hear a conversation, he shouldn't have it in a tiny, quiet house.

"I was just calling to say I can't make it tomorrow night. No, not a work thing, just busy." He chuckles. "That's very persuasive. Next week, maybe. Yeah, hopefully, the busy thing will be gone by then."

Oh, will I?

My stomach twists as I listen to his words. But I don't turn around, and I don't run away.

Mature. Grown-up.

Maybe the reason he put the brakes on was because he feels loyalty to someone else. It would make him marginally better than the other men I've fucked, although he probably shouldn't have kissed me or let me fuck his hand if he wanted to maintain any kind of moral high ground.

And whatever his deal is, he should be honest and upfront with me.

Since he's not doing that, I don't need to bare my soul to him.

When he hangs up the call, I clear my throat and move into the living room.

He doesn't react to my reaction. "You're up," he says blandly.

"I'm up."

"About last night—"

I wave it off. "Don't worry about it. You're right. It's too complicated. And before you know it, the crack team will have solved the small problem of someone stalking me, and we'll be able to get on with our lives. Go our separate ways and never see each other again."

He glares at me.

Someone doesn't like flippancy too early in the morning.

Oh. Fucking. Well.

I give him a bright smile. "I need to go shopping."

"No."

"Why not?"

"It's too dangerous."

"How can it be dangerous if it's spontaneous? Literally, nobody knows I'm here." Except maybe, probably, Wilson, I remind myself. I'll leave the pager here, though. He doesn't need to be able to track me to a mall.

"Too many unknown variables."

"Like what?"

"A store clerk recognizing you. Contacting the paparazzi. Your stalker has a Google alert for your name and the next thing we know, boom."

Boom.

I ignore the tremor of fear that runs through me. No. There

has to be a way to keep living my life. "We can go to the mall in the suburbs. Where it would take paparazzi too long to find us even if someone did recognize me, which they won't because you're a master of disguises."

"I'm not."

"You said you're going to go undercover."

"That's not what that means."

"Come on, Luke. We don't need to go anywhere I usually go. I want retail therapy. Given the circumstances, I'm not picky about what that looks like."

"Maybe I'll take you to Walmart."

Sure. I smile. "That sounds great."

It is not great. I take slow, non-judging steps down the moisturizer aisle. Well, it's not really a moisturizer aisle. It's a single aisle for everything facial, and bubble bath, and foot cream. Also, something called Bag Balm, which I've read about in magazines but definitely thought was a joke.

It's not a joke.

"Find anything you like, princess?"

I pick up the Bag Balm. "Yep."

It's hard to read his face from beneath the brim of his baseball hat. Or out from under mine—the limit of his masterful disguises, which is what he called the hat when he jammed it on my head. But then he put us both in his track clothes, and that actually was masterful. We look younger than we are, and our faces are well obscured. If he does go undercover, he'll be good at it.

Even though the thought of him living as someone else, surrounded by criminals, makes my chest hurt.

But I won't know him then. The chances of us running into

each other—

Next week, maybe. Yeah, hopefully the busy thing will be gone by then.

No, Luke doesn't want to run into me once he's done with this task of protecting me.

"I think it would be better if I buy a new bathing suit," I say, turning on my heel.

From behind me, I hear a choking sound. "I'll, uh, catch up with you in a minute."

It takes him more than that, and by the time he's found me in women's clothing, I've found the most conservative one-piece in the entire store. High neck, low on the legs, and covered in layers of ruched fabric designed to cover all lumps and bumps.

I don't have any interest in showing Luke any more of those.

At the checkout, I pay with cash; painfully aware my cards don't work. I will have to start keeping track of how much I spend. I'll have to keep a budget. I'll have to pick between Botox and Brazilian...everything. Waxes, blow-outs.

Maybe I won't be able to afford any of the above.

I don't make a lot of money, and there's a solid chance I'm not getting my trust fund back. Maybe I'll have to sell my jewelry.

You could write a book.

I won't, though. Not unless I get desperate. I do get a small paycheck from my counseling position—knock on wood that's still available to me when all is said and done. So when I return to work, I'll have a bit of an income.

But in the short term, I have limited funds.

Very limited.

Welcome to the reality of literally everyone else, Taylor.

Thanks, conscience. Thanks a bunch.

I clutch my Walmart shopping bag in my hand.

No more Botox. Hello Bag Balm. It's a brave new world.

[23]

LUKE

WHEN WE GET BACK from shopping, Taylor retreats to her room, only coming out for dinner, which we eat in polite silence.

It's hell.

Each time I think I might bring up last night—how fucking hot it was, how I want to do it again, how sorry I am that we didn't talk first, or after, or even during—she silently shuts me down. She has that *hell no don't try it* glance down pat.

Dismissive, cool, and rock solid.

Cool. That's the best word for it. She cooled on me, hard, after I hurt her feelings. And that's a boundary I need to respect. If she doesn't want to do anything again, if she wants to be done with me as soon as humanly possible, then so be it.

I'm not going to try to persuade her to touch my dick. I don't want to be that guy. She's probably had enough of that guy for a lifetime.

"Have you finished?" She looks at my plate. It's the first question she's asked me in hours. "I'm done. I'll do the dishes."

I've barely eaten any of my chicken and rice. Her plate looks the same.

"I'll help," I say. "And I'm done, too."

Without another word, she gets up and goes into the kitchen.

Silently, I pack up the leftovers, labeling hers with her name. Taylor, in a big black Sharpie scrawl across the top of the tin foil. Then I grab a dishtowel and start to dry.

There aren't a lot of dishes, so it doesn't take long.

I wish it would take longer. Long enough to figure out the right thing to say to thaw this silence between us.

It doesn't.

"I'm going to go to bed early," she says after pulling the plug on the sink.

"Thanks for helping tidy up." I get a small smile and a glance that doesn't quite meet my gaze.

"It's good for socialites to get their hands soapy, right?"

Fuck. "That's not what I meant."

"No. That's just me being jaded." She sighs. "Good night."

After she goes upstairs, I call McBride. They're still waiting on flight records for Lively. "The judge wasn't impressed with being pulled away from his dinner last night and made us re-do the request for a warrant, but we got it. Now it's just a waiting game with the FAA records."

"That's if he filed properly."

"We can request cell phone records next if there's any evidence he didn't. Thank you, social media and paparazzi, for keeping a creepy eye on literally everyone in the world."

"Get Twitter to do some of the timeline work for you."

She snorts. "We'd get more conspiracy theories than we could ever handle."

"Truth."

"If and when we know something, I'll loop you in. Go have your fun."

That's her second hint at knowing there's something between Taylor and me. "No fun being had here."

"Then you're not trying hard enough." She laughs and hangs up.

That's probably true.

———

I head upstairs at midnight, after checking the doors and my layers of security. I'm just about to get into bed when I hear a panicked whimper.

"No, please don't touch me, no-no-no. I'll be quiet..."

Grabbing my Glock from my drawer, I move silently and quickly into the hall. Taylor's crying now, and I pause at her door long enough to gauge a gut check on what's on the other side.

If she's not alone, swinging the door open could put her in harm's way.

If she's alone and having a nightmare, me busting in with a gun could be the last thing she needs. Her private terror is none of my business.

But if she needs to be rescued—

Before I can make that judgment call, her door swings open and she bursts out, falling into my arms.

"Hey there," I say quietly, lowering my gun.

She buries her face in my chest.

My bare chest.

I take a long, sobering breath.

"Shhh." I wrap my arms around her and hold her tight. "What do you need?"

She shakes her head and doesn't answer.

"Was it a nightmare?" Stupid question. Of course, it was a nightmare. "How about some water?"

A slow nod, then she pushes me gently out of the way and goes into the bathroom.

I scrub my hand through my hair then return my piece to the drawer in my bedside table where it belongs.

I'm wearing a shirt and sitting on the bed when she returns, her face scrubbed and her expression more rueful than scared.

"So, I get nightmares," she says, shrugging her shoulders up and down.

"You said that."

"Yeah."

"Yeah."

"What do you need now?"

"Nothing. It's fine. It probably won't happen again now. I'll go read for a bit."

I point to the TV mounted on my wall. "We could watch something. Here, or downstairs. I'm on vacation," I tease. "I can stay up late."

She shifts from one foot to the other. "No. I'm okay."

But she doesn't go away, either.

"Do you want to talk about it?"

A shake of the head.

I roll the dice. "Taylor, do you want a hug?"

She bursts into tears, and I go to her.

"This is so fucking stupid," she mutters into my shirt when I wrap my arms around her again.

I hope it feels good for her. It feels damn good for me.

"I can usually deal with them better than this."

"You've been through the wringer."

She exhales roughly and nods. "Sorry."

"You don't have anything to be sorry for."

"No, for...yesterday. I came on too strong."

Fuck. "No, princess. You really didn't. I wanted what you wanted. I just need to make sure I'm not taking advantage of you. We can't go full blast like that. Not if—"

I cut myself off. Now is not the time.

"If what?"

I pull back, putting a little bit of space between us. Just enough so she can see my face and I can see hers. "Is now really the time for this conversation?"

"Probably yesterday was, but I'm not very good at being honest, so..." She shrugs inside my arms. "Whatever. Now is as good as any time. Unless you don't want to."

I want to. "Last night was hot. Like, really fucking hot. Hotter than I expected, which sounds all kinds of wrong. You are amazing. A beautiful, sexy surprise. And I think it could have gotten really out of control there. I would have regretted hurting you."

"You can't hurt me."

"You *wanted me* to hurt you." Did she not realize that? Fuck, maybe she didn't. "And that can be hot. But given everything you've been through... Fuck, Taylor. I don't know. I just don't want to accidentally trigger something horrible and not be prepared to deal with the fallout. I want you to be able to trust me completely. To be honest with me about what you want, what you can't handle, and that doesn't happen by instinct or by ESP. You know?"

Her eyes are wide. "No. I don't. What are you talking about?"

Jesus. "Okay. How about we start here. I like kinky sex. Sometimes, really fucking kinky shit."

Her expression is almost comical now. Eyes as big as saucers, perfect little mouth dropped into a classic O. Perfect to shove my fingers into and make her gag—if that's her thing.

Which it probably isn't because of the sudden innocence I've just discovered.

Damn it all to hell.

I pull back further, and her hands wrap around my arms, stopping me. "Tell me more," she whispers. "I'm not stupid. I know what kink is. Tell me more about what you're talking about."

"Have you never thought of yourself as kinky?"

She bites her lip, her brows pulling tight and raising in a perplexed expression. "No. I mean, let's be honest, I think of myself as slutty and confused and problematic, and then I beat myself up for that because I know better up here," she taps her forehead. Then her hand slides over her chest and stays there. "But not here."

I gently tap my fingertips against the back of her hand. "What's there?"

Her breath puffs out in a shallow, excited exhale. "Lots of things." She twists our hands around and pushes them both against my chest. "What's there?"

I grin. Fucking hell. "Lots of things. Do you want to make a cup of tea and talk about them?"

She pauses. "That depends. Do you...do those things with other people right now?"

"No." We don't even need to talk about this in code. "There's nobody else. Hasn't been for a while."

Another pause while she searches my face. "Do you have anything stronger than tea?"

"I sure do. But if we go that route, we're not going to have sex tonight."

She drags in a deep breath. "That's okay. I mean, you've got a week of vacation ahead of you, right? Depending on what we talk about, it might be good to sleep on it."

I cup her face, my thumb brushing against the corner of her mouth. Her eyes dilate then her lashes flutter gently against her cheeks. "I like that plan." I lean in, hovering my mouth over hers. "I like you. And time is on our side this week. Let's start with a conversation."

She turns and leads the way downstairs, where I pull open

the kitchen cupboard where I keep my booze. A bottle of Jack, two bottles of white rum my oldest sister brought back from a vacation in Jamaica, and a questionable tequila of unknown origins. "Tennessee whiskey or the Caribbean's finest rum?"

"Do you have ice?" I point to the freezer. She checks and pumps her fist in the air. "Yes! Whiskey, please."

Grabbing two glasses, I pour us each a generous two fingers over ice, then hand her one.

"Okay, so... to dirty discoveries?" She holds it out.

I clink the rim of my glass against hers. "To kink."

Straight. Clear.

She takes a big sip and swallows. "To kink," she whispers.

I take a drink, too.

Her eyes are bright as she looks over my face. Down my body, then back up again. "Are you some kind of Dom?"

"I wouldn't use that word, but I like to be in charge." I hold out my hand, palm up. "To the couch? Let's get comfortable."

She slides her fingers over mine. Hers are cool from the ice in her glass, which she transferred to the other hand. I feel like I'm going to burn up, and the way she lets me lead her around doesn't help.

I had a girlfriend when I was in the Marines who was super submissive. She called me Master, and it got me hard, although in hindsight I didn't know fuck all about any of it. Over the years, I've been curious, read a lot online, and done a fair bit of dating inside the scene. L.A. is ripe for literally any kind of sex, so it's not hard to find.

"First of all, sex is sex. I don't want you to think I'm harboring any kind of weird secrets here. But one reason I put the brakes on yesterday was because I've learned a lot about healthy boundaries from kink."

She curls up tight, leaning back into the cushions as she looks at me over the rim of her glass. "The only healthy boundary I've learned is to move far, far away from the people who want me to have unhealthy sex."

"That's good. That's great."

She nods. "It is. But now I'm wondering just what you see in me that makes you think of kink. I don't want to be degraded."

"Fuck no. That's not my thing, either. But I don't judge those who like that—in a consensual, it works for everyone kind of way. Anyone who gets off on degrading people against their will needs to be taken out back and taught a lesson."

"You'd be busy in Washington."

"I'd be busy here, too, if I believed in vigilante justice."

The ice in her glass makes a pretty sound as she takes a couple more sips. Slowly, thoughtfully. "What would that look like? Consensual degradation?"

"Humiliation kink is...whatever you would want it to be." My mind races, trying to layer this in a way that doesn't assume what she might like—or not—and pass any judgment, but also not one that drops a too-much-information bomb on her either. This was not the middle of the night conversation I planned to have. "Kink is a power exchange, right? All sex is, really, but a lot of vanilla sex is an equal power exchange. An agreement to share the power in a relationship. So if you wanted to be humiliated, or degraded, that would be power you'd freely give to a partner. And they would cherish that power and use it for your pleasure. If being called names was your pleasure, for example."

"No." She sucks in a wobbly breath. "No, I don't think that's it."

"That's okay. Think about it. That's not my kink, either."

Her voice drops to a whisper, but I don't miss a word of what she says next. "I've been called a lot of names over the years."

Rage rises fast and swift inside me. "And you didn't like them."

"No."

"How do you feel when I call you princess?" I find and hold her gaze. Whatever her answer is here, it's okay. I repeat that out loud. "If I've hurt you with that, I'm sorry."

She smiles slightly. "I like it. It's...hard to explain."

"Sure. I get that."

"What do you like?" She licks her lips, then takes another drink. "Wait, can we get refills before you answer that?"

If she needs liquid courage for this conversation, I'm probably dragging her in way over her head. But I'm not going to touch her tonight, not more than a hug and a kiss goodnight when all is said and done.

So I go and get the bottle of Jack, and a bowl of ice cubes so we can refill from the coffee table beside us.

Grabbing the bottle, she tops up her own drink, then wiggles it at me. "More?"

I hold out my glass. "Bring it on."

She smiles. "Only if you tell me what you like."

"I like you. I liked last night."

"You made me stop." She pouts.

I wait until she pours my drink, then I put my glass down, lean in, and gently pinch her lower lip between her thumb and forefinger. "I like this lip," I growl. "And I would like it if you would listen to me."

Her eyes flare wide, then she pulls back and laughs.

Laughs.

And I fucking like that, too.

"Is that why you called me a brat?"

"Maybe on some level."

She chews on her bottom lip. "Tell me more."

"I like being aggressive. Consensually so. I like being

pushed, and I like to push back. It feels like fire in my veins. I love the little sounds you made when things got rough. I'd like to play with those limits and see where you get the most pleasure."

"I don't know how I feel about all of that. I've spent a few years trying my damnedest to be healthy and not indulge in my worst instincts. No offense."

"None taken. If you just want to have hot vanilla sex, without doing a deep dive into secret dirty desires, that's okay, too. But I'll keep some clear boundaries up when I feel like we're getting into fuzzy areas where consent and conversation really matter." I grin. "Which honestly should be all of it, but sometimes my dick thinks for me. I'm human."

"Aren't we all." She swirls her drink around in her glass, then drains it in one big, must-definitely-burn kind of gulp. "So is that what you want? To be more aggressive with me? To pin me down and hurt me?"

[24]

TAYLOR

I don't mean it to sound like a challenge, but that's how it comes out.

"Is that what *you* want me to do?" he asks evenly. "It would be hot if you want me to do it, sure. And not if you don't."

I snort. "That's too good to be true. You can't be that flexible."

"You want to know what I really want?" He tops up his drink and leans back, taking up way too much space with how good-looking he is. "I like it when kink flows beyond the bedroom. When it's foreplay and aftercare, when it's cuddling with an edge, because the dirty stuff is just a part of who you are. It's a part of who I am, and when I meet someone like you who seems to spark in the same direction. I like that. A lot. The details of how we fuck are secondary to that."

"That feels like the PG-13 explanation."

"There's nothing PG-13 about how I want to cuddle with you." Something deep in my belly zings at the rich, low promise in his voice. "Or how I might, for example, have done today's shopping trip differently."

Now he's got me hooked. And excited, and nervous. Inside

me is a weird mess of fluttery feelings and I think I like all of them. Even the nerves.

Maybe especially the nerves. "How so?"

"When you took off to go look at bathing suits, for example." He reaches out his hand. "May I?"

I put my fingers against his, and he tugs my arm forward until he's got my wrist circled. My pulse jumps at the warm, sure contact.

"What would you think if when you turned away, I caught your wrist like this and stopped you? Tugged you close to me, touched your chin, your cheek. Some gentle caress. And then I might whisper in your ear, *You forgot to ask me if you could go.*"

Fuck.

Every part of my body tightens up, gets heavy. "That's..."

He watches me.

I swipe my tongue against my lower lip. "Ah... Okay. So that's hot. I feel turned on when you say that, here, now. The idea of it is hot. But I don't know how I feel about it actually happening." I search his face. "Would you actually stop me from going shopping?"

"Fuck no. No. But that pulse, that momentary control thing...I think it's hot, too." He shrugs. "It's just an example."

But when he drops his fingers from my wrist, it doesn't feel like an example. And I feel bereft, if only for a second, like something really interesting has been snatched away.

He bumps his knee against my foot. "Okay, here's another one."

I lean in, eager for more. "Gimme."

"Since you liked your trip to Walmart so much today—"

"Like is a very strong word."

He blinks innocently at me. "You don't enjoy your Bag Balm?"

Actually, I really like it. That's not the point. "You want to take me to Sephora next time?"

He ignores that. "Since you liked getting out of the house, I considered—for a brief, hot second—taking you to a thing tomorrow night. And then I realized it was a bad idea, for a bunch of reasons. One of those would be that I think our chemistry is too obvious. McBride has picked up on it."

I wince. "Really?"

"Sarah's cool. It's fine. But my sisters are more obnoxious."

His phone conversation from yesterday. My brain stutters over the new facts, rearranging what I'd thought he'd been talking about—having to break a date—with what it actually was. A family obligation. The logic record in my brain skips and screeches.

"What?"

A ruddiness climbs his cheeks. "I know it's really not appropriate. I promise I don't take women home to meet my mom after making out twice. But that's just...another example." He trails off, and it's kind of weirdly endearing how embarrassed he looks.

"Because your family would see that we like each other?" God, that sounds so high school. Is that where I'm at? Entry-level, teenage-emotions level of kink and relationships?

"Because this thing I'm talking about—kink, power exchange, me being in control—it's who I am. And the PG-13 level stuff is some of my favorite parts. There's a lot of that in a social setting, and as dorky as it sounds, my family is a good chunk of my social life."

That doesn't sound dorky. It sounds sweet, and so far from my realm of understanding that I can't even imagine it.

And he's still talking. "It's always a big fucking crowd, and I've taken women before. Which sounds wrong. I mean, I've taken dates sometimes as a one-off...which sounds even worse.

It's no big deal. My family never thinks I'm going to settle down..."

This time when he trails off again, and I burst out laughing.

"Wow. That hole just kept digging itself, didn't it?"

"I'm good at a lot of things," he growls. "Explaining family dynamics and admitting how my sisters think I'm a fuckboy and it's kind of okay is not one of them."

I raise my eyebrows. "Are you a fuckboy?"

"No." He pauses then doubles down on that. "No. *No.*"

"That sounds like a yes, Luke. It sounds like you are admitting that you are a kinky fuckboy, and this conversation just took a very honest turn."

He pokes his tongue into his cheek, looking adorably drunk and honest. I think this might be my favorite Detective Vasquez yet. "Fine. I like sex. I have sex. I'm honest about that. I don't really have relationships, because of my job."

"Mmm."

"Come on, Taylor. You get it."

"I haven't had sex for three years. What do you think I get?"

His mouth drops open.

And then closes.

Good. Now we're both having record skips in the brain.

The woman he was talking to about canceling plans was a sister. For fuck's sake, neither of us are good at this communication thing.

"Three years?"

I wave my hand. "I had a lot of fuckboy sex before that, don't you worry. I mean, you know about a lot of it. Some of it was on the evening news."

"That does win top fuckboy status between the two of us," he says dryly.

"Well we can't all be discreet fuckboys, now can we?" I tilt my head sideways. "When was the last time you..."

"A few months ago. And a few months before that. Last year I had a casual relationship that was off and on for most of the year. She came to Sunday night dinner twice, but then not again, because it wasn't really our dynamic. The relationship before that one was the closest to what my family would like to see me have, but it was crazy messy in other ways. We worked together."

"Another cop?"

"A lawyer, an assistant district attorney who didn't love how I sometimes do my job, and that came home with us. We lived together briefly when I sold my house, before I bought this one. It proved we weren't compatible."

And would we be compatible? What would our dynamic be? So many questions. And then there's the whole *way-too-fucking-soon* element. "I don't know how I feel about meeting your family. Plus won't they recognize me?"

"Sure." He frowns. "Are you worried about your safety, or me being embarrassed by you?"

"Both?"

"They know I'm a cop. I trust my family with my life. They would never expose you to any danger. And there's nothing about you that I'm embarrassed about, Taylor."

"My past."

"Is in the past, right?"

"There's a video of me..." I'm not going to describe it. He's aware. The whole world is aware.

"There are millions of websites full of videos of people doing that same thing. And I'm pretty sure every adult in my family has done that thing, too. Not that I want to see it. I bet they don't want to see you do it, either, so they're not going to watch that video. And I only want to see you do it to me, so we're all good on leaving that thing in the past. Clear?"

No. Not clear at all. And yet, I believe him.

"Anyway, I know we can't go to tomorrow night's dinner." He studies me over his glass. That's supposed to be my move. I return the look, and he chuckles. "But if you want to know what I really want, that's it. Social stuff, where we subtly flirt about power exchange all night long, in public. And it gets you all worked up so you ride my hand like a banshee when we get back. Plus I like the idea of getting to know you better."

"And then hurting me?"

"You're stuck on that."

"Yeah. Because you said that I want it."

His right eyebrow slowly curves up.

I smile. "And you might not be wrong."

A wicked grin spreads across his face.

Oh, lord. I drink, and then I drink again. When my glass is empty, I lean my head back and stare at the ceiling. "You have a nice house," I finally say. "I don't think I said that when I first saw it, and I should have."

"You looked kind of horrified."

"It's small."

"We can't all have mansions."

Mansions are overrated anyway. Full of filth and terror—and not the good kind like Luke seems to be promising. "That's okay."

He appears above me, and I realize I'm still staring at the ceiling. Which means Luke is standing over me. "Hey."

"Hey."

"You're suddenly drunk."

"Yeah." I try and snap my fingers at him. "That is what happens when one drinks whiskey, Detective Vasquez."

"True."

"Do you like being hurt?"

He shakes his head and smiles. "Prefer to dole out the spankings rather than receive them."

"Okay." I lick my lips. "Can I ask you for something?"

"Anything."

"Can you find a way for me to see my sisters?"

His smile blurs a bit. All of him is blurry now. Maybe I'm crying.

He disappears, and then reappears beside me because he's knelt down next to me. I'm definitely crying. He wipes my cheek. "Give an inch and you'll take a mile, won't you?"

I clumsily wave my hand at his face. "I thought it couldn't hurt to ask."

"Yes, princess. I'll find a way for you to see your sisters."

———

The next morning, I wake up where I last remember being, still on the couch. I hear clattering in the kitchen and the events of the night before flood into my mind. The nightmare. The talking. The drinking.

Oh, God, my head.

Nobody has ever seen me have a nightmare. Nobody except Luke, now.

That realization makes me want to pull the blanket over my head and go back to sleep.

The clattering stops, and then a strong pair of legs clad in snug denim appear in my field of vision. "Good morning."

He doesn't sound hungover at all.

Wincing, I look up. All the way up, because he seems extra tall today. "Is it?"

"I think so." He sets the glass of water in front of me. "Do you need a painkiller?"

I make a face. "I need to brush my teeth."

The corners of his mouth twitch, and he gestures to the stairs.

Gingerly, I push up, relieved to find out my head doesn't fall right off. Then I climb off the couch and go upstairs to sort myself out.

When I come back down ten minutes later, he's sprawled in my spot on the couch. "Good morning," he says again.

Suddenly I feel shy. It's a strange and foreign feeling.

He stands and moves closer, coming to me when I clearly can't come all the way to him. He brushes his fingertips along my jaw, from my ear down to my chin, and then lifts my face up. "I said—"

"Morning," I whisper, cutting him off.

"That's better." He leans in, soft and gentle, and kisses me right on the mouth. It just about knocks the wind out of me.

If talking about kinky hurt-y sex late at night means romantic kisses the next morning, who wouldn't want that?

"You're being sweet." I tap my fingers against his chest. "Why?"

He laughs. "Oh, so suspicious."

"Always. Born and bred."

"Because you make me sweet," he murmurs, tangling his fingers in my hair. "And you taste good, and I want to stretch out this feeling for as long as possible before I accidentally say the wrong thing and you're hissing and spitting at me again."

"I've never spit." I sigh happily and give in to the warm, intoxicating caresses. "Tell me nothing is happening today."

"It's Sunday. Nothing is happening."

"Good."

"Except—"

I groan.

"Sorry. You said I should tell you that, so I wanted to do as commanded. But it's not really true. I have a list of questions from McBride. Background stuff, not on the record."

I groan. "Okay."

"Just to fill in some holes. And then, if you're a good girl..." He nips at my jaw, making me gasp.

"Are you bribing me with sexual favors in exchange for being a police informant?"

"I am if you're into that."

I am now. "Okay, officer," I say breathily. "What do you want to know?"

LUKE

It would be too fucking easy to sink right into that role-play. Pin her down and "question" her until she screams my name. Sadly, McBride actually did send a list of questions, so we need to be semi-serious as we go through them. I get the email on my phone, then sprawl on the couch with Taylor curled up on my lap.

It's wild how comfortable I've gotten with having her here—on my lap, in my house, in my life—in a few short days.

"Are you sure you're okay with this?"

"Yeah. I mean, I've learned that secrets destroy me. So… bring it on. I have a lifetime of shit to unpack. What's one more set of squirm-worthy questions?"

"Hopefully, these won't be so bad."

We start by confirming how long she's lived at her address, if she's had any neighbor changes in the last six months, and the date she started working as a peer counselor at LAST.

"Why do you need to know that?" she asks after she tells me the information.

"Sometimes a change in behavior can grab someone's attention. Any life change is worth making a note of, looking around at that time. Did you meet someone new? Rebuff any attempts to date you? That kind of thing."

She shakes her head. "Nothing like that. I put out a pretty strong *not interested* signal into the universe."

"It didn't work on me."

Leaning back to better look at me, she tips her head to the side and gets a puzzled expression on her face. "No, I don't think I had the same shields with you. Huh."

I can't help but grin. I try to hold it in, but my lips twitch, and the smile spreads against my will.

"What about new co-workers?"

Here she hesitates. "I don't feel comfortable talking about the work that we do at LAST and who does it. But that has always felt like a very safe space to me—no spider sense tingles, no creepiness. And I'm the only new hire in the last year. Our clients are all women or people who identify as non-gender conforming. Don't you think this is a man?"

We do, so I let that go for now.

"New friends?"

She shakes her head. "I don't have any friends. I know that sounds horribly lonely, but I've been really focused on myself for the last couple of years. My only friend is my youngest sister, really. And she has her own life in San Francisco."

"You don't trust easily."

"Or at all. I'm a messed up girl, Luke. Never forget that."

"I won't." *You're safe with me, Taylor.* I kiss her softly, my lips dusting against hers. Against the corner of her mouth, then again on the soft, sweet swell of her lower lip, and to the other corner. Back and forth. I've got kisses for days. "Did you ever go up to San Francisco, then?"

"Once. Ali is more likely to come here for a visit. Her husband is a Mayfair."

"Of the New England Mayfairs, I assume."

She giggles. "Of the Mayfair Enterprise Mayfairs. Micro-conductors? LaunchX? They're going to send the first manned mission to Mars."

"Oh. Those Mayfairs," I tease right back. I don't follow business news. "I thought he looked more like a special forces operator."

"He was, in the past. Newly returned to the family fold. They have an office here, and he sometimes comes for work, and brings Ali with him."

"Nice. So when she comes down, where do you go? We're looking to push some pins into a map, basically. See if we can find a trend." I'm not going to tell her that McBride will overlay Taylor's social map with the victims of the reservoir murderer and try to find points of commonality.

She rattles off a list of high-end spas and shopping areas. Then she lists a plastic surgeon. "What? You don't think I look like this naturally, do you?"

I hold my hands wide. "No judgment." But a small amount of curiosity, because whoever did her work did a great job. "Can you remember dates? Procedures?"

"Is that really necessary?"

"You could talk directly to McBride if you'd rather. Cut me out of this conversation." I kiss her again, on the corner of her mouth, then the tip of her nose. "But I don't care. You're gorgeous. Whatever makes you happy."

"Botox every four to six months. Last appointment was three months ago. I had a tummy tuck last year, after I gained and lost some weight after the move. And a little lift here," she touches the outside corner of her eye. "Two months ago."

I lean in close and kiss her there, too. "No scars?"

"They're in my eyebrows. Dr. Jain is a genius." She touches my mouth, then the little scar on my cheek from a bad collision with a t-ball stand when I was a kid. "You're not vain enough to get work done, are you?"

"I'm vain enough to go to the gym five nights a week when I don't have a house guest."

"I do that, too. But the gym doesn't help with skin sag."

She's stunning. Youthful, sexy...but it's not for me to say what makes her happy. So I pause for a bite-y, growly kiss that makes her squirm. Then I go back to my list of questions from McBride. "Tell me about that gym. Address, clientele. Any guys there start to pay a lot of attention to you?"

"No. I'm a frigid bitch, remember?" She tells me the address. It's in Beverly Hills, which is a bit of a drive for her.

"Why do you go that far for the gym?"

"Privacy. It's secure, the staff is well-paid, and nobody gawks at me. Frankly, in some parts of Beverly Hills, nothing I've done is shock-and-awe worthy of attention."

"But you don't live there."

"No. I prefer to live in a more...generic neighborhood? That sounds bad." She fiddles with her fingers, trying to find different words. "I want to be anonymous. That's part of it. But also, I don't want to build any critical relationships here that could be weaponized by my mother. No connections, no leveraging. I'm so over all of that. It's toxic. And I have a lot of regrets that I didn't pull out sooner. Or in a saner fashion."

"Does your mother still have that kind of hold on you? You said you haven't seen your parents in a year."

She pinches her hands tight, stopping the fidgeting, and takes a sobering breath. "That's right."

"Where was that? Back in Washington?"

"No. They came out to L.A. for the Oscars last year. My mother was one of the executive producers of that horrible movie about the snuff film fanatics that was nominated for best picture. We had drinks at her hotel the day before the ceremony. It was a reception of sorts, and I went because she sent an embossed invitation and it didn't feel like the invite was optional."

I tap those dates into my notes. "Did you meet anyone that night that gave you the creeps?"

"Everyone that was there? I've never heard so many people call a movie about depravity *sexy* in my entire life." Her cheeks turn pink. "It's not the good kind of depravity."

I know what movie she's talking about. A dark, twisted thriller that had a solid NC-17 rating, big with the can't-get-laid-voluntarily crowd. Not my thing. "Nope, it's not. And how did the interaction with your parents go?"

"Awkward. Distant. I didn't hear from them afterward, and that was just fine by me. I think I disappointed them. They'd hoped I'd show up with a movie star on my arm, and instead, I was alone, and left alone—another great disappointment. My mother likes to trade in secrets, and you don't learn those by going to bed lonely."

I set my phone aside because that sounds heavy—and personal. Beyond the scope of the investigation, unless her parents slide into focus as suspects—but the murder connection makes that less likely.

The profile is clear. We're looking for a man who targets women, and who has targeted Taylor in a different way, for a different reason.

"This isn't for McBride and Singh. This is just me asking because I want to make sure I don't hurt you as a partner by tripping over some of that history. How old were you when your mother first used you like that? Sent you into the lion's den to be sexual prey."

She drops her head, her hair curtaining off her face from my too-curious, too-rough question.

Fuck. "Shit, I'm sorry, Taylor. It's none of my business."

She shakes her head, her face still down. "It's just more complicated than that. She didn't just start one day. Not really. It permeated everything. I grew up watching things that weren't quite right. And some things—secret things—that were very, very wrong."

"Do you want to tell me about them?"

"No."

My heart cracks for her, for that little girl who saw too much. "Okay."

Slowly, she lifts her face and gives me a sad smile. "I don't remember the first time I saw something I shouldn't. Probably I was a toddler. I remember quietly storing that kind of knowledge away, though. Like nuggets of information that might one day be useful. I learned that secrets are powerful. Once they spill out, they're just messy and hurtful. And it hurt enough keeping them inside, I wasn't sure I could handle what it would feel like if they scattered all over the floor."

"How many secrets did you keep like that?"

"More than I could ever count."

I gently stroke her cheek, desperate to keep her gaze on me. For her to see that this is safe, that I'm here for her no matter what she says. "You sound like a spy forced into service against your will. Like you were a small, scared Harriet the Spy, but it was a very real, very grown-up thing and not a game at all."

"I guess I was. And no, it wasn't a game. The consequences were clearly life or death. I knew that as a teen, for sure, and probably sooner."

"Have you ever told anyone?"

"Never."

"You've been holding this in forever?"

"Yes."

That's horrifying. How lonely. "Thank you for telling me."

"Do you believe me?"

"Of course."

"Why?"

"Because you said it happened."

She blinks, slowly. Appraisingly. "That's a good line."

"It's not a line."

"People lie about bad things happening to them all the time."

"Not all the time. And when they do, it's usually for a reason. Something else that happened. A need that's not being met. In a very rare instance, it's to manipulate the system."

She curves one eyebrow up in an elegant *gotcha*. But she doesn't have me caught with anything, because I'm not fooled by her act. She's still very much that scared little girl thrust into an adult mess.

"And even though I've told you I'm a manipulative bitch, you don't think that's me?"

"You keep saying that, but I don't feel manipulated, I promise. For example, you didn't mean to kiss me the first time, in the kitchen. That knocked you off-kilter just as much as it did me. I think you've cultivated this image of you being manipulative to get people to stop playing with you, not for any other reason. And I've done my best to show you I'm straight up here. I'm not playing you, Taylor. So I don't think you're playing me. I just think you don't mind *me* thinking that so you feel like you've got the upper hand."

Blink. Blink. Then she smiles. "Okay. Maybe."

"And of course..." I trail my fingers over her thigh, then settle my hand on her hip. I squeeze. Hard. "I prefer to have the upper hand. And I think you do, too."

"Have we reached the reward part of the interview, Detective?"

"We have, princess. We have." I dump her sideways onto the couch, crawling after her as she shrieks in mock-protest.

Bracing my hands on either side of her head, I hold myself above her and make sure the parameters are clear. "Nothing too intense. This is just a little stress relief. Whatever you need. Whatever you want. This is safe. And just between us. You and me, okay?"

"Please."

"Whatever you want."

"Kiss me again." She laughs weakly as her tongue darts out to swipe her bottom lip. "I can't get enough of that, and I don't even like kissing that much."

"What do you like, then?"

Her eyes glitter, then she blinks. Once, slowly. A sweep of dark eyelashes against her cheek. Bright eyes again, staring right into my soul. "I liked being fingered."

"You want to fuck my hand again, princess?"

"Aren't you're the most romantic person in the world," she gasps as she hauls me close. "And yes. Please."

"I like the way you say that. So polite. So proper. Such a good girl."

"I'm not."

"I know. You're my bad girl, aren't you?"

"The worst." Sharp words. True words.

"Are you warning me?"

"I don't need to warn you. You know exactly who I am."

"I do. And I like you, exactly as you are."

She laughs and leans back. Presenting her pussy, as if it's the only part of her I'm interested in. Hardly.

I hook my fingers over the waistband of her jeans and lazily rub my thumb against the button. "You don't believe me."

"No, I do." She bats her eyelashes at me again. This time more coyly. A flirtation. "I know you *like* me, Luke." Her gaze drops to my crotch, where my appreciation of her is on full display. "You like the way I push your buttons, for example. You like that I'm smart. Street smart, at least. I know the ways of the world. I'm no Pollyanna."

My chest squeezes tight. She's not, and that's just fine. I'm not interested in some innocent ingenue. "You're a survivor. You're a fighter."

"That's a way to pretty up the reality of it, sure."

"Wow, do you talk to your counseling clients with that negative little mouth?"

She pouts, her lower lip jutting out.

I want to bite it. I want to make her bleed, make her cry, make her gasp and shout and admit she's perfect just exactly how she is.

I curl my fingers into her pants more, my fingertips grazing the top of her mound. "No panties, Taylor?"

She shakes her head slowly from side to side. "Nope."

I lean in. "I like that, too." Her breath hitches as I brush my lips against hers. "Now be a good girl and come on my hand."

[26]

TAYLOR

HE DOESN'T EVEN UNDRESS me. He just works his hand into my pants, like touching me is enough. I don't think I've ever been with a man who didn't want to look at me all spread out. And now this is two for two where Luke stays pressed against me, kissing and touching and just being in the moment.

It's nice not to feel like a sex Barbie.

It's even nicer to give in to the dirtier, stickier parts of second base. Grinding and sliding against his hand, letting him be rough because I know he'll stop if I want him to.

Giving in to the roughness with that safety net is exhilarating. Like this is what sex was always supposed to feel like, and my efforts to separate it into two parts—the rough and awful side of sex I let happen to me because it was better than the alternative. And the safer, sweeter sex I desperately tried to have with other people that never felt quite right.

This is better than all of that put together. This is hot and fast and hard—God, so hard, with Luke's weight pressing against me in all the right places, his hand the perfect violation between my legs. And when I come, it's a rush of good and bad feelings, like it always is, but this time the good ones are the ones that linger.

I never want to wash off the residue of Luke wringing that feeling from my body.

When I finally stop shaking, he licks off his fingers, then kisses me. Slow and sweet.

Then he lets me wrap my hand around his cock and jerk him off—what I missed out on the first time. He's big and warm in my hand, throbbing as I rock my fingers up and down his length.

Again, he's pressed right up against me, like he likes it when we don't have quite enough room for this. When he comes, it's in a messy spray against my skin, my belly. And that feels good, too.

————

Later, Luke and I work out together. He's got some heavy weights in his basement, and it feels good to lift them, to test my body in a good-stress kind of way.

And the whole time, I think about what he's put in front of me.

Kinky sex. Hurt-y sex.

Nice, happy, healthy sex.

And how much of an idiot am I that I genuinely didn't realize the two could go hand in hand?

I don't miss how his eyes smolder when I make little unhappy noises at the end of a set. Push myself to lift a little more, tax my body to the limit.

He wants me to make those noises for him, because he hurts me because I want him to hurt me, and *I do.*

The kernel of what I might confess to him, what I really want more than anything else, has started to form. The words seem still so far out of reach, but for the first time in my life, I can see a path between where I am and what I secretly want more than anything else.

"Having fun?" he asks as he collapses on the mat next to me.

"Yes." And it's the truth.

He showers first, while I'm still stretching out, and when I finish going through my whole body routine, I find him already in the kitchen prepping dinner.

"I'll be back to help you soon," I promise before I head upstairs. But when I stop in my room to grab my shower supplies, there's a message on the pager from Wilson.

Watch the news tonight if you can. Video leaking of Gerome Lively and Victor Best. Chatter says leak is internal Secret Service. Timing is suspicious. Cole is still in L.A. if you need him.

If I need him for crisis management. If I need him to twist the world's perception of me...again.

My stomach rolls over.

I never want to be in the public eye ever again. But definitely not tonight, not when I'm so close to a real thing with Luke.

Maybe I should try to go back to thinking of him as Detective Vasquez.

If it's on the news, it'll be there later, too. It'll loop for days, and racing back downstairs without a shower is not a good choice for my mental health. I cannot succumb to the sick feeling in the pit of my belly to go and see what the video is. First I need to take care of myself, recenter myself as fine and whole and healthy, exactly as I am.

Who I am has not changed. If something from my past is

dredged up, that's still in the past, even if for others it is in the present.

I am a good person.

I am a kind person—at least most of the time. I try, and that's all anyone could ever ask of me.

But the whole time I stand under the hot water, the panicked worry refuses to budge from the base of my throat.

Finally, I give in, get out, dry myself off, and pull on leggings and a t-shirt.

When I open the bathroom door, Luke is waiting at the top of the stairs. Extra casual, like he doesn't want to alarm me. *Oh no.*

"What's up?" I ask as normally as I can.

"There's a video you should see. From a few years ago, before the election campaign. Victor Best was a guest on Gerome Lively's yacht."

I desperately try to do the math. "Oh?" I make it sound like I'm trying to make a joke, even though I know it's not funny. And it's not really a joke. "I'm not in it, am I?"

"No."

"Did you think I might be?"

He hesitates. "Yes."

Well, that's honest.

He holds out his hand, and I take his phone. The video is looping on the screen. I tap the corner of the app, and the volume comes on.

Yep, that's Gerome's yacht all right. I know it well enough. And there's the President of the United States, before he was POTUS, sprawled out on a couch, a young woman probably not even old enough to be called a woman on his lap.

"I could be in this video," I admit. "I've been at parties like this."

"But not this one?"

"I don't think so. It's past my time in his social group."

"Have you ever been in a situation like this with Victor Best?"

I hesitate. "I don't think so."

"But you aren't sure?"

"Gerome likes his girls to be high." My stomach threatens to purge itself, but I keep going. "There's a lot I don't remember."

Luke's jaw flexes, his eyes sharp and unwavering. "How long have you been clean?"

I bristle. I can't help it. There's a limit to my openness and being accused of being a junkie is past it. "Excuse me?"

"Let me rephrase."

"Please do."

"He forced you to do drugs?"

"Yes. It was never something I used outside of his company. I'm lucky to not have an addictive personality, I guess. It's my only redeeming quality, though, so it doesn't count for that much."

"You have many redeeming qualities. When was the last time you..."

"Years ago. Gerome also likes his girls to be girls, or at least to play at that. There's nothing innocent about me, as you know."

"I don't know that at all," Luke says, his voice silky. "I think in many ways you are too damn innocent for your own damn good."

"Are you mad at me?" I glare at him, because what the fuck?

"Fuck no."

Okay, so that's both of us on edge and angry now. But not at each other.

"Come here." He takes my hand, his fingers warm and strong, and leads me downstairs. "Do you want a drink?"

"No."

"Tea? Coffee?"

"Any chance you have the makings of a banana split?"

He laughs. "Sorry. But you—Ms. Turns Her Nose Up At Everything—love banana splits?"

"Rude. And yes, of course I do." I roll my eyes. "What's not to love about them?"

He shakes his head. "You surprise me at every turn."

He stops in the living room, and we curl up on the couch. He cups my face in his hands. "We all have stuff in the past. It's how far we are from it now that is worth judging."

"Let me guess. You were a Boy Scout, and now you get the stink-eye from your federal law enforcement counterparts for playing fast and loose with the rules, so you get it?"

He ignores my sarcasm. "Exactly. Look how far I've come with my understanding that it's more about what feels right inside than what the letter of the law says."

My bristle softens a bit further. *Tell me more about what feels right inside, Detective Vasquez.*

"Dinner?"

"Mmm. Yeah. But can we check the news first? It's a fine balance between ignoring it because it doesn't matter, and staying on top of the chatter because it's even worse to be caught flat-footed."

He hands me the TV remote, kisses the top of my head, and stands up. "I'm going to finish cooking. Knock yourself out, but turn it off if it gets upsetting. Deal?"

"Deal."

I take a deep breath before turning the TV on. It's the headline story on the first news channel I find.

"The video was sent to all the major news networks, using a digital encryption that protected the sender. It seems to depict President Best in the company of a young woman. Billionaire Gerome Lively, who has had many brushes with the law over the last few years, is visible on the boat, and it is believed that if this is authentic, that it is his yacht, pictured here in an undated photo..."

They drone on, repeating the same facts over and over again. They have a guest on to talk about video manipulation software, and if it is possible for someone to have fabricated this video to embarrass the first-term president, who is embattled against a Republican Congress who want nothing to do with his protectionist rhetoric.

How far we've come with video scandals. Nobody questioned whether or not mine was authentic.

As if I had conjured the subject change with my mind, the news anchor pivots. "The last time video was leaked of this nature from the executive branch, it was a salacious sex tape, recorded by the former Vice President's mistress, the much younger Taylor Dashford Reid, a Washington socialite—"

I turn off the TV. "Cram it all in there, guys."

But if that's the extent of the ways they'll cover me, then it's fine.

I go into the kitchen. "My name hasn't been released to the press, has it? About the bomb attack?"

Luke looks up from the salad he's making. "No. Were you worried about that?"

"It's weird timing that this video would leak. Why would the Secret Service—" I cut myself off, but he doesn't miss it.

"How do you know it came from the Secret Service?"

"I assumed. Who else?"

"Anyone else on that boat? A hacker? Your brother-in-law or any of his cohorts, who are all obsessed with bringing down Lively?"

"Because he's a bad person and has committed an insane number of crimes, none of which *your* cohorts have been able to nail him for."

"Don't change the subject. You knew the Secret Service leaked this. How?"

"How did you know?"

His jaw cracks to the side as he looks at me, once again livid. Great. Finally, he exhales. "Your brother-in-law is the one who sent it to me."

"Cole?"

"He thought you should know the context in which it was being leaked."

Damn it. The Horus Group needs to coordinate their messaging, so I don't land flat-footed with the good detective. "Okay."

He shoves the salad bowl aside and prowls toward me. "So how did you know about the Secret Service?"

I turn red. "Uh…"

"Taylor." He catches me by the wrist and pulls me close, his other hand trapping my chin.

The truth spills out. "Wilson gave me a pager. He promised he wouldn't use it to violate my privacy, and I believed him."

"What the fuck?"

"It's fine."

"It's not. You have a pager here after I expressly told you no electronics?"

"If it's from 1993, does it really count?"

"Yes." He glowers at me. "You are fucking lucky that Cole seems to genuinely have no idea where you are."

"Good."

"Go get it for me."

"It's—"

He lets me go and points upstairs. "You need to get me that fucking pager right fucking now."

I run, my feet slipping on the stairs. My heart is pounding, out of control, but as I rifle through my bag to get it, I realize I'm not scared.

Luke isn't going to hurt me, no matter what I do.

I'm upset because I've disappointed him. He's shaking mad because he thought he could trust me, and he was wrong.

Stricken, I take the pager to him.

He clicks on the button. "Where are the messages?"

"They delete after they're read."

"And he gets a digital read-receipt of that, I'm guessing?"

"Something like that."

"Does it have a GPS tracker in it?"

"I don't know."

"You don't know? Do you care?"

"No? I don't, I guess. I also thought...this was a way for him to kind of know that I'm okay."

"He's a hacker."

"And you've never met a principled crook before? He has a code. Hurting me is not in it."

Luke turns the pager over, then takes it apart, carefully looking it over for any electronic additions. Finally, he puts it back together and hands it to me. "There you go."

"You aren't going to smash it to bits?"

He shakes his head. "It's fine. You need a little tether to that world. That's fine. You don't trust me. That's fine, too."

"I *do* trust you."

"Really?"

"I've told you more about my past than I've ever told *anyone*, Luke. Yes, I trust you. And it's fine if you don't trust me. I'm used to that. But this is my life that's on the line, not yours. So I also trusted Wilson, and you'll just have to deal with that."

"Is that so? I'll just have to *deal* with it?"

Now I'm pissed off again, too. "How much of your anger is jealousy?"

His jaw flexes. Ah, my old friend the angry tick is back.

I lean in, my breath dusting his cheek. "You worried I'll have to fuck him to pay for this protection?"

Before I know what's happening, I'm pressed up against the wall, Luke heavy and big against me. "I would kill him if he tried," he growls. "Nobody forces you to do something like that ever again."

"Except you?" I push against him, wanting him to push back. Wanting him to kiss me and take me, show me that I haven't ruined everything between us with my secrets.

But it's the wrong thing to say.

The absolute worst thing, because I'm the worst person.

His face goes white. "No, Taylor," he grounds out as he pushes away from me. "Fuck." He turns and heads for the hallway.

"Where are you going?"

"Out," he tosses over his shoulder.

Worry twists ugly in my chest. It doesn't go away even when he stops and slowly turns. The look on his face is inscrutable, but not good.

"You're right. I am jealous. And that's not okay. I'll be back, but I need to do some thinking on my own right now."

I stare after him as he leaves, arming the security system on his way out.

Well, fuck.

[27]

LUKE

I don't go very far. I feel so fucked up right now that driving
would be a bad idea.

On the one hand, I know it's just a pager from a trusted
friend.

On the other, that trusted friend is one step removed from
being a criminal, part of a vast international conspiracy ring to
manipulate governments. To people like them, Taylor is
completely disposable.

Why would she put her trust in them?

Why wouldn't she put her trust in me?

But she didn't know me a few days ago. When we went to
Washington, I was a stranger who judged her for everything she
was and everything she'd done. Of course she grabbed on to any
small crumb a known element could give her.

I head up the canyon behind my house, climbing the path
that leads to the open hills. There's a rock up here that I sit on
sometimes, to go and think, to talk to the memory of my dad, or
to be alone. Today it's the last one. No good thoughts come to
me. I don't know what I'd say to my dad, either.

Sorry I held a woman against a wall. You would have taught me better than that. You'd kick my ass for that.

I'm coiled up tight. Restless. There's something not right about this video leak. The timing is suspicious, Parker was right about that. *She trusts them.*

Maybe I need to read the dossier they have on Lively. Maybe I need to ask if they have one on President Best.

And now we're getting into dangerous territory.

The kind of territory that can lead to charges of treason.

I pull out my phone and call McBride.

"How's vacation?" she asks. Then laughs. "That never gets old."

"I'll return the favor the next time you pretend to take time off. Are you at the station?"

"I will be soon, just on my way back from the gym now. Ram is grabbing us dinner. We've taken over the conference room and are going to pull an all-nighter, going over all the murders from the beginning. See what we've missed."

"Text me when you're done in the morning. I'll meet you for coffee on your way home."

"Is everything okay?"

No. My whole world has been upturned. "It will be."

When I hang up on her, I call my sister's house. Everyone is there for dinner, and I just want to hear their voices for a second. A familiar chaos, instead of this out-of-control mess. "Ma," my sister shouts as she answers the phone. "It's your baby boy!"

She doesn't even greet me, just hands over the phone.

"Luke," my mother says in my ear, her voice warm and soft. "What is it?"

"Nothing, Ma. Just wanted to say hi since I couldn't make dinner."

"Are you on a case?"

No. Yes. Sort of. "It's complicated."

"What does that mean?" She laughs. "Is it a woman?"

Yes. No sort of about that. "Maybe, yes. I thought about bringing her to dinner, but it didn't work out."

"Maybe next week."

Except she might be out of my life by next week. If everyone does their job, hopefully she will be.

And the restlessness in my chest gets worse.

The thought of losing Taylor disturbs me. Twists hard in my chest and threatens to shatter bones.

"We'll see, Ma. I love you."

"Love you, too." She laughs as a kid climbs into her lap and demands the phone. "Uncle Luke has to go, baby. Next time."

Next time. So many promises of next time. I've missed more family dinners than I've made over the years. Never really committed to any kind of relationship that would give me children, a spouse, a partner to bring with me on the regular. Someone who would get to know my family and learn to love/hate the chaos just like I do.

The call gets disconnected at the other end. I put the phone away and stare up at the late day sun, still hot on my skin.

Then I glance down the hill to my house—and see Taylor sitting in the backyard, watching me. I can't even be mad at her for being outside when it's daylight.

Fuck.

I stand up and wave, then make my way back down the path.

———

She's back inside when I return, finishing the dinner prep I'd abandoned.

"I didn't run away," she says, keeping her back to me.

"It was my turn to do that." I lean against the door jamb. "I'm sorry about grabbing you earlier. I shouldn't haven't have done that."

"When?" She turns, looking genuinely confused. Still a firebrand, still full of fight, but I've tripped her up.

"When I pushed you against the wall."

"Oh." She blinks. Then shrugs. "I goaded you into that."

No. Fuck. "Even if you tried, I should have walked away. I know how to de-escalate situations. I don't know why I can't with you."

"Maybe I make you feel things you don't like."

"The problem is that I like them too much."

Another shrug.

"Don't tell me you don't feel it, too. This out of control chaos, the chemistry that fucks with your head. Or is it just me? Do you think it's better to be numb? Frozen?"

"You tell me."

"What does that mean?"

"You're pretty chill, too. Are *you* frozen?"

Fuck. That's not what I meant. "Can I touch you?"

She frowns. "Why?"

"So I can show you that I'm not." I move closer. Close enough to touch, to grab, to pin hard against me, but I don't. I wait for her to turn.

When she does, I reach for her hand, asking her to give it to me. I press it to my chest, where my heart is thumping painfully. "Do I not feel hot-blooded to you? I have to keep my feelings contained, but—"

"Do you?"

"You'd rather I explode?"

"You can't tell me that you get to be battened down and I don't. Numbness is a coping strategy, and I think we both use it."

She's not wrong.

In my arms, she goes soft. Sweet. "We are a product of our lives. Everything that has happened has made us who we are. I just need you to remember that it's as true for you as it is for me." She exhales gently. "Don't push me any harder than you let me push you, okay?"

"That's pretty fucking smart."

"Three years of intense therapy and training to be a counselor. I've put the work in."

"And it shows." I kiss her temple, then her cheek, and finally her mouth. Soft and sweet here, too. Giving. Warm.

We're both hot-blooded in all the ways that matter.

Feelings are overrated.

"Do you want to eat?"

"I'm not hungry for food right now," I growl.

She tugs at my shirt, wanting me naked. The feeling is mutual, and I strip her out of her t-shirt, baring her breasts. For my hands, my mouth. I lift her onto the kitchen counter then cup her perfect swells, pushing them together so I can go back and forth, sucking on one peak and then the other, until she's grinding against my cock. Making helpless noises and begging me to do all the filthy things to her.

"Fuck me, Luke."

Those magic words. I've said no enough. Held her at bay enough. We still need to talk about kink boundaries, but right now, I just want to be inside her. Simple. And oh so complicated, in so many ways safe words and the like could never touch.

I tangle my fingers in her hair and tug, manhandling her just enough to keep that edge. She gasps as I move her back, so we're looking each other in the eye.

"I want to take you to my bed. I want to hold you tonight."

I'm asking for a lot. I'm asking for more than sex, and if she says no, that's fine. I'll deal.

She goes still, then nods. "Okay."

I surge forward, grabbing her under her ass and behind her back as I lift her into the air. I don't want to waste another second. She clings tightly as I mount the stairs, and doesn't let go until I lay her down on my bed.

As I strip down and grab a couple of condoms from the bedside drawer, she shimmies out of her leggings. And finally—fucking finally—I have Taylor naked in my room. Naked and ready for me to do my best and worst to her.

I stop at the foot of the bed to appreciate her lush, naked body. Her legs spread open, wide for me. A wanton offering I take, dropping to my knees. Falling forward to feast on her swollen, slick, sweet pussy.

She smells like the best kind of sex, sultry and sweet. And her taste is even better licked right from the source.

"Luke," she begs. "I need you inside me."

I give her a finger, then a second, as I lift my head and look at her. "Come for me first, baby. Come on my face, then I'll fuck you so hard."

Her lips part in a prolonged side as I thrust into her. But she's intent on getting her way here, and who the fuck am I to argue? "Please," she whispers. "I want to feel you stretch me with that big thing."

The big thing throbs in eager agreement.

I groan and slide my fingers out of her, sticky with her clear juices now. I wrap my fist around my cock, jacking it for her appreciation.

"Yeah. That. Put that big hard thing inside me," she gasps. "Take me."

"You want this buried deep?"

"All the way." Her eyelids droop, fluttering shut as I push

into her, as I imagine myself tearing her in half. *Making her mine.*

That's a fucked up thought right there. And it gets me even harder. So much for feelings being overrated. That's a huge fucking feeling and it's surging through me.

Mine.

Mine.

I groan her name. She blinks up at me, the most beautiful vision I've ever seen beneath me, and smiles. "So good. More. Gimme more, Luke."

I stroke my hands down her legs and notch her thigh up high, pressing her open for me to fuck her harder.

Her breath catches in her throat as I fill her up. Deep. Hard. I love the wild-eyed, sex-drunk look that rolls over her as she twists tighter toward an orgasm. "Gonna come for me, baby?"

She gasps.

I like that. I like that so fucking much. I'm throbbing, ready to fill her up. "I'm going to come, too," I growl. "So hard. Wanna come together? Wanna milk it out of me with your clutching pussy? Or do you want me to pull out and spill my seed all over your thighs? I'd like to see that. My come on your skin."

She whimpers and whines, her fingers skittering down her body to find her clit.

I grin at her. Wicked. Hot. "Yeah. Touch yourself. You can't fucking help it, can you? You need to come. You need this dick, this big, hard—"

With a strangled shout, she wraps her legs around my waist, jerks her hips up so her clit jams hard against her fingertips, and comes so hard around me I feel it in my balls. Like a bull let loose in a china shop, I fall into her, rutting hard as I chase my own release, as I let the filthiest thoughts take over and the base, raw need to fill her up be finally, blissfully satisfied.

When my own climax retreats, I find myself wrapped tight around her, my face buried in her sweet-smelling hair.

And she's giggling like a schoolgirl. "Wow," she whispers as I slide out of her, grabbing the condom to get rid of it.

No fucking shit.

I take care of business, then wrap myself around her.

"That was wild," she murmurs.

"Very." I kiss her softly. "I'm sorry about before."

"Me too."

I close my eyes and sink into the bone-deep satisfaction of having just fucked, and fucked well.

[28]

TAYLOR

Monday morning, Luke is up before dawn. "Go back to sleep," he whispers. "I'm heading out to have coffee with Sarah McBride. I'll bring breakfast back with me."

I wonder if I won't be able to sleep without him next to me, but I roll over and snuggle into his pillow, and the scent of him quickly drags me back into slumber.

When I wake up again, he's back and sitting at the end of the bed, holding a brown paper bag.

"What's that?" I ask groggily, rubbing my eyes.

"Banana split supplies."

"For breakfast?"

"Why not?"

I can't think of a single reason. "I'm up."

After I pee and brush my teeth, I find him downstairs. It's a familiar, happy feeling now, skipping down the stairs to find him in the kitchen.

Downright homey, I hear my mother sneering in my head.

She wouldn't know, of course, and she can't intrude here.

"Okay, I'm here to help," I say.

He turns around, clapping his hands together decisively. "You want a banana split, princess, you get the world's best."

"The world's best? That's cocky. I've had some amazing desserts. Including the banana split at—"

He raises an eyebrow as I cut myself off, and an uncomfortable heat crawls up my neck. His eyebrow curves exponentially higher when he realizes I'm embarrassed. "Where?"

"The White House," I mutter. And it was a flirtation point between me and the target of my most embarrassing affair. Not my finest hour.

But Luke doesn't blink when he gets the dirty truth from me. Maybe that's why I give it to him. Even if I'm embarrassed about my past, and I am—oh God, I am, more and more each day—he doesn't judge me for it.

"But you've never had The Luke." He smirks deliberately. "Now I'm going to need some assistance."

"Oh. I see," I smirk right back. Sparring is a good, safe ground to retreat to. "You need *help*, but sure, this is going to be the *best ever*."

He hands me the brown paper bag.

"I've got full confidence in you, detective," I say dryly.

"If my lovely assistant wouldn't mind unloading the groceries while I get started," he says as he opens a cupboard and pulls out a jar of sugar.

"I guess I wouldn't mind." I'm grinning now.

"I'll take the pineapple juice first."

I blink at him. When he points at the bag I'm still holding, I set it on the counter. Inside I find pineapple juice—proof the man is crazy—as well as ice cream, chocolate sauce, whipped cream, and bananas—getting closer.

He sets a sauté pan on the stove, and uses the juice and sugar to start a caramel. Once that's bubbling away, he adds the bananas, sliced lengthwise, cooking them just long enough to give them a sticky caramel coating. Then he deftly scoops them out with an oversized spoon, putting them in two bowls.

"Stick those in the freezer," he says as he turns down the heat.

I do as he instructs, and when I turn back, he's got all the other supplies ready.

"Come here," he murmurs, tugging me close. "We've got a minute while those cool. I haven't gotten my good morning kiss yet."

I give it to him, a long slow taste, and then I fetch the bowls from the freezer.

He serves up a scoop of ice cream, drizzles on chocolate sauce, adds a spoon of warm caramel from the pan, then he slides it across the counter. "Last bit is all up to you, princess. Add your whipped cream and blueberries to make it perfect."

He goes to the bag and pulls out a pint of blueberries I missed.

"Unconventional." But I still take a nice big handful and scatter them on top of my sundae.

"They were the first things you ate out of your salad when we went to Washington."

"That's a weird thing to notice."

"It was a weird conversation. I latched on to the blueberries like a canary in a coal mine. I figured, if you were still eating them, you were okay to keep talking."

I give him a somber smile. "I'm always okay to keep talking."

"Sure. I see that. But it hollows you out. I see that, too."

"Thank you." I grab two spoons and hand him one. "Speaking of talking...how was your coffee date?"

He frowns. "Not a date."

"I know."

"Do you?"

"It's just a phrase. What's the latest? Can I ask that?"

"Sure. Eat your breakfast."

I laugh and dig in. The caramel sauce is freaking amazing, and totally not what I expected. "This is yummy."

"But is it the best?"

I lick my spoon slowly, grinning. "The best I've ever had."

"Damn fucking straight." He winks, eats his own bite, and then launches into a run down of the progress on the case—which isn't very much, it sounds like. "We're still in a holding pattern on getting Gerome Lively's travel details. And this video leak feels like a shot across the bow in some ways, like someone knows that he's on our radar, and is trying to mess that up."

"How would that mess it up?"

"The higher profile a case, the harder it is to do the investigation properly. Evidence gets tainted, tip lines get flooded. And that's even before the celebrity trial if it gets that far. He's dodged the bullet more than once. Now he's cocky, and that can work to our advantage, but only if we keep the upper hand."

"Shit."

He drops his gaze to my mouth. "Language."

"Really?" I laugh and lick up another mouthful of ice cream. "You don't want me to swear?"

He drags his attention back to my eyes. "Maybe I want you to swear and like the idea of punishing you for it."

"Interesting. *Fucking* interesting."

His pupils go dark, and I squirm in my seat.

"Very interesting," I murmur.

Then he grins, and the moment slides back into comfortable chatter. He gives me a little more of the update, but then cuts himself off. "I don't want to talk about work. I'm on vacation."

"Sure, vacation for you," I tease. "But someone still wants to kill me."

As far as jokes go, it's pretty dark. Luke doesn't think it's funny. "And very smart people are working on that. I promise I never lose sight of that. But I'm supposed to be distracting you."

"Are you? Is that your official task, to wave orgasms and spankings in front of me?"

He grins. "Spankings? So is that something that you want, princess?"

"Maybe."

"Say it."

"I want you to spank me."

"Tell me more."

"I want you to spank me for saying *fuck* and *shit* and *damn*."

"Finish your ice cream, and then we can talk about this more on the couch."

He watches me eat, the promise of what is to come clear in his gaze. I watch him, too. Curious about how he turns the heat on and off like that in the middle of this madness. How he can switch it on for pleasure, and off when he needs to be serious or gentle.

The control there is a huge turn on, I realize. Like that's the thing that's been missing in my life.

Control.

Real power, not misused and abused power. Power with limits.

When we finish eating the best breakfast ever, he leads me to the couch. Instead of putting me over his lap, he sits down and tugs me on top of him, my legs spread.

I've quickly figured out this is his favorite position.

"Before I give you that spanking you so clearly need," he growls, "we need to have a clear conversation about limits. Hard limits, soft limits, and just as importantly, things on your yes-please list. Have you thought about that? Kinky things you really want?"

I nod. This has been cycling through my mind already, and I

know what I want to say. "I want you to pull my hair. Hold me down. I've been thinking about...the hard push of your hand against my back. My neck."

"Your neck?"

My face flames. Does that reveal too much?

He rubs my legs gently, his gaze glued to mine. "Do you want me to choke you, princess?"

"Maybe." It's a whisper. Like I can hardly believe I'm saying that out loud, and that's true. It's such a dangerous thing to admit.

"There's no maybe with stuff like that. I need to know what you want."

"Yes." Barely a sound. I nod as well. "I like that idea. And...I want it to feel real." My voice cracks. "Is that possible? Is that okay?"

He pulls me in close, his hands running up and down my spine. "Shh," he says. "Yeah, that's okay."

I know it is. I *know* it is. But I'm crying anyway. "I just want to be normal," I whisper.

"You are. There's nothing wrong with figuring out what feels good for your body and your brain."

"What else do *you* like?" I ask him. I need to know. I need to not be the only one to say something truly out there.

He shifts beneath me. He's turned on. A big, hard erection. I squirm against it.

"That. I like that. Turning you on." His fingers skate up my back and settle on the nape of my neck. Warm, firm pressure. "Look at me, Taylor."

I lift my face.

His face is soft. And then, ever so slowly, ever so carefully, his grip is not. He squeezes the back of my neck, and then twists his hand up, tangling his fingers in my hair.

I gasp at the first tug, and moan at the second.

His face stays soft, his eyes gentle. "I like being rough *if* it turns you on. It's not the only way I like to have sex. But if you like it, I'll love it. Get that? I'll be all in."

All in. An excited tremor jolts through me. I lick my lips, and his gaze drops to my mouth. "How all in?"

He blinks, and his gaze is locked onto mine. "You want it real?"

I gasp again. Hot, wet, angsty need pulses between my legs. "Yes," I whisper.

He twists his hand, pulling my hair tight.

Whimpering, I arch my back, trying to follow his movements. The heat in my pussy spreads, blooming hard and fast in my belly, making my breasts ache with heaviness.

With his free hand, he traces my jaw, then rubs his fingertips against my lower lip. I want him to shove them into my mouth and make me gag.

What is wrong with me?

Nothing.

It's a simple and yet terrifying thought. I've spent so long knowing that I'm horrid and rotten to the core.

Luke taps my mouth to get my attention. His lips twitch as I refocus on him. "With me?"

"Oh, yeah," I breathe. *Just fantasizing.*

"We need a way to make sure it's not going to far."

"A safe word?" I know some things. I just never thought they would apply to me. All kink I've been exposed to in the past has been extremely non-consensual, which is hard to think about.

"More of a safe question. A double-check that you're in. And yes, a safe word too. So either of us can hit a big, red stop button any time we need to."

"Okay."

"There's a basic set of words, common to all in the kink

community for the most part. Red, yellow, green. If you're good to go, then you're green. If I need to be cautious, then it's yellow. And if you—or I—want to stop, then it's red, no questions asked."

I nod. "Okay."

"But if you want it to feel real, then we need to be a bit more clever. And work up to it, starting with some practice rounds. So I want us both to memorize a question. I'm going to ask you if you want me to stop. And you need to say the magic words that will tell me that we're all good, you want me to continue—even though you're saying the exact opposite."

A wicked thrill slices through me. "That sounds really hot. Like if you say, *I don't think you want me to stop.* I would know that's a question."

"Let's practice that. I don't think you want me to stop, do you?" He says it hard, with a nasty edge, and it's so freaking hot I can't even handle it.

My breath puffs out hard and fast, little desperate pants. "You don't know what I want."

He grins hard and feral. "Oh, yes I do, you brat."

Squirming against him, I make an embarrassing noise that's part moan, part whimper, and all sex.

His attitude drops away, and he cups my face. "Yes?"

"Oh, yes."

"Let's do that again." His eyes shift, his gaze turning black. Fierce. "I don't think you want me to stop, you little brat."

I whimper. "You don't know what I want."

"Good girl." He pulls me in for a kiss. "We'll put that into play soon. We'll talk about it again. You're so brave, thank you for sharing that fantasy with me. That gets you a reward. Take off your pants."

I get naked, and he perches me on the edge of the couch, my legs spread wide. Then he kneels in front of me, his eyes on my face until the very last second, when he ducks his head, and all I can see is dark hair.

His tongue slides against my folds, a wet, delicious exploration of my skin, and then I feel a soft suck against my clit. My hips push up off the cushions, and my hands drive into the strands of his hair, holding him in place.

Yes, God, yes.

His tongue never stops, but he's not fast. Nothing desperate about how he goes down on me. He's taking his sweet time tasting me, coaxing me higher and wilder until I'm grinding against his whole mouth, and it's perfect.

So perfect.

And not kinky at all, but I still don't have any problem climbing the hill to my orgasm. I'm eager for it, happy to come for him. I want to shatter into a million pieces and have him lick me back together again.

Because once I'm whole, he's going to tear me apart, and I'm going to let him.

Tonight, I'm going to act out my dirtiest, most depraved fantasy. And Luke is going to help me.

———

Before we get back to the dirty, dirty things I want my captor to do to me, he makes contact with Cole and tells him that I want to see my sisters. Are they going to be around until the end of the week?

I like that he pushes it off like that. It gives me some breathing room. I said I wanted to see them, and I do, but the guilt and shame that always burble up whenever I think about my family and what I dragged them through is a lot to deal with.

Luke nods as he listens to something Cole is saying on the other end of the line. "I agree, there's a bad actor messing with things behind the scenes. Let's give it a few days, if you are going to stay in the city."

And then panic surges in me at the thought of my sisters leaving without seeing them.

Totally irrational.

I don't want to see them because it's upsetting. I can't bear the thought of them leaving without seeing them.

I'm twitching by the time Luke gets off the phone. He looks at me across the room and instantly—like a psychic—gets that I'm worked up. I can see him size me up and judge me as... needy. He crooks his finger.

Come here.

Wordlessly, I cross the room and stop in front of him.

He strokes my cheek. Softer than soft. Sweet. And then he tangles his hand in my hair and tugs. Not soft. But still sweet, in his own way.

I shudder and rise up on my toes, following the tension. My eyelids flutter shut and the tension slides out of my body.

"Mmm. That's better." He kisses my mouth and slowly releases me. "You looked like you need a distraction."

"I did. I do."

"Tell me what you want, and I'll make it happen."

"How much time do you have?"

"All afternoon, princess. And all night if you'd rather."

It's dark when I creep out of bed. The only light in the room comes from the flickering television, and for a moment, I think he's asleep.

But then he turns and looks at me.

No words are exchanged.

None are needed.

I walk toward him, my pulse thumping. Nerves jangle as I stop in front of him, my bare knees brushing against his sweat pants.

God help me, I'm a mess. *I want it to be as real as possible.*

I swallow hard. He looks up at me, his eyes hooded, his mouth slick like he'd just licked his lips before I appeared. *I want to lick his lips.*

I want to crawl into his lap and seduce him. A forbidden, off-limits fuck in the middle of the night. Turn the big, bad cop into a rutting, fucking machine for my pleasure.

It's hard to read his expression in the dim light. Dark eyes, hard jaw. Impenetrable. Maybe this is a bad idea.

I step back, and that's when he strikes, his arm whipping out to grab me by the wrist. "What are you doing out of bed?"

A gruff, hard question.

It makes me wet between the legs. Slick and hot and bothered.

So bothered.

I wrestle against his hold. "I wanted some water."

"No water in here."

"Stop," I whisper. A test.

His eyes narrow in on my face. I lick my lips.

You mean like a safe word?

Maybe more of a safe question. A double-check that you're in.

"I don't think you want me to stop, do you?" He growls the words. Identical to when we practiced them, a secret code offering me the chance to unlock depravity.

I'm shaking, and it's not from fear. I give him my practiced response. "You don't know what I want."

I'm yanked into his lap so fast I don't see it coming. His free hand shoves up underneath my loose t-shirt, his shirt, which he gave me before I went to bed.

To wear for this moment.

He palms my ass roughly. "No?" He laughs in my ear. "Pretty wet for a scared little kitten. Pretty fucking soaked for someone who claims she doesn't want me to roughly shove my fingers up her tight, hot little cunt."

She's got a hot little cunt. I freeze.

Instantly, Luke releases me, his grip going from punishing to protective in a split second, his hands loose on my hips. "Yellow? Red?"

I can't answer.

"Red. It's okay," he whispers. "Sorry."

"No." I swallow, my mouth painfully dry. "No. It's... Yeah, okay. I'm fine. Probably a yellow, really. I just..."

He tugs me in against his body and pushes up, standing in a fluid motion. "Come on into the kitchen."

Like I have any choice. He's carrying me like a rag doll.

He flips on the light, and I bury my face in his neck. It's too bright, too much. I don't want to have the conversation we're about to have, because he's not actually an asshole, he's just playing one because it turns me on.

"Taylor," he murmurs as he sets me on the counter.

I hold on tighter, not letting him go.

He leans into the embrace and sighs. "If you tell me what it was, I can nix it next time."

Next time. I laugh hollowly. "Will there be a next time?"

"Sure." He swears under his breath. "Of course. Babe, why wouldn't there be?"

I lift my head a little because my face is getting hot pressed against his skin. And also, maybe just a little, because I want to see his expression. "I don't know."

He scowls at me, and that makes me so happy I can't even stand it. "Taylor."

"Luke."

"Stop that."

"Stop what?" I grin at him. Sad, scared, dopey. But happy.

"We're playing with fire here. It's okay to take it slow and make sure that it's safe." He grips my face in one of his hands and squeezes.

I suck in a startled breath.

He smiles. Slow. With intent. "There's my girl. I like the way you shake, Taylor. I like the way you shiver. I *don't* like saying the wrong thing and making you freeze up. I want you hot and achy and needy. Not scared in a bad way." He leans in and grazes his teeth against my jaw before brushing his lips against my ear. "Scared in a good way. Got it?"

"Got it," I whisper back. "You promise there will be a next time?"

He holds his hand up between us. "Pinky promise."

Oh, that does weird things to my heart. Weird, good things. I wrap my little finger around his, and we shake on it.

"So what was it?"

"One of the men that fucked me early on, when I was..." *Too young.* "A teen. He said I had a hot little cunt. To someone else. I don't really remember."

He pulls back, his face murderously flushed. "Fuck him. Fuck anyone who ever took a piece of you that wasn't theirs to take. I'm sorry, baby. Let's work on the language piece. I'll make it fucking hot. We'll reclaim what you want to reclaim, and burn the rest to the ground. Okay?"

I nod.

"I want to hear you say it."

"Okay," I whisper.

"Louder, princess. Shout it."

"Okay," I say louder. I tip my head back and project it to the ceiling. "Okay!"

He kisses my neck as I shout it over and over again, and then he pats my bum. "Good girl. Now let's get you upstairs and tucked back into bed."

I grin. It's not going to be exactly what we practiced, but it's still going to be hot.

And there will be a next time.

He pinky promised.

[29]
LUKE

I WAKE up the next morning under a warm, sweet-smelling woman. Taylor is draped on top of me, and I close my eyes again.

This is fucking magical.

We have a lot of work to do to get to a good, healthy place with kink, but fuck if I'm not loving the challenge.

It's a good distraction from the threats of the outside world.

From a case rolling on without me, from political drama ramping up.

Hopefully, none of that will touch us today.

She stirs, then climbs off me.

I reach for her and she giggles. "I'll be right back."

She disappears into the washroom, and I listen to distant sounds. The toilet flushes. Water runs in the sink. Then she's brushing her teeth—cute—and the water runs again.

When she gets back, I snag her by the wrist and roll her beneath me. "We have an important conversation to have about dirty, dirty words."

"Oh. So, we're going to do this now?"

"No time like the present. The sooner we hash out the

details, the sooner you can come and find me being a pervert in the dark again. That was fucking hot."

"Okay." But she doesn't say anything else. Doesn't lead, and I don't want to be guessing here.

I nuzzle her neck and kiss her jaw. "This is a safe space—"

"He says as he pins me to the bed."

"You like it."

"I love it."

"So as I was saying before I was rudely interrupted, this is a safe space. You can cry—"

She grins. "Mmm. I think you'd like that."

"Shut your sweet little mouth for a second, please."

"Shutting."

"You can cry. You can take ten. You can change your mind. You can be unsure. Literally, anything is okay. All I ask is that you do your damnedest to be honest with me."

"Can we start with something a little easier?"

"Than honesty?" I laugh. "You're cute."

"I'm stunning. Cute is for girls who can't afford the best plastic surgeons in the country."

"I don't believe you can afford them right now."

She looks horrified. "Now you can shut *your* sweet little mouth, Detective. That is a temporary situation."

"I'm sure it is. Focus."

"I don't know what I'm supposed to focus on."

"Off the top of your head, are there any words you don't like, don't want me to use again. Last night I veered a little too hard into cunt territory."

Her eyes flare as I say the c-word, but she's still smiling. "Cunt is actually okay..." She trails off, biting her lip. "But maybe better if I use it first. If I use it, then that's a cue that I'm feeling it. Because sometimes it's hot, and sometimes it's very much not."

"Got it."

"Pussy is nice. Slit is good."

Fuck, I'm getting hard. This is supposed to be a working session, not foreplay for me railing her hard and fast until we're all sticky with sweat and come.

"How about scared? Little?"

She nods, then shakes her head. "Scared yes, but little...that may have been the trigger last night. Same with..." She takes a deep breath. "Tight."

Those are both no-go words now, no question about it.

I cup her face in my hands. "Brave?"

She smiles. "I like that too, but kinda not the point."

"It's true, though." I kiss her nose and try something else, assuming a role. "*I bet you're frightened of me.*"

She smiles again, biting her lip at the same time. "Mmm."

"I bet you want me to show you just how mean and scary I can be."

Another nod, a shaky exhale.

I file that one away in the Definitely Use To Make Her Wet category. "And we've got those safe words, right? Remember that."

"I didn't want to use them," she admits, her face crumpling. "That just seemed like so soon, I wanted to give the role play a chance."

"You did. You came downstairs and found me. God, I was so fucking hard for you. Giving you that. That was a win, right? It doesn't matter if it didn't go exactly as planned for the duration. It started with a fucking bang, right?"

"Oh, yeah."

"I'm all in on this, if you're enjoying it. Don't worry about that."

"It's more than enjoyment," she says softly, gazing up at me. She looks impossibly vulnerable and endlessly beautiful. "I feel like this is giving me something I didn't even know I wanted, but I desperately need. It's wild. And wonderful."

"I will do whatever it takes to make you burn from the inside out. Whatever you need to be a phoenix and rise from the ashes of whatever fucked you up before."

"I need it all. I need it on my terms. I need you."

"I'm yours." A servant willing to do what it takes. I'm not going to heal her. I know that. She's going to heal herself, and maybe part of that will be through testing all sorts of bounds inside our relationship.

But damn it, I want to be a witness to that for her.

"You said I should be honest?" She drags in a ragged breath as she looks me straight in the eye. "I'm feeling kind of anxious right now, and I really think coming would make me feel better."

How can I argue with such unassailable logic?

"Your wish is my command," I growl, shoving her legs apart with my hand. As she trembles, I trail my fingers up the inside of her thigh. "What are your words?"

"More, please, and thank you?"

"Red, yellow, and green." I frown at her. "Where are we now."

"Super green."

"Did you like how I shoved your legs apart?"

"Uh...yeah." She squirms, trying to bring her sweet little slit in contact with my fingers.

I let her, because I'm easy, and I want to be inside her so bad I can taste it.

Just like last night, her pussy feels amazing. She *is* hot and tight, and the words haunt me. I hate that she has triggers. No-go places in the middle of her fantasies that wreck everything.

It's a fine line, walking through her nightmares and pushing only the right buttons. "Ah, you feel so good. You're fucking wet, babe. You must want more."

She shakes her head. No. "Be gentle." But then she smiles, and winks, and laughs.

It's unbelievably hot.

"That's not what your pussy is telling me. You're a greedy girl, aren't you? Hungry to ride my hand. Get off on me. Flood my fingers with your come."

She rocks against me, wet and slick. Always ready for more.

I breathe as much respect as I can into the next line, because it's fucking amazing. "You're insatiable."

"I've been starved of this." She licks her lips, her eyes wild. I love that truth that she's just served up, too. Maybe this is the only way she could admit it. "For far too long."

Forever, I realize.

My little firebrand has never been loved. Never been free to love.

"Too fucking long," I growl back at her. "But this is yours. I'm yours. Use me, baby. Get yourself off. Fuck my hand. You want more?"

"Uh huh." Her mouth is swollen, her lips red.

I ease my fingers out of her and cup her whole sex, my fingertips teasing the sensitive skin just past her pussy. Heading for her asshole, if that's where she wants me to play next.

"How much more?"

She shudders against me. "Luke..."

"Is that something that's hard to ask for, baby?" I kiss her softly. She likes that. She likes me to be big and bad and mean— and sweet. She loves the cajoling. "What would you say if I told you I've jerked off to the thought of fucking your ass?"

A sob tears from her body but she's not crying. It's a gulping gasp, desperate and horny.

Music to my ears.

"How would you want me to do it?" I croon the questions as I move against her, being heavy, holding her down. "Do you want me to take my time and stretch your bum? I'd enjoy that. Watching you ride my fingers there just like you do in your pussy."

Her eyes flare wide. "Or...?"

"Or I take you hard and fast."

Another cry slides over her perfect lips as she grinds her clit against the heel of my hand.

I don't have any lube, but she's slick as fuck from her greedy pussy. I slide some of that slippery goodness to her back hole and rub, ever so softly. I'm not going to fuck her right now.

I'd never fuck her raw, without being prepped, but she can get off on the idea of that if she wants.

It makes me rock hard. I know she can feel my cock against her hip, and when she mewls at my touch, I wrench her toward me. Holding her tight with one arm with the other hand ruthlessly rubs back and forth along her crack.

"Tell me to stop touching you, princess."

"Stop..." she breathes it out. And grinds her clit against me again.

I bring my mouth to her ear. "I don't think you want me too. You're too fucking horny."

"You don't know what I want." It's a prayer, a breathless plea. *Yes, this, keep going, more, unlock all the filth.*

My finger's on a quest now, a ruthless invasion of her ass, and every time she whispers for me to stop—all the while pushing against my touch, because she wants it so fucking much, we both do—I press a little harder.

It's the third stop, the third push back against me, that my fingertip breaches her tight sphincter, and I slide up to the first knuckle into her clutching heat.

"You feel so good, princess."

She cries out, and her pussy floods my hand with fresh arousal.

"Ah, yeah." I slowly fuck her with that finger, in and out, loving her whimpering moans as all those nerve endings light up. So sensitive. Perfect. "Come for me. Come while I violate your ass, against your will, come because you just can't help it, because the big, mean man is holding you down."

With a strangled cry, she clenches her thighs around my wrist and rocks hard. I feel her come, feel the orgasm start deep inside her and the muscles around my fingertip clench down hard.

I want to feel that on my cock.

"Such a good fuckdoll," I murmur, kissing her cheek. "Stay here for me. Don't move a fucking muscle. I'm not done with you yet."

I ease my finger out of her and roll off the bed, lightning quick. I wash up in the bathroom, then hurry back.

But before I can get a condom from the bedside drawer, my phone rings.

I see on the screen that it's the captain. This can't be good.

Seeing as Taylor is stretched out in front of me, I'm tempted to ignore it. But I don't, because duty, and I'm glad I answer—because it is good news, which shocks me to my core.

"There's been an arrest," she says. "We think he looks good for the whole thing."

"You're shitting me. Who is it?"

"I'm going to hold off on giving you any details because we might need Taylor to come in and pick him out from a lineup."

So he hasn't confessed. "All right. I'll talk to her. Today?"

"This afternoon if she's close enough by."

She's naked in my bed right now, and looking at me with a smile. My heart sinks. "I'll be in touch."

When I hang up, Taylor crawls over and kneels behind me, draping her warm, sex-soaked skin against my back.

"Was that about me?" she asks as she kisses my neck.

"Yeah." I take a deep breath. "They have someone in custody. The captain would like you to come in and look at a line up. If he's been stalking you, you might recognize him, and then we can go at it from that angle. Dates and times, places."

"What if I don't recognize him?"

I turn, giving her my most reassuring look. "That's okay. There's circumstantial evidence, too. No pressure."

WHEN WE ARRIVE at the station, the squad room is quiet. Captain Woods meets us by Luke's desk. "Just in time. The cavalry is on their way over, so I need to run interference there. They want to take our suspect before we do the line up, which is bullshit— Pardon my language, Ms. Reid."

"Literally the nicest thing anyone has said in my presence all day," I tell her.

She laughs. "I'll put them in the conference room. You take Ms. Reid to the lineup room. McBride is almost ready, and that's a quiet place to be out of the way, anyway."

"You don't want me in there?" Luke winks, so I know this is an in-joke between them.

The captain looks him up and down. "No offense, Vasquez, but the chances of you telling someone to get fucked is too high."

He grunts, and I suppress a smile. She's probably not wrong.

She claps him on the shoulder. "At least I know how to say it diplomatically."

"I'll keep on keeping our witness company, then."

"You do that."

She flits away to the elevators, and Luke leads me down a hall and through a keycard protected door. On the other side of that, there's another hallway, and I'm officially lost.

"So, who is the cavalry, exactly? The FBI?" My pulse jumps a bit at the thought of seeing them again after ditching them. I didn't do anything wrong, but a lifetime of being conditioned to face the worst judgment has made me jumpy.

"Probably. And the Secret Service has its thumb in this, too. They all seem attached at the hip. Here we go."

He opens another door, and we're in a dark anteroom, looking through one-way glass at something out of a movie or a TV show. An empty room with height lines painted on the far wall.

My pulse jumps again. It's pounding now.

"Have a seat," he says. "McBride will come in and do the official stuff for this. Until then, let me entertain you with terrible knock-knock jokes."

"Okay." My voice sounds faint to my own ears. Small.

Luke steps closer and wraps his arms around me. The hug feels good. "I'm here," he whispers. "Even if I can't hold you during the identification, know that this hug is very much continuing in spirit."

"Thank you." Over his shoulder, I catch a glimpse of a set of televisions, all showing different video feeds from around the building. "What are those?"

"This whole place was wired for telecom stuff. This wing is secure, for example, so if we want to stay here to stay close to an interrogation, but there's a meeting happening in the conference room, you can call in from here. Honestly, I don't think anyone has ever used it. But we do use the video conferencing there for task force stuff when a big manhunt is on, or when we sent the forensics from your case to Quantico for the FBI to process."

"Fancy." I watch the captain step into the conference room,

then turn back to Luke. "So, I guess this means our time together is coming to an end. I won't be your captive anymore."

He hauls me in close for another tight, squeezing hug. "Fuck, Taylor. We'll still be friends."

"Because it got complicated there for a while."

"It may always be complicated," he murmurs. "I don't mind that. I'm not easily scared off."

And I will try my best to distance myself. To push him away, because I'm broken and I like to test all the boundaries I bump up against, and then go brittle. Sharp.

Self-defence in the most dysfunctional way possible.

But before I can admit that to him, the door opens and Sarah McBride steps in.

"Hi, Taylor. Thank you for coming in." She smiles, and my panic eases a bit. "Have you ever done one of these before?"

I shake my head, giving her my full attention while she explains the process.

"You can turn around, look at the back wall, and after they line up, I'll get you to turn around again. It's important that you stay quiet. The glass isn't completely soundproof. But remember, they can't see you. And you are safe in here. Got it?"

I nod. "Yes."

"Good." She moves to an intercom and presses it. "Bring the lineup in, please."

I catch sight of a uniformed cop opening the door before Luke touches my back, and I turn around.

The television monitors are the only thing in my sight now. There's a group of men in suits with Captain Woods in the conference room. There's nobody in the lobby in the second shot.

And on the third screen is a straight on shot of a man in a suit, walking alone down a hallway.

I suck back a gasp and spin around, blindly reaching for Luke.

[31]

LUKE

As McBride waits for the lineup to get settled, she hands me the case file.

The suspect is a young guy who worked briefly as a nursing assistant at the plastic surgery clinic Taylor went to. One of the reservoir murder victims went there as well, and they found some evidence in his garbage from the last murder scene.

All circumstantial, but a good start.

Now we just need Taylor to recognize him, and they'll have something to really nail him on in interrogation.

"All right, Taylor, you can—" Sarah starts to give our witness direction, but Taylor has already turned around, her eyes wide.

She's reaching for me, full of terror.

"It's okay," I say, taking her hand. "Tell us who you recognize."

She shakes her head. Tears are welling in her eyes.

"No one in the lineup," she whispers, shaking. "The Secret Service agent. It's *him*. And he's coming this way."

I turn and follow her finger, pointing to the monitor on the right.

There's nothing there. It's an empty hallway.

"Who did you see?"

"I don't know his name." She swallows a gulp of air. "He was on the VP's detail, though. He creeped me out. And I've seen him around L.A. I know I have."

Behind her, McBride's eyes go wide.

Photo line up, she mouths at me. *Keep her here.*

Yeah, no fucking shit. We're not leaving this room if there's an agent in the building who has murderous intent toward Taylor.

My fingers itch to grab my Glock, to put her behind me and wait. But I don't want to alarm her any more than she already is, so I give her a reassuring smile. "Tell you what. Take a good look at this line up, just in case. And then Sarah's going to go dismiss it, and get the captain, and we're going to find out who it is that you saw. Okay? And in the meantime, we're going to stay here. Nobody knows where we are. It's fine. You're okay."

Taylor nods shakily, then looks through the one-way glass. She does it carefully, even though I know her mind must be racing. "No," she finally says. "I don't recognize any of those people."

Sarah chews on her bottom lip. I can tell she's trying to decide whether or not to explain that Taylor probably *has* seen at least one person there, in a medical setting. "How about number four?" she asks. "You don't recognize him at all?"

Taylor frowns and looks again. "I don't know. Maybe. Oh—wait! He works with my plastic surgeon. Sorry, out of context. But I've never seen him anywhere other than that office, and I don't think he was there the last time I went in."

Which means maybe someone is probably setting this guy up.

How did he find him? Has a Secret Service agent been running a shadow investigation, mis-using his badge? The captain is going to have to quietly talk to someone higher up that chain.

This is going to get messy.

"I'll be back," says McBride. "Thank you, Taylor. I know this is all very unsettling. We appreciate your cooperation. I'm going to find a uniform to stand guard outside, then I'll make a couple of calls and come back."

After she leaves, I lock the door.

Taylor's gaze follows my hand.

"Just in case," I say, as casually as I can. "But he's not going to try anything in a building full of cops."

"I hope you're right." She wrings her hands together.

I take two chairs from the back wall and put them at right angles to each other, hers close to the wall, out of line of sight from the door should it get busted open. Mine is looking at the door. "Sit. Let's find something interesting to talk about."

She gives me a faint smile. "Like kink?"

"Or just dating stuff in general."

"Dating?" Her eyebrow raises. "Detective, do you have something you want to ask me?"

I grin, ignoring my own angsty worry. It serves me no good right now. "Sit and you'll find out."

She folds herself into the chair, and I sit beside her, relaxed and open, but ready to grab my weapon from my holster if I need it.

"So I was thinking," I tell her. "I'd like to take you dancing."

"Oh?"

"How about when this is all over, we go out on a date. I'll pick you up at your place, take you out for dinner, show you a good time."

Her eyes twinkle. "A good time, huh?"

"That's how I was supposed to spend my vacation time. Sleeping in, dancing all night."

"Sounds fun." But she sounds wistful. Or reluctant, it's hard to tell.

Now's not the best time for this conversation, but it works as a diversion tactic, so I press on. "I'll wait until you're free of me as your captor to ask you out officially."

That gets a real smile. "I kind of like having you as my captor."

Before I can reply to that, my phone rings. It's the captain.

"This is Vasquez," I say as I answer the call.

"We've reviewed the security footage. I believe the agent Ms. Reid saw was Newcomb. He was here, and he asked the sergeant on duty where Taylor was. He's left the building now."

"Are you sure?"

"There's video footage outside of him getting in his car. You stay where you are. McBride is going to bring a photo array with his face in it for Ms. Reid to identify. We're going to do this by the book. And if he's our guy, we'll nail him to the wall."

I disconnect the call.

"News?" Taylor asks, searching my face.

"McBride is going to come back and show you some photos. Let's keep talking about your fantasy for me to lock you in a birdcage while we wait."

She bursts out laughing. "What?"

"It's a thing." I wink at her. "I bet you'd like it."

"How big of a birdcage are we talking? Is there a lovely pillow for me to recline on while reading?"

"As big as you want. And of course there would be pillows. Only the world's finest comforts for my captive princess."

She shakes her head and laughs lightly. "Amazing."

It really would be. One day maybe I'll take her to a dungeon full of cages and she can have her pick.

There's a triple knock, then a slight buzz as McBride uses her keycard to unlock the door.

Ram is with her. He turns the bolt again once they're inside. So—they aren't sure Newcomb has actually left the building, either. The tightness in my gut twists harder. This could turn into a dangerous shooter situation in a dozen different ways.

"Okay, Taylor. Another line up for you to look at this time. In this folder are a set of photographs. If you recognize anyone, please be as specific as you can." Sarah hands it over and pulls out her notepad.

By the book.

Taylor takes a deep breath and opens the folder. Her face goes white. "That one," she says immediately, pointing at Newcomb's photo. "He was on the protective detail for the entire duration of our affair. And now I realize I've seen him around L.A., although I couldn't place him those times. He wasn't in a suit. Seeing him here, in the suit, on that video monitor—that's when I recognized him in context."

"Can you tell me specifically, if you can remember, where you saw him here in Los Angeles?"

"He was at the plastic surgery clinic once. That was the first time I noticed him. He was awkward enough about it catch my attention. And then I saw him twice more, shopping in the same area of Beverly Hills. He didn't seem to notice me those times, but I recognized him as the weirdo from the clinic."

"Was he a client there?"

"I assume so."

"Okay. Thank you, that gives us something specific to track down. Really good."

I look at McBride. She looks at Singh. And we all nod at once. It's not much, but it might be enough to get a search warrant.

I squeeze Taylor's shoulder. "Good girl." I don't even fucking care if they know how I feel about her. "Here's the thing. I'm going to help Sarah and Ram with this now. So I need to take you somewhere safe."

She blinks at me. "My sisters?"

I nod. As much as I hate it, Cole Parker is the only person I would trust right now to keep Taylor safe.

She closes her eyes and takes a deep breath. "Okay."

"They're going to make sure that it's safe for us to leave. And we need to talk to the captain first. So we'll hang tight here for a minute—"

There's another triple knock at the door. This time, it's the captain. She jerks her head for us to join her in the hallway.

Taylor nods as I excuse myself.

In the hallway, Sarah gives Woods a rundown of the ID, and the probable cause. "That she ID's him at the clinic gives him the connection to the person he set up—and his access to the case gives him the means. Him asking about her here today, combined with the threats and the encounters in the past, is a solid case for him being the stalker. From that, we could build a circumstantial case that connects him back to the murders, but I don't have anything direct there. Should we give this to the FBI, since the stalking is technically their case right now?"

The captain shakes her head. "That's why I came down here. Ferdinand just left. He's got a clear profile and it's not a law enforcement agent. He won't pursue this."

I see red. "That's fucking bullshit. Pardon my language, ma'am, but he's protecting the Secret Service here."

She nods. "I agree, Vasquez. It doesn't smell good."

"So who do I have to blow to get a warrant for a Secret Service agent's apartment?"

She looks at Sarah, her face grim. "I know a judge who will grant this. You get the application going while Vasquez gets Taylor the hell out of here. Then I'll get the warrant while you begin the stakeout."

[32]

TAYLOR

Luke leads me to the garage, to where he parked his car, and I'm freaking out the whole way.

Memories are slamming into me. Of that guy—Newcomb, they said, and that rings a bell. Agent Newcomb watching me with the former VPOTUS. Seeing him again here, and not knowing where I recognized his face from.

And now they think he's the guy who blew up my car.

Why? It doesn't make any sense. And that is terrifying to me.

Men wanting sex, that's normal. I grew up with that and feel like I can control that situation to some degree.

I can't control a stalker. He's not working with a full set of...anything.

As we stop beside Luke's car, he wraps his arms around me for a tight hug. "We'll get him," he promises me. "And you'll be safe with Cole until we do."

I shiver inside the circle of his arms. "I know."

"Still scary." His voice cracks a little. Just a little, but it's reassuring. "For me, too. And that's not something I usually have to admit."

———

We go in the service entrance of the Beverly Wilshire. Luke flashes his badge and people get out of our way.

The elevator takes us straight up to the top floor, and when we get out, there's a big guy wearing an earpiece who stops us. He doesn't accept the badge, either, not just on good faith. He looks at it, really looks at it, and calls in Luke's name.

Only after he gets the okay from Cole, inside the suite down the hall, does he let us pass.

"You'll be safe here," Luke promises.

I know.

I don't know if I'll be treated well, but I'll be kept alive, and given the circumstances, that seems like something to be grateful for.

The door to the suite opens before he knocks.

Instead of my formidable brother-in-law, it's his wife standing there.

My sister Hailey, who hasn't wanted anything to do with me in years.

Her eyes are as big as saucers and her lips are pulled tight together, but she steps aside and swings the door wide for us.

It's more welcoming than I ever thought I'd get from her.

"Hailey, Luke…"

"We've met," he says from behind me.

"Right." I stop inside the foyer and give my sister—the middle one, the very good one, the judging one—a small smile. "Hi."

"Oh, for fuck's sake, Taylor." She throws her arms around me as she growls in my ear. "What the fuck is going on?"

"So much," I whisper.

From somewhere else in the suite I hear a squeal, then quick footsteps.

"Incoming," Hailey whispers back.

I laugh as Ali plows into us. The little one, the sweet one, the smart one.

And then there's me.

The fuck-up. The slutty one. The one in danger, now and before and maybe always.

I hear Luke talking to Cole beside us. Excusing himself, because he has to go. Then his hand is on my back, and I twist around, almost hugging him before I remember we're not alone.

"Thank you," I say instead. Two simple little words. Easy. Polite. "And good luck."

He holds my gaze, then nods. "We don't need luck, princess. But I'll take it."

Then he's gone, and I'm being dragged deeper into the suite. Ali has a big plan to watch Queer Eye and not talk about the criminal takedown that's about to happen on the other side of the city. Hailey is reassuring me that Cole will be on top of any updates.

And all I can think about is the detective who just walked out that door and took a part of me with him.

[33]

LUKE

IT TAKES the captain less than an hour. When she arrives with
the warrant, we're waiting in a surveillance van a block away
from Newcomb's apartment, a low-lying nondescript walk-up in
a low-rent neighborhood.

We have an undercover team playing basketball right
outside his window, and to the best of our knowledge, he isn't
home.

"The warrant is pretty tight," Woods says. "We're looking
for evidence of stalking Taylor. That's it. If we don't find that,
we can't keep looking for murder evidence, not unless it's lying
in plain sight. Got it? We can't fuck this up. He might be just as
smart as he is dangerous. If we don't find it now, we need to
leave room open to find it later."

"Yes, boss."

"All right. On my signal, let's go."

We radio for a last update on his whereabouts then head in.
The van drops us as close as humanly possible without driving
through his wall.

McBride and Singh go first, with the warrant. They find the

superintendent, who likes the piece of paper more than he likes his tenant, and immediately lets them in.

The captain and I follow as soon as they're at the door.

Inside, it's a generic one bedroom with rent-a-room furniture and a vague smell of single man. Cologne and too-strong lemon Pledge.

"Nothing visible in the living room," Singh says. "Sarah, you take the bedroom. I'll check the kitchen, such as it is."

"Not a problem," McBride says, stopping in the doorway of the bedroom. She turns around, whipping her hand out and planting it in the middle of my chest.

Holding me back because...holy fuck.

The place is a shrine to Taylor. Her photos are everywhere.

And so are photos of the reservoir.

Every murder victim photographed. Taylor's head imposed on each of the bodies.

Behind me, Captain Woods swears under her breath, then calls in the update. "Suspect should be considered armed and dangerous. Let's keep this to the tightest possible comms channels. Suspect is a Secret Service agent. Repeat, he should be considered armed and dangerous. Last known whereabouts was the Northeast police station approximately ninety minutes ago."

When she finishes, she looks at me, then to Singh and McBride. "What next?"

Right.

This is their case. I was brought along as a courtesy. But I'm a good cop, and an extra body. I'm still in this, whether they think they need me or not.

Ram gestures at the bedroom. "I'll stay here until Forensics arrives to document and bag up this psychotic mess. Captain, you and McBride go back to the station and work the comms fan out. We may need federal assistance to find this fucker."

"Cole Parker has resources," I say, my throat tight.

I'll fucking use them even if the LAPD can't.

The captain coughs. "One thing at a time, Vasquez. Let's hope it doesn't come to that."

But if it does, I know what choice I'll make.

I'll protect Taylor, every fucking time.

"Are you going back to the hotel?" Sarah asks me.

I should. I will. But first, I need to go through this scene quietly myself. I need to know who this guy is, what makes him tick. "I'll keep Ram company until Forensics arrives."

———

Once they clear out, Ram closes the apartment door and gestures to the bedroom. "Have at it. Just don't touch anything. Or torch anything."

"Was I that easy to read?"

"It's what I would want if I were head over tits in love with a victim."

"I'm not—" I cut myself off. I wouldn't pretend that I'm not wrapped around her. Denying how I feel is all kinds of wrong. "It's complicated."

He waves his left hand at me, where his wedding ring sits. "I get it, man."

I pull out my phone. We'll have proper crime scene photos to pore over later, but right now, I want to have a working sense of the scene at my finger tips. I take video first, then photos, from the angles I imagine he'd look at the wall.

From the bed, which I'd like to light on fire.

Up close, where I can see fingerprints on the photos.

Fucking sloppy motherfucker.

I pull on a pair of gloves and nudge the drawer on his bedside table open. Nothing exciting in there. Same with his dresser. He's fastidiously clean, and boring on the surface, except for the creepy murder wall.

But under the bed, I find pay dirt. Dude has a box of international passport blanks and a slick looking printer, embosser. "Ram, in here."

I carefully flip through the stash.

"That's touching shit," he warns me.

"The Feds are going to want in here now for sure," I say. "Call the captain. I bet this guy has been crooked his whole time with the Secret Service. It probably doesn't trump your murder charges, but this is a weird side business for a federal agent. Who's in the market for..." I hold up one of the blanks. "A Moroccan passport, for example. Or a New Zealand passport."

"Mercenaries. Spies."

"Right."

Our radios whisper-squawk at the same time. *"Team 1, suspect is approaching the building. Advise on action. Should we arrest?"*

Ram looks at me and I shake my head. If I have the option of taking this asshole down, I want it.

"Let him enter. We'll arrest him inside." He releases the call button on his radio. "Where do you want to wait for him?"

"Behind the door out there." I return the passport supplies to where I found them and jump to my feet.

I pull the gloves off as I move swiftly to the entrance, then I slide my Glock out of my holster and take position.

On the other side of the door, I hear Newcomb stop and slide his key into the lock.

My pulse jacks up a beat. Three, two...

The handle turns, and the door swings open, temporarily covering my location. When it shuts, revealing Newcomb's back to me, I silently bring my weapon up, aiming at his centre of mass. "Freeze, asshole. I've got you covered. Don't move."

He moves. Of course he does. He twists around, dropping to kick my legs out from under me.

I'm ready. I jump, driving my knee into his skull before I tumble on top of him. I'm not sure what part of his arm I grab, but he screams as I wrench it behind his back and shove, twisting him to find the other motherfucking wrist so we can get him in cuffs.

Ram is right there, ready to slap them on as I wrestle my way clear.

And when I stand up, I'm breathing hard, even though it all happened in an instant.

I shrug at my colleague. "I told him not to move."

"You did," Ram says blandly. "I heard it with my own two ears and everything."

I search him quickly, and find he's carrying in a shoulder holster. Ram puts gloves on and removes the weapon before I continue, but the rest of my search is boring. His pockets are empty, and his wallet doesn't produce anything interesting either.

"Perry Newcomb, you disgusting piece of shit, you are under arrest. You have the right to remain silent. Anything you say can be used against you in a court of law. You have the right to speak to an attorney before we ask you any questions. You have the right to have your lawyer with you during questioning. If you cannot afford a lawyer, one can be appointed for you if you wish. If you decide to answer any questions now without an attorney present, you have the right to stop answering at any time. Is that clear?"

At our feet, Newcomb doesn't say anything.

"Maybe he didn't hear me," I say to Ram, conversationally. "Should I repeat it louder?"

"I heard it just fine. We can move on to asking him those questions now."

"We should stand him up, then." I grin as I reach down and grab him forcefully by the arm. "Up you get, asshole."

But the Secret Service agent isn't interested in talking. He stares at me in silence once we get him upright.

"This is all pretty damning evidence," I say softly as I move around him. "You probably only have a small window here to affect what happens next. Once the D.A. is involved, all bets are off." Nothing.

Ram tries next. "You look like a serial killer with this room, Perry. I know you probably aren't." He waves his hand at the wall. "This is all about Taylor Reid, isn't it? You don't want to kill indiscriminately. You just want her. Right?"

Cold refusal to speak.

Heavy footsteps sound in the hallway outside. "All right. Crime scene team is here. Let's get this asshole to the station." I turn around so the uniforms will see my badge when they come in through the door Ram propped open.

We hand over the scene to the forensics team and haul Newcomb out to a marked car. I leave Ram to ride with the suspect, and go around the block to get my own car.

After I take off my bullet-resistant vest and stash it in my trunk, I text Parker a brief update, then head straight for the station.

"You're on vacation," Captain Woods reminds me when I stalk into the squad room. "You don't need to be here for this."

"I'm the arresting officer."

"I saw that," she says dryly. "I trust that you didn't leave any bruises on him?"

Probably not. "It was by the book. Has he lawyered up yet?"

"Yeah, as soon as we fingerprinted him."

"Is the D.A. on the way?"

"The D.A. is in the house," I hear from behind me, and I

turn around at the sound of a familiar, but no-longer-friendly voice.

Assistant District Attorney Nora Vance.

Ex-girlfriend.

Ex-friend.

By-the-book fanatic.

She stops in front of me, a tall, cool drink of professionalism and disdain. "What do we have?"

"I should let McBride and Singh field this one," I say, stepping out of the way.

She closes her eyes like she's saying a silent prayer I haven't fucked up a case.

That makes two of us, but I know I didn't.

"Executed a warrant looking for evidence that the suspect, Perry Newcomb, was stalking Taylor Reid, a woman he knew from Washington, D.C. He did not disclose their previous relationship—"

"Relationship? Is this a domestic violence case?"

"Sorry, I misspoke," Sarah explained. "Their previous relationship was tangential. He provided protective detail for the Vice President—the former Vice President—and Ms. Reid was... an acquaintance of VPOTUS."

Nora blinks. "Wait. The same Reid family who were in the news last week for financial crimes? The ones who are connected to the current POTUS?"

"The same."

She holds out her hand for the case file. "I heard a bit about this case. I thought the Feds had it."

"The local connection is the reservoir murders." McBride's face is beyond grim. "When we executed the warrant, we found photographic evidence that Newcomb was responsible for those as well."

"Is that why you went there? Because you connected the two cases?"

McBride and Singh exchange a wary look. "Yes. But we stuck to the scope of the warrant. He had the murder evidence glued to his wall in plain sight."

"All right. Thanks. Obviously, I'll be arguing against bail. You can transfer him to booking since he's lawyered up and won't talk. Has his attorney shown up yet?"

"Right behind you, counselor." I don't recognize this guy, but he looks expensive.

Nora knows him, though. They greet each other cordially, although he doesn't hide that he's a pit bull. "Your detectives had no right to be in my client's apartment, A.D.A. I've reviewed the warrant. It was an overreach, based on nothing but the wild accusations of a woman whose reputation for lying has international reach. We'll see you in court, and this will be thrown out." He gives McBride, Singh, and me a dirty look. "My client was working the same case as your detectives, clearly, and they wildly misinterpreted the information they found in his apartment."

Working the same case. I can't stop myself from storming across the squad room. My colleagues get me before I punch him, McBride grabbing one arm and Singh putting his entire body in front of me on the other side. "Get out of here," I growl. "Your client isn't going anywhere tonight, so your dirty work is done, you piece of shit."

"Detective," Nora smoothly says behind me.

I shrug off my friends. "He's not fucking worth it."

"There's a process here," she reminds me. "Please don't interfere with it."

"I'm out. I'm out," I repeat. So fucking out.

"Good." She turns to the lawyer. "Bring that argument to court. Don't air it in front of my detectives. And Vasquez is right. Your client poses a clear danger to the population. I'm confident the warrant was executed appropriately, and the rest is up to a judge to determine."

He leaves, and she gives me a pointed look, like, *this better be clear cut.*

Aw, fuck it. I jerk my head toward the empty conference room. "Can we talk for a minute?"

"Sure." She glances over at McBride. "I'll be right back so we can go over my response to his ridiculous motion, all right? I need to know everything—and I mean everything—about how the warrant came about."

Sarah nods, then gives me an awkward thumbs up when Nora turns around again.

I laugh despite myself.

Once in the conference room, I push the door shut and get right to the point. "I need to disclose a personal relationship with the victim of the crime here, Taylor Reid."

Nora groans. "Really, Luke?"

"I'm being upfront about this."

"Why were you involved in the arrest? Jesus Christ, you always need to be such a fucking hero."

I don't have a great answer for that. She's not wrong. Still, I regret nothing. "We didn't know he'd return to the apartment."

"That seems like splitting hairs. You shouldn't have been involved in the investigation to begin with."

I wasn't involved with Taylor when the investigation started, but I'm going to leave that detail out. It doesn't matter now. "Nora, you know I'm a good cop."

"I know you like to break rules when they get in your way. Try not to do that anymore." She jerks her head in the direction of Sarah and Ram. "Do they know?"

"Yes."

Her face softens, shifting from prosecutor to ex-girlfriend. "Do you know about her history?"

Something twitches painfully in my neck. "Of course I do. And she knows about mine." I say this pointedly, because Nora can't think she has the emotional upper hand when it comes to interviewing Taylor. If this goes to trial, it's going to be messy and public.

I've reconciled myself to that fact.

I don't like it, and Nora will know that. I've always been intensely private. From her perspective, there's no way Taylor and I make sense.

Frankly, I don't care if it makes sense to anyone other than us. "She's been through a lot in the last week, in her whole lifetime, and she's been brutally honest with me." Even if it took some cajoling and threats-slash-promises of punishment. "There's more, too. It's for her to tell, and a lot of it is out of our jurisdiction, but she could bring down empires."

Tension radiates from Nora's gaze. I can practically hear her competing thoughts. *But is she a reliable witness? What a challenge, though.*

"Meet her with an open mind," I say, my voice low and thick with urgency. "She busted this case wide open for us by putting herself out there on the ledge. It's going to feel fucking precarious for her right now."

[34]

TAYLOR

Cole brings us takeout for dinner and passes on an update that Luke arrested Perry Newcomb at his apartment.

I let out a breath I feel like I've been holding since I arrived at the Wilshire. "That's great," I say, truly relieved. "Is Luke coming here?"

"He's heading to the station," Cole says.

I try to hide my disappointment, but I do a crap job, and my sisters notice. As the evening progresses, Ali gives me a look every time I say Luke's name. Maybe because I say his name every third sentence despite trying really hard to talk about anything else.

Maybe also because I turn a little pink when she calls me on it. "Fess up. What's going on between you and the hot cop?"

"Uh..." I look back and forth between my sisters. Hailey's gaze is dark and unreadable. I hate that I'm worried about her judging me. I've done a lot of hard work to get out from under that shame monster. "We're sleeping together. We've talked about dating once this is all over. It's not ideal, we both know that, but we're honest about it. He's big on talking and boundaries. He's a good guy," I say, ending on what sounds like a weak note. Like I need to defend him. "It's not—"

"It's okay," Ali says.

Hailey stays quiet.

"I know it's okay. But it's not ideal." I repeat the lines I've told myself a dozen times over the last few days. "Maybe I'm not cut out for doing anything quite the right way."

"There's no such thing as a right way," Hailey finally says.

I'm so shocked you could bowl me over with a feather.

She gives me a rueful look. "There are better and worse ways, don't get me wrong. But Cole and I weren't an ideal match when we got together. I didn't trust him, didn't like him. But he fit right up against me, and that was hard to argue against when my heart got involved."

Fits right up against me. That's Luke. He sees all my damaged, broken pieces, all my jagged sharp edges, and molds himself around them. When he's wrapped around me, I feel whole.

"He makes me feel good," I whisper. "Really good."

"That's hard to find," Ali says, rubbing my knee. "Hang on to that."

I'm going to try. "He might not want anything to do with me once this is all over."

"You said you'd talked about dating, though."

"Sure. It might just be talk." I shrug, needing to protect my fragile heart a bit.

"I hope it's not," my youngest sister says softly.

That makes two of us.

"Me too," says Hailey.

Three of us.

"He made me the best banana split ever," I confess. "For breakfast, after we had a fight. And then makeup sex. It was really awesome."

Hailey grins. "Cole brought me ice cream when I was having my period. Ice cream is such a good move, more men should know about it."

"Remember when Scott brought me cupcakes to try and woo me after we broke up?" Ali leans in. "The way to our hearts is clearly through sugar."

I think of what Luke said. Safety. "Sugar and security, maybe. We need our men sweet and tough at the same time."

Hailey blinks. "Yeah, that's probably true. Have you ever dated a guy like Detective Vasquez before?"

I shake my head. "Have I ever dated before? For real? No. But the men I went out with in D.C. weren't anything like him. I didn't know he was what I needed until he found me."

"Need is such a powerful word," she murmurs. "Be careful."

"I will. I am." I take a deep breath. "If we don't work out, it'll be okay. He's giving me something amazing right now, and I will always hold that close. As awful as it's been to be so scared —and I still am, don't get me wrong—this has also been a weird time of getting to know myself better than I ever thought I would."

"You've changed so much."

"Not completely," Ali hastens to add, shooting Hailey a look that says *be nice*. "He's good for you, but you are good all by yourself."

I haul my little sister into a tight hug. "Shut up, you. You're so fucking smart."

She giggles inside the circle of my arms. "Language, Taylor."

I flop back on the couch, laughing. "That's what Luke says, too. Then he threatens to spank me."

A shocked silence follows.

I realize I've said too much.

And I start laughing even harder.

Hailey starts in with me, then Ali finally joins in until tears are running down all of our faces. "Sugar, security, and spank-ings," she finally wheezes. "It's the magic recipe for the perfect man."

"I don't need to know that about my baby sister," Hailey says. Then she pauses. "But she's not wrong."

I don't know why I'm shocked. I've learned so much about healthy sex in the last three years—and then even more in the last three days from Luke—that I know even straight-laced good girls like my two sisters might be into happy, kinky sex in private.

But for so long, I've felt like a freak with them. The dirty one, the slutty one. The whore. The fuck up.

And now my tears aren't from laughter. My shoulders shake, and Ali wraps herself around me. Hailey grabs tissues then takes up vigil on my other side, but I can't stop the sobs from racking my body.

After what feels like ages, they pull away, but their arms are replaced by two others. Luke is suddenly in front of me, his body warm and strong against mine. I fall into him, snotty-faced and swollen-eyed.

"I've got you," he growls into my hair. "It's okay."

———

Leaving the hotel is a blur. Luke tells us about the arrest. My sisters promise they'll be at the courthouse in the morning for support, and then he ushers me downstairs, holding my hand tightly in his.

His car is parked next to the valet station this time. No need to hide at the service entrance. He gives a twenty to the kid working there. "Thanks, man."

"No worries, officer."

I feel so wrung out, like I'm empty and drained.

At the next red light, Luke squeezes my knee. "It's okay."

I nod. I know that.

"Do you want me to take you home?"

I turn and look at him. "Pardon?"

"Would you rather go back to your place? You're free to go home now. I was going to take you back to my place for the night, because I have food, but—"

"I don't want to go home," I say quietly. The thought of being in my apartment, either alone or even with Luke, fills me with terror.

I'll have to get back on that horse, but not tonight.

Tomorrow. After the arraignment, after I know dude is going to stay in jail.

The rest of the drive to his house passes in silence. As we climb up the canyon roads, and onto his street, his private oasis on the edge of the city, a new feeling takes over inside me.

I want him.

He got me off this morning—and oh my God, was that only this morning?—but we didn't have sex. I want us to be together, as much as humanly possible, tonight.

Smashed bits, hot breath on skin, aching muscles kind of together.

I need him.

Oh, that makes me shiver, because I can't need another person. That's too much, but it's also true, and I'm too fucking tired to lie to myself tonight.

I need Luke.

When he pulls into his garage, I wait until he comes around to open my door. Once upon a time—maybe a week ago, who knows—I thought about how I could manipulate this man. Best him with hubris and sexuality.

Now I just want to serve him, to use my lifetime of seductive abilities to give him a night he will never forget.

He opens my door and I step out, sliding against him as I stand. I can feel the heat of his body, the tension in his limbs, and I tilt my head up so we're looking at each other. Face to face, ever so close.

"Thank you," I whisper, a slight smile playing at my mouth. Tentative. Innocent. It's not an act, not in a bad way. Just...me, amplified. Me, dressed up for dirty play.

Me, getting a chance to be the innocent seductress I never got to be.

He strokes my cheek, brushing a strand of hair back behind my ear, and I exhale, letting my eyelids flutter shut.

He groans and his mouth crashes down on mine.

Yes.

Oh, yes. Please, more, *Luke*...

The car is hard against my back, but Luke cradles me in his arms as he presses against me. Hard against my front, too. I'm pinned in place, his captive princess, and my heart feels so full it hurts. His mouth trails over my jaw, down my neck, then back to my lips.

More kisses, endless kisses.

Safe, dirty, special kisses.

"Take me to bed," I breathe, and he groans again, his cock thick and hard against my belly.

When he wrenches away from me, we're both gasping.

I touch his face and smile before I head for the door. He follows hot on my heels, his attention burning against my back.

Inside, I set my bag down and kick off my shoes as he resets the security system. Even as he does that, I can feel his gaze keeping me in his peripheral vision.

I like that feeling that he can't let me out of his sight again.

Way too fucking much.

Stop overthinking this. We need to reconnect. It's been a

long day. Stressful and scary, but done now. We need to fuck the pain out of our system.

It doesn't sound quite right, of course. It's probably not right.

I don't care.

And when he turns and pins me down with the full-force of his attention, once again, I stop thinking about it.

"You," he says, prowling toward me.

I smile. "Yes?"

"Come here."

My heart skips a beat as he catches me in his arms and lifts me up. I wrap myself around him, tighter than tight, as he takes me upstairs.

To his bed.

We strip together, working back and forth. My top, his top. His pants, my pants. I ditch my panties as he grabs a condom, and then we're fused together again, rolling and kissing and biting—oh God, the biting, so good—until he pins me down.

There aren't any words for this. There's just raw, hungry need. I need him inside me, I need his weight on top of me, and he gives it all to me.

His gaze is hot and hard as he pushes my legs apart and finds me wet. Ready. The tension ratchets up between us as he teases the heavy head of his cock through my folds, then presses deep inside me in a single, piercing thrust.

It's right there, on the tip of my tongue. I can feel the words, and they don't even feel wrong in my mouth. *I love you*, I want to say. But it's too much, too soon, and not at all realistic.

I love the kink.

I love the friendship he's given me.

The safe space.

I crave safety, and Luke has given it to me in spades when he didn't need to.

Of course I think I love him. Of course I actually love him, because he is lovely. That shouldn't be confused for long-term commitment.

And God only knows how he feels about it.

So instead of saying something, I kiss him. I give him my tongue, my mouth, my surrender. I kiss him as he fucks me hard and slow.

I kiss him as the arousal shifts inside me, from a gimme gimme feeling to something more heady, more overwhelming. To the twist and climb of an impending orgasm, where all I can feel is the size of him inside me—big, heavy, thick—and the bursts of pleasure that come with each thrust and grind.

I kiss him as I begin to shake.

As he shudders on top of me, his grip getting almost too tight, but still perfectly right.

And he kisses me back.

Fiercely.

Demandingly.

We kiss each other as we come, together, and we kiss each other long after we disentangle our limbs. We kiss until he's ready to go again, and then our kiss only breaks apart long enough for him to roll me on my stomach. Once he's inside me again, he finds my mouth.

Never enough kisses.

Never enough touch.

Never enough.

But we're going to try our damnedest to fill that aching need.

All night long.

[35]

LUKE

First thing in the morning, we go to her apartment so she can dress appropriately for court. No more leggings and tank tops, no more acres of bare, tan skin for me to tease and touch and love.

She puts on a severe-looking black pantsuit, with a simple black t-shirt underneath.

And now I have a fantasy of bringing the bossy lady CEO to heel.

She could wear a burlap sack and I'd find it filthy and full of potential.

She picks up her phone from the couch where we left it a week ago and wiggles it at me. "Now we can sext, Luke. That'll be fun, won't it?"

Glad I'm not the only one with dirty thoughts on my mind. "Absolutely fun. I'm looking forward to it."

Her smile is a little too wide, a little too bright, but I can't blame her for trying to push away the fear of what's about to happen with a bit of play.

I'm always game for distraction.

When we arrive at the courthouse, we find her sisters

waiting for her in matching suits. Together they make a formidable wall of polished socialite attitude. Nothing will fuck with the Reid sisters. Not a stalker, not the paparazzi, not the federal agents they all have good reason to distrust with every fiber of their being.

And the Feds are out in force today. Once we're inside the courtroom, a team of federal prosecutors identify themselves to the judge and ask for standing in the hearing. Apparently while we are sitting here, another group of them are filing a sealed indictment against Newcomb related to charges around leaking the video of President Best and Gerome Lively, but for privileged reasons they expect that case to be delayed and ask that this proceeding be put on hold.

The judge is having none of it, much to Taylor's relief. "That is a motion you can make as we progress further through this process. However, what I see in front of me today—murder, attempted murder, stalking, threats—all of that is very serious. And we will be proceeding today with a reading of those charges and entering an initial plea from the defendant. What happens in federal court is a matter for a federal judge, not for me, unless I'm directed by that judge. Do you understand?"

Beside me, Taylor exhales quietly, her eyes bright.

Her relief grows as the arraignment proceeds. The judge first refuses Newcomb bail, then accepts his pleading not guilty, and warns his lawyer that she won't have much patience for playing games.

By the time he's remanded back into the fine custody of the Los Angeles County Sheriff's Department, Taylor's cheeks are wet with silent tears.

Beside her, Ali is leaning hard on her shoulder, and on the other side of the youngest Reid sister is Hailey, glowering fiercely at Newcomb.

Nora gathers up her notes, tucks them in her briefcase, then comes through the barrier between the gallery and the lawyer's desks in front of the judge.

"Ms. Reid?" She stops in front of us. "I'm A.D.A. Nora Vance. Today went well, as I hope you saw."

"Yes, thank you."

Nora glances at me, then down at where my hand is tangled in Taylor's. Just a beat, but from the way Taylor tenses up, I don't think she missed it.

"I have time this afternoon. I'd like to go over your statement while it's all still fresh."

"Of course."

She hands over a card, like we both don't know that I know exactly where her office is. "One o'clock?"

Taylor nods solemnly. "I'll be there."

We go back to the Wilshire with her sisters for a light lunch and a lot of debriefing, then I drive her to the DA's office on Broadway. It's stop and go traffic the whole way.

Once we're parked, she reaches across the gear shift and puts her hand on mine. Her eyes are cool, calm. "Is Nora Vance the lawyer you dated?"

"Yeah."

"Okay." That's it. She drops her gaze and unbuckles her seat belt.

"It was a while ago."

"I know. You said that."

"You remember everything, don't you?"

"Probably." She sighs and leans back against the head rest, her gaze sliding down the street. Into the distance. "This is going to sound weird, because of course I'm a little jealous—like a normal amount, that weird little twinge inside—but I like that you have a bit of a complicated past here, too. It's kind of balancing."

I laugh. "I like that take."

"I thought you might."

"I told her about us. You aren't a dirty secret to me, Taylor. Or any kind of secret at all."

"Oh."

"I didn't tell you about her because we had more pressing things going on yesterday, and then...we weren't talking at all. It just slipped my mind because she's just a colleague now. Has been for ages."

"It's fine." She draws in another breath, a deep one, then claps her hands together. "Okay, let's go upstairs so I can bare my soul once again."

"Your favorite thing to do," I murmur, leaning across the car to kiss her.

She rubs her nose against mine. "Only with you."

———

McBride is in the waiting area when we arrive upstairs.

I sit down next to her. "What are you doing here?"

"Ferdinand and I just had a very interesting lunch."

"Dining with the enemy, Sarah?"

She laughs.

But she doesn't expand.

I pick up on her hesitance and drop it. Once Nora comes out to get Taylor, I pick it up again. "What did he say that you didn't want to tell me in front of a witness?"

"She's more than a witness."

A fuck of a lot more. That's not the point. "Fine. What did he say that you don't want to tell me?"

"He got a weird pushback from somewhere up high on our request for flight data on Gerome Lively."

"Huh."

"Yeah. He brought it to me, cop to cop. I don't think he's our enemy."

I rub my jaw. What the fuck does that mean? "Why would they want us to drop that, when we'd drop it anyway because we got the guy? Newcomb is our guy, right? He set up the nurse from the clinic, but he wasn't set up by someone else, right?"

"He's our guy. Newcomb knew where the investigation was going. He had the inside track for knowing what—and who—to put in our path that would look right. That kind of insider information wasn't really available to Lively, anyway. And actually, I was able to use the flight data to rule him *out* as a suspect, because he was elsewhere. The records alibi him. So no, I don't get it. But I'm wondering if there's something else I would see, if I watched that long enough."

"But you can't."

"I can't." She presses her lips together, then leans in close. "But Taylor's brother-in-law could," she whispers. "If someone told him about this."

———

When Taylor emerges from the back rooms of the D.A.'s office, she looks...different. Tired, yes, but that's to be expected. There's something else there, something that looks a bit like anger. The quietest anger imaginable, just a bare flicker.

But I see it.

She shoots me a look like, *don't hug me, I might break*, so I fall in step with her and we head back to my car.

As soon as we're alone in the vehicle, she explodes. "The legal system is totally fucked. Totally, completely fucked. Can I say that? No offense to you, Mr. Cop."

"None taken."

"This isn't about Newcomb. That part went just fine. Luckily, I'm not really needed to convict him, because if it hinged on my testimony, we'd be lucky to nail his ass."

"Did Nora say that to you?" I will go back up there and tear her a new one.

"No." Taylor swallows hard, fighting back tears. "No, she was fine. Extra nice, maybe, considering that she knows we're sleeping together. But the questioning turned to Gerome Lively, and that's where it went off the rails."

My mind flashes to Sarah. To Ferdinand and what Nora might know, and how she might know whatever that is.

But I don't need to guess. Taylor's unloading isn't done.

She stares out the front of the window. "I told her that he raped me when I was thirteen."

Fuck. No.

I mean, she'd basically told me in Washington. And I should have seen this coming. I know that survivors minimize their experiences to keep the disclosure safe. Measured.

"I'm sorry," I say. The words sound hollow and not nearly enough. "That's awful."

We're sitting in a parked car on a busy street in downtown Los Angeles. In theory, life is swirling around us. All I see is Taylor, holding her head high even as she cracks open on the inside.

She's so fucking brave. Especially if she's already told Nora this, and been warned there won't be anything that can be done about it.

It's not the first time I've seen a witness dig deep into their fear and find astonishing strength. It's not even the first time I've seen someone I love do it. My mother sending me off to boot camp when she'd lost her husband on the same base. My sisters at varying times being rock-star moms.

But this is the first time a woman I am in love with has had to bare her soul, share her most secret pain, and have no fucking idea if it will pay off.

"I thought maybe it might be connected," she whispered. "Or even if it isn't connected, it still seems like the right time to say something. But it's too late. She said it would be up to the US Attorneys in Miami, the same office that gave him a deal last time. They won't want anything to do with me." She looks at me, pain radiating from her eyes. "I kept that to myself all these years. Because I thought it was keeping me safe. I thought all the secrets I kept close to the chest were like armor. Instead they were just weighing me down, slowly drowning me."

"You were right to share."

"But nobody will believe me."

"I believe you. I told you that before. That hasn't changed. Did Nora believe you?"

"Yes."

"Okay. That's two of us. Have some faith. Not in the legal system, necessarily, but in humanity."

"That's a big ask, Detective."

I give her a crooked, weak smile. "I'm full of those, Princess." I squeeze her hand. "Can I take you back to my place and make you dinner?"

She looks off into the distance. "Dinner sounds nice. But could we do it at my place? I think I want to go home. I couldn't last night, but I need to sooner or later. Do you want to come over? Stay a while, then tuck me into bed?"

And then leave her alone for the night?

But I can't push myself onto her. And she's right. She needs to get back to her life.

If I give her space, she'll let me be a part of it, too. "Whatever you need."

Putting the car in gear, I head to her end of the city.

We stop for groceries, then I escort her up to her apartment, both of us painfully vigilant. That will pass in time, but it's hard right now.

I kiss her senseless in the kitchen as we put away the food we bought, and then hold her on the couch for a long time. Kiss her again after dinner, many times over.

But we don't have sex. We talk. We sit in silence. We talk more. For the first time since our chemistry spilled over into explicitly needing each other, another need has taken top priority. A sweet, dependable shoulder to lean on.

I want to be that, too.

She starts yawning early, which is my cue to leave. Once she's tucked into bed, I take my leave. "I'll call you once I get home."

"Good. I want to hear you say good night one more time."

"You like that?"

"Love it."

I brush my lips against hers. "Good night, Princess. Tomorrow, do you want to go the beach? Go dancing? I still have a few days left in my vacation."

"Yes." She yawns as she tries to say something else, then she scrunches up her nose. "Okay, I'm tired."

"You are. Go to sleep."

"Call me when you get home! I'm not going to sleep until you call."

I grin the whole way to the car. It was a long day, and a rough day. Brutal for her in so many ways. But that bit right at the end had been pure sweetness, and it carries me all the way home.

It takes me fifteen minutes to get up into the canyon.

I have my phone out as soon as I'm in the garage. Time to say goodnight to my girl.

[36]

TAYLOR

I'm smiling like a dope as I answer the phone. "You made it safe and sound?"

"Yep." Luke's voice is low and warm in my ear. "Now close your eyes. It's dreamland for you."

"Night," I murmur. *Love you.*

He doesn't answer.

"Luke?" I blink my eyes open and realize the call has disconnected. Maybe he hung up after I said *night*. Did I fall asleep as I imagined saying *love you*?

Wait, did I actually say it?

Mortified, I sit upright in bed. Oh, shit.

My fingers shake as I dial him back. He doesn't answer.

Fuck.

But that doesn't make any sense. This is Luke. *Luke.* Mr. Talk Shit Out. Mr. Feelings Are Fine.

There's no way he's ghosting me because I said something too emo, and I'm not even sure I said it. The more I think about it, the surer I am that I didn't.

I dial him again, and this time the phone goes straight to voicemail.

Something is wrong. *Something is wrong,* and I don't have a car, because a mad man blew it up, and Luke's house is a solid twenty minutes away anyway.

He once told me to call 911 if anything happened. If I had a worry for any reason.

I'm sure, sickeningly so, that something terrible has just happened. My fingers shake as I dial.

"911, what's your emergency?"

Oh God, oh God, oh God. If Luke's phone has just died, I'm going to be very sorry about this. "I was talking to a cop just now, and his phone went dead. Now I can't reach him. His name is Luke Vasquez and his address is..." I fumble over it, forgetting the street number. My words are spilling out too quickly, not making much sense, but I'm sure in my head that there's a problem and I can't fix it by myself. "He just arrived home. He called me from his garage, and then we got disconnected. And I know that sounds crazy, but he arrested a Secret Service agent for stalking me, and there's a solid chance that someone isn't happy with him. Can you check if Perry Newcomb is still in jail?"

I hear myself.

I hear that I sound crazy.

"Ma'am, please stay on the phone. We're dispatching a police unit to that address right now."

Fuck this shit. Stay on the phone. I jump out of bed, my legs just as shaky as my fingers, and I run into the living room. I need my purse, I need a hoodie, and I need to get to Luke's house. "I have to go," I say out loud. To myself, to the dispatcher.

"Ma'am—"

I hang up and go into the Uber app. Is it wrong to ask a complete stranger to drive you to a crime scene?

Well it wouldn't be the first time I've done something morally ambiguous.

But my fucking credit card doesn't work, so I call Cole, crying.

"I'll get you a ride," he says. "We'll meet you there."

"I'm not waiting for your guys, Cole."

"I have Uber, too. It's okay. Go downstairs. Someone will be there soon. Do not go into the house even if police have arrived. You don't want to see it, Taylor."

It. A crime scene.

Luke maybe killed because of me.

I'm sobbing by the time I get to the lobby. My Uber is waiting for me, a nice-looking guy named Muhamet who offers me tissues and turns down his radio. "You are not Cole?"

"It's complicated," I whisper through tears.

It's probably better if he thinks I'm running away from a break up or something rather than toward a—

My phone rings again. I don't recognize the number, so I don't answer it.

Then Cole calls back. "I'm in the car," I say.

"So are we."

"Who's we?"

"Me and one of the guys." One of his goons. "Your sisters are at the hotel. You could go there. I can deal with whatever's on the scene."

"No." I swallow around razor blades in my throat. I need to go to Luke. "I'll see you there."

I hang up the phone.

Then I turn it off. Back on again. Another unknown number call. Maybe that's the police telling me not to be an idiot, that Luke is fine. I wait until the strange number goes away, then I try his phone again. Still no answer.

When we arrive in the canyon, there's a cop car blocking the street before we get to Luke's place. Muhamet gives me a look of concern. "This is as close as I can get, miss."

Miss.

I give him a weak smile. "I'll be fine."

"Are you sure?"

"Yeah. Thanks. I'll give you five stars for sure."

He watches as I get out, then doesn't drive away. He rolls down the window, listening, as I approach the officer blocking the street.

Nice guy.

Nobody needs to worry about me, though.

"Hi," I say quietly. "I know something is happening at Luke Vasquez's house. I called it in to 911. I'm his—" I don't know what he is. Am I his girlfriend? I'm his dirty sex partner, but I don't think this is the time or place to identify as such. "He was on the phone with me."

The uniformed cop doesn't give a fuck. "This street is closed, ma'am."

"I get that. To, like, everyone else. But I need to get to his house. I need to see him."

There's a growl of an engine behind me, and I turn to look.

Two oversized black SUVs arrive. It could be the FBI. But it's not—it's my brother-in-law. I don't miss the fact that Muhamet is now staring at the scene we're making. I wave at him, my heart pounding. "We're good here. Promise."

"Your Uber ride?" Cole asks, like this is all no big deal.

"Can you bribe this guy or something?" I jerk my thumb at the cop behind me, who protests. I don't care. I'm about to run up the street screaming Luke's name.

"Don't need to." Cole looks past me at the cop. "Sarah McBride is up there. Get her on the radio. She'll authorize us to come closer." Then he looks at me again. "You should answer your phone. She tried to call you. Luke's stuck in his house with someone, but the situation is under control. Get in."

He's alive. My heart leaps into my throat and I scramble for the back door. By the time I've got it closed behind me, we're moving again, given the all-clear.

When we turn the corner onto Luke's street, it's a mess of cop cars, marked and unmarked. Lights all over the place, uniformed officers going door to door. And pretty close to his front door are two ambulances.

Waiting.

I start to cry.

"Hold it together, Taylor."

Really not possible. I don't respond to Cole.

"My understanding is that this is basically a hostage situation."

My mind races. "Who is in there with him? Is it Newcomb?"

"They have no intel on that yet. But no, Newcomb is still in lockup."

"How do you know it's a hostage situation then?"

"He appeared at the door long enough to tell the cops to go away. He said it in a way that told McBride he was in danger. They have codes."

Codes. Secret languages. God bless his kinky cop soul. He has to survive this so I can ask him which came first. I jump out of the car and run toward the front line, ignoring Cole shouting at me to stop. Screw that.

"Sarah!" I yell.

She appears from behind the ambulance and steps out into my path, her hands up. "Hey hey hey. Slow down. It's going to be okay. Luke is smart. He's going to be able to talk his way out of there, because there is no winning for whoever is inside. He'll get them to see that in time. We just need to give him that space."

I start sobbing again, which is why I'm a civilian and she's a cop. "I thought maybe his phone just died, but I knew that wasn't the case. Oh my God."

"I know." She wraps her arms around me, and holy fuck, I've been hugged more times in the last week than I have in my entire life, and it's really fine.

Luke broke me.

In a good way.

And now he's locked in his house with a crazy person. "Who is it?" I whisper. "Tell me. You know, right? He told you in code?"

She shakes her head. "I don't know. We're negotiating with him via notes right now. I want you to stay out of sight, though. He can't know you're here. You get that? It will fuck him up. He thinks you're at home, asleep. We did not tell him you called 911. We'll do that once he's safe. He'll be fucking proud of you. You did the right thing."

My heart wrenches hard.

She leads me back to Cole, who fires a bunch of questions I don't really follow. Then he takes me firmly by the arm and leads me back to his vehicle.

The next two hours drag by. At quarter to midnight, there's a flurry of activity, and I go to leap out of the SUV, but the goon stops me.

"I'll go find out," Cole says, his brows slashing across his forehead in a stern, don't-fuck-with-me expression. "Stay."

I can't believe my sister likes this man.

I throw myself back against the seat and pout until he returns three and a half minutes later. I timed him.

He jerks his thumb at the goon. "Take a walk for a few," he says before climbing into the back seat with me.

"What is it?" I ask as he rocks his jaw back and forth. Clearly something went wrong. "Cole..."

"You're not going to fucking believe it."

"Try me," I say faintly.

"It's your crackpot mother."

"What?"

"Inside with Luke. It's your *fucking mother*. Amelia has come unhinged, clearly, and thought she could kill Luke without anyone finding out. Now she's trapped in the house with him."

"My—" I'm speechless. Absolutely, what-the-fuck-do-you-mean-my-mother speechless.

"I know."

"She's dangerous," I whisper. "And connected. Cole, we need to make this stop, now. She has the power to summon mercenaries here."

"She must not anymore. She wouldn't be doing this if she could have sent mercenaries to do it, Taylor. Think about it for a second. I don't know what kind of changes have gone down in PRISM, but maybe she's been booted from the council because of your father's criminal indictments."

"But if she— I mean, why would—" My mouth goes dry. "To hurt me. To shut me up."

We'd considered it a possibility with the car bomb. I should have known that if my mother wanted to hurt me, it wouldn't be a near miss like that.

Amelia Dashford Reid doesn't miss.

But now she's in a hostage situation with the LAPD, and maybe she doesn't know how to end this in a Dashford kind of way.

She's gone off the deep end.

Maybe she was always there. But this is bonkers mad. What was she thinking? What *is* she thinking?

My brain spinning, I grab Cole's arm. "You need to tell them to tell her that someone has called this whole thing off. Not my grandfather. Someone else..." A Rolodex of powerful people spins through my mind. The President would be too obviously a false promise. She wouldn't believe that. "The Attorney General has intervened. Tell them to tell her that. They are friends, but not really. And she has dirt on him."

She has dirt on everyone.

Including me, but I've shared all of that with Luke now. Which makes him a liability to her.

Cole nods. "Smart. Stay here."

He lets himself out of the car. I watch him stride quickly toward the front line, and then when I'm sure he's out of hearing range, I quietly open my door and slip out the other side.

It is smart. They'll think it's a good idea.

And it might even work.

But I'm not going to leave it up to chance. Slowly, I creep up the outside of the line of cars. Nobody is watching me, so I get pretty close before I need to break across the lawn.

Then I wait.

There's a fierce discussion going on between Cole, Sarah, and a big, burly guy I assume is the incident commander.

I see my opportunity, and I race for the front door. Behind me there are shouts for me to stop, but that's never going to happen.

I'll trade my life for his in a heartbeat.

[37]

LUKE

There's shouting outside, and Amelia flinches.

I'm not sure she's ever fired a gun before, but she's pretty comfortable pointing one at my chest. "Ignore them," I say quietly. I give her a smile, too.

I've smiled a lot in the last few hours. Nothing like getting to know your girlfriend's mom at gunpoint.

It turns out Amelia's had a hard week, too. Her husband was arrested, she was in tough negotiations to not get arrested herself, and the extra governmental powers that be who should have come to her rescue did not. Instead they fired her. She's slightly grumpy about that and has decided to take it out on me.

I don't actually have any sympathy for her. Mommy dearest is crazypants, and has zero idea of appropriate boundaries. Like, for example, don't point a loaded weapon at a police officer. As Taylor would say, that's freaking rude.

"You were telling me about—"

There's a thump against the door, and someone tries to open it.

My pulse jacks up.

Amelia aims her gun at the front door. "Answer it. Tell them to go away, or I'll start shooting."

I go to the door and raise my voice enough to be heard through it. "Stand back, I'm turning the deadbolt."

Pressing my hand against the wood, I unlock it—and a ball of fury pushes through, knocking me down.

The gun goes off, smashing the light bulb over our heads.

"Do not shoot," I yell out as loud as I can. "Everyone stand down, we're fine in here. Right? Amelia? We're fine."

The ball of fury pops up, and my heart stops.

Taylor has crashed my hostage scene, and that is so not fucking okay.

"Mother," she says coldly. Now I know where she gets that tone. I like it on her—and hate it on Amelia. "What the actual fuck are you doing?"

Way to calm down the lady with a gun, Taylor. Between her overt hostility and the tumbleweed entrance, I think it's safe to say that my princess makes a terrible commando.

She turns to me, giving Amelia a wide target on her back. My heart starts again, racing triple time now.

"Sarah said I couldn't let you know I was here," Taylor says, the words tumbling out fast and furious. "But when I found out it was my mom, I needed to trade places with you."

What the fuck? "No," I growl out, shoving her behind me. I lock the door again, a show for her mother that this is fine. We're fine.

"No," Amelia says coolly. "Get away from the door, both of you."

Taylor tries to get around me and glares at her mother. "Yes," she says. "Let him go. He doesn't know anything. He's no use to you. I'm your vessel of secrets, right, mother? I'm your dirty little girl, just like you. So here I am. You've got me. You can let him go."

"I think I'd rather hang on to both of you." Her mother sneers, and my heart breaks for Taylor.

She really thought that would work.

But I know that's not how it goes. Hostage takers don't trade people. They shoot people. Especially when startled.

Amelia's finger trembles against the trigger. "Or maybe I don't need either of you after all," she says softly.

Fuck, no. That's the sound of someone giving up.

I twist around, throwing myself at Taylor, taking her down to the ground as the gun goes off twice. I hear it, I feel it, and then the whole house erupts in noise as darkness takes over.

[38]

TAYLOR

I'm still screaming. The window exploded over my head, the door behind me was busted open, and the room is full of cops in body armor and face masks. Dark shadows swarming, but I can't focus on them. All I can see is Luke, still on top of me.

"Officer down," one distant voice says. "Repeat, we have an officer shot on the scene. Suspect is shot. Two gunshot victims. Send in the medics, stat."

Gloved hands roll Luke off me and I scramble to my knees, sobbing as I realize he's been shot in the side. His hoodie has a hole in it, and I reach for him, but I'm dragged back.

His face is white and he's not breathing.

He's not breathing.

I scream again, his name now an agonizing prayer hanging on the air. No. No. *Luke.*

Different uniforms rush in now. Paramedics. They block my view, and then instead of getting busy saving his life, they just stop.

They just stop, and then they stand up again.

Why aren't they working on him?

I sob uncontrollably as they move aside.

Luke holds out his hand and gives me a weak smile. "Come here, baby. I'm okay."

I surge forward, falling on my knees at his side.

"Vest," he whispers, his eyes closing again. He tugs at the bottom of his hoodie. "I'm okay. Hit my head on the way down, that's all."

That's all.

Oh my God.

I'm moved out of the way again as the paramedics take over again. Another team is working on my mother, across the room, and I try to stand up, to go to her and see, but I can't walk.

I turn to the cop holding me back and say something, but it's garbled.

"We have another gunshot wound here," I hear someone say.

It takes me too long to realize they're talking about me.

[39]

TAYLOR

THE NEXT THING I hear is a beep.

Beep, beep, beep.

My mouth tastes like ass. Dry ass, the worst kind of ass.

I try to open my eyes, but those feel like sandpaper, and that's not happening. I crawl back into my sleepy hole, because it's easier there.

I think I might hear Luke's voice, for a second, but then it's gone.

————

Someone is touching my hand. Cool fingers.

I groan.

"Taylor?" That's Luke's voice. I try to find him, but my eyes are gummy now. Is gummy better than sandpaper?

"Here." A woman's voice. "I'll turn off the light. Is that better?"

"Ye—yes." Oh. That's me. I try to smile, but my lips crack. Ow.

"Shh. You're a bit dry, dear." I blink again, and this time my eyes open all the way.

I'm in the hospital. Luke is on one side of me—looking like absolute shit, and gorgeous at the same time—and there's a nurse on the other side. She's holding a cup, and a washcloth.

"Water?"

She nods and daps the cloth at the corners of my mouth. Oh, Lord, that feels good.

I try to sit up, but Luke stops me.

"You're covered in monitors, baby. Stay still."

"I'll get the resident on call." The nurse disappears, and then we're alone.

"Hi," he says, his voice crazy soft.

A tear slides down my face. How can I make tears when I'm this freaking dried out? "Hi."

"You gave us a good scare."

"Back at you, Detective."

"Yeah. Sorry about that."

"What happened?"

"Shhh. I'll tell you everything later. Right now, just stay still. They won't let you sit up and move around if you set all the alarms off."

It's coming back. My mother. God. My *mother*. How could I be born to that hellbeast? "Is Amelia dead?"

He gives me a stricken look. "Yes."

"Good."

"Taylor—"

"She tried to kill you. Because I love you. That's fucked up." My voice cracks. I sound super rough, but I need to get this out. "I'm not going to pretend to be sad about that, Luke. I don't care if the alarms go off, so you can tell me—"

The door swings open and a troop of medical professionals

stroll in. "Nice to see you awake, Taylor," says the person in front. A woman. Maybe the resident. "I'm Dr. Jackson. I did your surgery, and everything went well. You're going to make a full recovery."

I look at Luke. I had surgery? Full recovery from what?

He squeezes my hand. "It's been a long few days. You needed some serious sleep, apparently."

One of the other doctors introduces themselves as a rehab specialist and asks if they can look at my toes.

"Sure, but I need a pedicure like whoa," I mutter.

That gets a laugh.

Hey, maybe I'm funny now. Does getting shot by your own fucking parent make you funny?

They poke my toes and ask me to push against that touch. "Good."

"Where was I shot?"

Dr. Jackson sits on the side of my hospital bed. "The bullet went through your side. It nicked your kidney and got pretty close to your spinal column. You had a lot of swelling, and we were worried—were, past tense—about mobility."

I shift my legs, relief coursing through me. "I'm going to be okay?"

"Full recovery."

"Can I drink some water, then?"

She laughs. "Yes. And you can eat a little bit today. Soup, jello. Let's ease you back into things. After you eat, we'll get you up and try some walking."

They all leave, and Luke just sits there. He's looking at me strangely.

"What?"

"Nothing. I'll get you some water."

He disappears and returns with an oversized mug with a straw sticking out the top of it at the same time as a different nurse, a guy this time, comes in with a small bowl of jello.

I wait until he leaves to make a face at Luke. "That's disgusting."

"I'll get takeout for you. What do you want?"

"A salad."

"Soup?"

"Is this a negotiation, Detective?" My voice goes gravelly and rough on the last word, and he hands me the water. I take a long sip and close my eyes.

When I open them, he's giving me that same, strange look again.

"You're staring at me."

"I like to look at you."

"Stop it," I whisper

"Why?"

"Because it's weird. I don't know how to translate looks like that."

The corner of his mouth twitches. "Because you're not built for emotional intimacy?"

I laugh a little, which hurts. I frown instead. "Sure. Maybe I think you're about to pick a fight with me."

"Have I ever done that?"

Jesus. I don't know. The last week seems like a blur of hostility and fucking that ended in us both being shot, but it's all buried under an overwhelming sweetness that matches the way he's looking at me. "No?"

He laughs. "You aren't sure, are you?"

"I'm a fighter. It's all I know."

"Not true. You knew I was looking at you with fondness."

I groan. "Oh God, that sounds awful."

His laughter gets worse, and he's grinning now. Big and bright and happy. "The absolute worst? Me being *fond* of you?"

"It sounds like something grandmothers feel."

"Terrible."

"You're mocking me."

"Absolutely. What would you rather I say? That I love you?"

I freeze.

I mean, I did say it first. But I'd just woken up from practically being dead.

He shakes his head, his eyes soft. "I know it's hard to hear. I know for you this is more dangerous than anything else we've been through. For you, my beautiful princess, love is a form of edge play, isn't it? Lean into it. Let yourself ride that edge. Because I do love you. I'm fond of you, and you make me laugh, and you make me *happy*, which is quite the fucking feat. And most of all, I like you. I like everything about you. And when I thought you were going to die, I wanted to die, too. I made them take me in the ambulance with you, and I fucking cried, okay?"

"No..."

"Also, I haven't showered in days. Or shaved. So maybe this isn't the right time to tell you that I love you, even though you said it first. I went with fond instead. It seemed safe, but then you went and decided to be rude about it."

It's so much.

It's *too* much. It's too nice, too lovely.

Because I'm fucking fond of him too, and *that's* rude.

"This wasn't the plan," I say quietly. "I left all my big feelings behind in Washington."

"Those were different feelings. Nothing like this."

I shake my head. No. Nothing like this. "This is different."

He grins. "So different. This is *wild*, baby. This is love."

———

It takes another three days before I'm discharged.

The FBI agent, Ferdinand, comes and explains to me that

for reasons that are none of my business, the whole incident is going to be covered up.

He didn't say it was none of my business, of course. He used other language. Smooth words that mean the same thing.

I don't care.

I'm going home with Luke. Nothing else matters.

———

I've only ever known one kind of date. Dinner—late, always late in Washington, because people don't finish work until eight or nine. And then back to their place to screw. Sometimes a cocktail reception subs in for the dinner.

And that's if there was even a date. Let's be honest. Few of the relationships I had were healthy enough—or legit enough—to be able to go out in public together.

But even with all of those caveats, going on a date with Luke is something special.

We get ready together at my place. He's basically moved in with me, because his house is still a crime scene. While I was still in the hospital, he went and picked up a bag of stuff.

Then he dropped it at my apartment and came straight back to my bedside.

It's been a rough week.

Last night was the first night we've actually been able to sleep together in what feels like forever. And I slept like the dead—pun definitely not intended, way too soon.

Luke fussed over me all morning. "Are you sure you're up for going out tonight?"

"I'm sure," I reassured him each time.

I don't know how much dancing I'll do. Or he'll do, for that matter. Last night was the first time I saw the massive bruise on his side.

"It's nothing," he said. "Pretty much healed up."

"I thought you were wearing a vest? Did I imagine that?"

"Those things slow the bullets down. That's all. This one still felt like a pretty good kick to the side."

I traced the bruise as gently as humanly possible. "Holy shit, Luke. It's such a good thing that you were wearing…" I looked up at him. "Wait, why were you wearing your vest?"

"Don't worry about it," he'd said.

As we get ready for the date, side by side, I'm still worrying about it.

"Luke?"

He looks over at me, mid-shave. "Mmm?"

"Last night you dodged my question about why you were wearing a vest when you got home."

His face tightens up. "I know, baby. I'm sorry."

"Why?"

"Because I spent every minute sitting by your hospital bed wondering if I should have handled that differently. You were smart. You called 911. I could have done that. I didn't, and I'll always regret that."

Shock rolls over me as I realize what he's saying. "You knew someone was in your house?"

"I wasn't lying when I said my security system was good. She was hiding in the shadows, but yeah, I knew. As soon as I got home. I saw the alert on my phone."

"But you called me to say good night."

"I promised you I would. And I didn't want you to worry."

"I did anyway. I knew something was wrong."

"See? I should have known that would be the case. And if I'd been smarter, you wouldn't have been shot. Maybe it could have gone down differently." He wipes off his face and comes to stand right in front of me. "No, baby, don't cry."

"I can't help it."

"I'm sorry."

"Why? I'm sorry. Fuck, this is all my fault."

He presses his forehead against mine. "I don't want you to feel that way."

"Well, I don't want *you* to feel that way."

"We're a pair, huh?"

I sniffle, and he wipes my cheeks.

"What's done is done," I whisper.

He nods.

"I've really brought the mood down for our date."

"You're the counselor. You know that we're going to be processing this for a long time."

I blink up at him.

He's smiling.

"You're right." I kiss him right on the mouth. "Finish shaving, Detective. You promised me some dancing."

We head out of town, to a place in Malibu, and the drive is lovely.

Quiet. Peaceful.

Warm and full of hope, because I'm sitting beside Luke and he's breathing and smiling and alive.

Our table is outside, under strings of white lights and overlooking the Pacific Ocean.

After we eat, he offers me his hand. It's not the raucous club scene he promised. That will come later. But it's still hands-down the sexiest dancing I've ever done. He moves me through a few steps, then spins me around, my back to his front.

"One two three. One two three." He presses his hand flat against my belly, careful to avoid my incisions as he guides me through the steps he's probably been making since he learned to walk.

"Dancing is in your blood, isn't it?" I ask, twisting my head to see his profile.

He smiles. "So is lust."

My breath catches.

"No rush, Princess."

I'll be the one to rush things. I miss him.

Spinning in his arms, I show him that I'm okay. Battered, but not broken. Hurt, but not harmed. I can move. I can be moved.

And when we're ready, I'll want everything he can give me. Rough, passionate lust. Everything that is in his blood, in his soul.

But I get winded by the time the song is over, and he makes me sit for dessert.

When we're finished, we drive to a beach access point that Luke knows.

"You know I've never come out here? Not once in three years. I've never explored up and down the coast at all."

"We're going to rectify that. One little hidden treasure at a time. Careful here." The sun is setting, and it's glorious. I'm not watching where I'm stepping, but it's okay because Luke is watching for me.

He sits on a log someone dragged down to the beach, and I sit in front of him, leaning my head against his knee.

We watch the sun set over the ocean, and as darkness sets in, the waves get rougher.

"A penny for your thoughts," he murmurs.

I take a deep breath. "I was thinking I feel like the ocean right now. Stormy and full of churn. I'm like the ocean inside, but with the sound turned off. All the roiling around inside and I still feel numb."

"That's normal."

"I know that. And yet I don't believe it. It still feels surreal. I thought when I came out here three years ago that I'd gone through my trauma and it was all behind me. Now it's happened all over again. I was fooling myself, Luke."

"Or protecting yourself. Retreated to fight another day."

"I don't have any more fight left in me."

"You don't need to do that ever again." He strokes my hair. "We can run away if you want. Go into hiding."

"I thought about that. When I left Washington. Disappearing to an island somewhere."

"Would you do that now?"

I shake my head, lost in thought as I stare out over the ocean. "No."

"Why not?"

"Because trouble has a way of catching up to you anyway. Might as well stand and fight. I'm just not sure I'm up for the next one."

[40]

LUKE

I DON'T WANT there to be a next fight.

But that's her call to make, not mine.

"I can't keep quiet any longer," Taylor murmurs, her gaze locked in the distance. It's taken me a long time to realize that's what she does when she's thinking. Beautiful mind-ing, I call it now. She looks away from the conversation, from the here and now, and lets her brain churn.

And she sees some amazing things.

She knew I was in trouble from the way a phone conversation ended.

Her whole life, her ability to see in three dimensions has been undervalued. Not valued at all, actually.

I lean in. I could listen to her talk for hours. "About Lively?"

Good thing we have the rest of our lives to discuss anything and everything.

She nods. "And it's going to have ripple effects. I know that. It's ironic, actually. I tried to destroy the last administration. Not for any good reason. They were perfectly reasonable politicians, but I needed my out, and that was the path I saw in front of me. I tried to create as much damage as I could. And here, almost by accident, this administration may tumble instead. I don't want to do that. And maybe I should have because they're not good people at all."

"But it's not who you are anymore. You used to be a chaos agent because it was all you knew. And now it's not."

"No." She turns back to the here, to the now. To the conversation, and me. She gives a beautiful smile. A from-the-soul smile that's happy and gorgeous. "It's not."

"I see you," I whisper as she stands up and brushes the sand off her legs. "I see how good you are."

"You helped me realize that."

"Did I? When?"

"Sometime yesterday, maybe? It took a while."

"Bite your tongue," I growl as I ease her into my lap.

"I'd rather you bite it."

I kiss her instead. Gently. Biting will come later.

"This is going to be rocky," she whispers. "However I find a way to tell my story, it's not going to be easy."

"I'll be there. Every step of the way."

"It's okay if that part of my life is separate. I can quietly come and go from here. If you're going to be undercover—"

"No." I cut her off with my words, and then my mouth. "That's not happening. That was some insane wish I had when I didn't know what else I wanted from life. I'm more than happy being a detective. I'm ecstatic to come home to you every night. I will put in leave time to go with you to Washington, and hold your hand in a big, scary courtroom. Or in a television interview if you go that route instead. Whatever you want."

She wraps her arms around me and leans into me, pushing her face into my neck. My ribs ache a bit, but they can fucking deal.

I have Taylor back in my arms. I don't care how much it hurts. I feel invincible right now.

"I kept a lot of secrets from you," she whispers.

"They were yours. You didn't need to crack your heart open for me."

"No. But I needed to do it for me." She kisses my neck and sighs.

The moon is rising now, and the path back to the car is pretty well lit. "We should head back."

"Don't want to," she mumbles. "Let's stay here forever and share all our secrets."

I chuckle gently. She doesn't need to convince me. "Deal."

She carefully stands up and walks down to the water.

Then she turns back and waves at me. "Come on," she calls. "Let's dip our toes in."

Deal.

TAYLOR

A week after I come home, I'm cleared by the doctors to go back to work.

It's surreal to return. Luke drives me. I still don't have a car.

I still don't have any money, really, and I won't for a while. When your mother shoots you and then dies, any effort you might have been able to put toward convincing the FBI that your money isn't dirty gets a touch more complicated.

Everyone is there. The executive director, the volunteer coordinator, the coordinator of counseling services, and they have flowers and an edible arrangement.

"We were worried about you," my boss says. "It was so scary to think of someone targeting one of our own."

One of their own. Not one of the Dashford Reid daughters, not a socialite, not a fucked up sexpot.

A fellow crisis worker. A fellow woman. A colleague.

I belong here. I wanted to, desperately, before the attack. I did my best to be social and friendly, but I was never sure they liked me back.

Tears slide down my cheeks. "Thank you," I whisper. "I missed you all so much."

"It's okay if you want to take some time before you get back to peer counseling. There's lots of admin work."

I shake my head. "I can do this. I want to do this."

"Great."

And that's it. Back to work.

Surreal.

But wonderful.

———

The next shoe drops a week later. Luke and I go car shopping—for a used car, which is wild. And fun. I sell some jewelry, and it turns out that you can absolutely buy a car for a rough trade-in value on a gaudy diamond bracelet and three pairs of earrings, if the earrings are big enough and the car is old enough.

To celebrate, I go window shopping on Rodeo Drive. Luke has to work tonight, until midnight, and I'm happy to fill the time with something fluffy.

But when I return to my car, there's a woman standing next to it.

My pulse picks up. I don't like the way she's looking at me.

"Ms. Reid, I'm Melinda Gray. I'm a journalist."

"No comment."

"You don't even know what I'm going to ask."

"The answer won't change."

"Do you want to talk about Gerome Lively? Did he rape you?"

I jerk backwards. How could she know that? I look her over. She's generically pretty, in a never-had-plastic-surgery kind of way. Ordinary. Straight brown hair, polite smile that reveals neat white teeth. She had braces probably, and her clothes are decent quality. Not wealthy, but not desperate. "Who are you?"

"I told you. I'm a journalist."

"Lots of people call themselves that these days."

She holds out a card. "I'm only interested in the truth, Ms. Reid."

I'm not going close enough to her to get it. But I also don't want to have this conversation in the middle of a busy shopping area. "Then you haven't been around for very long. The truth doesn't sell magazines."

"Actually, I've been around long enough." She pushes a strand of hair behind her ear, and there's something familiar about her face now. That gesture.

"Have we met before?"

"A few times."

I try to place her. "Here? Or in Washington?"

"Back east."

I frown.

"I worked with the Horus Group." She smiles. "Back then I went by Ellie. I was the receptionist there for a while."

"Quite the career shift."

"Not exactly."

Ah. The pieces are falling into place. A sick lack of surprise twists in my gut. "You were undercover there."

"Something like that."

"What happened?"

A cloud passes behind her gaze. Enough of a clue that I know I don't want any part of her revenge plot, whatever it is.

I shake my head. "Still no comment. I'm sorry I can't help you. You're barking up the wrong tree."

"I'm not," she says firmly. "Gerome Lively has a long track record of abusing women. Young women. Girls, even."

She's not wrong. But I'm done showing people my hand and getting nowhere for it.

"If you ever change your mind. If you ever want to tell any part of your story—on your terms, I promise—my inbox is open."

"How can you promise that? My terms only? You don't know what those terms are. You don't know if you can trust me to be honest with you."

"I think I can."

"Why?"

"Because you went to ground. And even when your car exploded, you did everything in your power to keep that quiet. You don't want to be found. So if you decide to speak up, I'll know it's for different reasons than before."

Would it, though? The bitter, angry nugget deep inside me feels the same. And how could I tell any story about Gerome without talking about my mother, who has now been scrubbed from my life, but not my past.

And forever more I will have to lie about her. How she died, where she is.

With a painful jolt, I realize I resent what I'm caught up in now more than I ever suspected, just as I resented my life then. "Don't assume anything about me, Melinda. I will absolutely disappoint you."

"I'm sure that's not the case. Your story could be quite inspirational."

I shake my head. "Either way, it's not good for me. I don't need to put myself front and centre for judgment or false validation. I'll get both, neither will feel right, and it will destabilize any progress I've made toward a healthy, real life. You get that? I'm just living now, and it's great. I don't want any part of the performative bullshit you people trade in."

She sticks her tongue into the corner of her mouth. Thinking. "What if it were anonymous?"

"What?"

She shrugs. "What if the story is exactly what you just said? Once upon a time, there was a scandal. The details don't matter. They can't be shared, anyway, because the woman at the centre of the scandal very much wants to stay out of the public eye—forever. She's had a bitter taste of it, and now spends her days wrapped in a cloak of privacy. And inside that cloak, she's found happiness. But there was another scandal. A secret one. Way back when, when she was a child. Too young to be culpable."

"I don't think so."

"That's a better answer than no comment."

"No comment."

She grins. "Too late, Taylor. I know that you're considering it, and that's *awesome*. If there's anything I can do to prove that I'm a trustworthy journalist, you just give me a shout. My secure contact details are on the card."

Which I still haven't taken.

Damn it.

I move closer, and she puts it into my hand. Then she steps away from my car.

Giving me space.

"Think about it," she says. "And I'm really glad to hear you're doing well now."

Fuck. If only she really knew. I nod.

"And Taylor?"

"Yeah?"

"If you talk to Cole, or Jason...any of them. Don't tell them about me. Okay? I'm going to trust you with my secret first. And then you can decide if you want to trust me."

[42]

LUKE

I GET BACK to Taylor's apartment at half past midnight. And when I open the door, I can smell cookies.

I find her in the kitchen, drinking a glass of wine and staring at the working oven. Behind her is a rack of clean mixing bowls. "You baked."

She nods, still staring at the oven. "Yep."

"Is something wrong? Something's clearly wrong." I close the gap between us and kiss her gently. "Hi. Love you."

"Hi. Love you, too."

"What happened?"

"A reporter found me. A reporter who once went undercover in the Horus Group, which is really weird, but it's not the weirdest part. I think she actually had a good idea, but it scares me, and I don't know what to do."

I kiss her again. "Let me tuck my gun away and wash up. Are those going to be done soon?"

"Five minutes."

"Pour me a glass and we can talk about this over a plate of warm cookies. Deal?"

She nods.

I change into a pair of sweatpants and a t-shirt, then return to the kitchen. It's not a far walk. Her apartment is nice—rich girl nice—but too small for both of us.

I should move back into my house soon.

But the thought of sleeping apart from her tears me in two, so until we've been dating long enough for me to suggest that we buy a new place, a place that is truly ours, I'm going to continue being a squatter in her small space.

I help her plate up the cookies—chocolate chunk and walnut, delicious—and then I settle in with a snack and my listening ears. "Okay, tell me everything."

She takes a long sip of wine, then a deep breath, and launches into the whole thing. "I've read some of her pieces tonight. She's a really interesting journalist. Nobody knows who she is—she wasn't kidding when she was telling me that she was trusting me with her secrets, too. She's super anonymous, and she pulls these pretty incredible sources out of nowhere to drop truth bombs on Washington."

"This might be what you were looking for. A chance to tell your story, on your terms."

"That's what she said."

"But?"

"But it's hard for me to trust her. Or anyone."

Yeah. There's the rub. "Ah, I'm sorry."

She shrugs. "It is what it is."

"Cookie?" I hold one out to her.

She takes a giant bite direct from my hand. "The rest is yours," she mumbles around the crumbs.

"I didn't know you could bake."

"First time for everything. Apparently, I can follow a recipe."

"You're very good at following instructions," I agree.

Her eyes spark. "Am I?"

"No."

She groans and swipes at me. I catch her and spin her around, pinning her to the counter so I can mock frisk her. "But I like it when you struggle."

"Mmm."

"It's been a long couple of weeks." I skate my fingers down her sides, making her shiver. We've made love a lot, but always gentle. Always careful.

"It has."

"If you're feeling up to it—"

She shudders. "Yes."

"You don't even know what I'm offering."

"Yes to all of it."

"Ball gag?"

"Deal."

I laugh. "Do you have one?"

"Improvise with my panties."

Fuck, that's hot. "Do you need a distraction tonight?"

She nods. "Yes."

"A big one?"

She inhales shakily. "Is that a cock joke?"

"I would never joke about how big my dick is, baby. That's super serious conversation right there."

"Of course." She twists in my arms, turning around to look at me. "Yes, I want a big distraction tonight. Don't be gentle with me. I'm healed up now."

"Okay. I'm going to put the cookies away. You go get ready for bed and I'll join you in a minute."

When I get to the bedroom, I find her stretched out on her side, naked.

Looking at me.

There's something feral in her eyes, like a challenge I want to rise up to meet. A matching heat sparks to life inside me. I can be a tiger for her. A lion.

I prowl across the room and pounce as she rolls away, landing on top of her, my legs and arms bracing on either side of her trembling body.

"Tell me," I growl. "Tell me what you want."

"Hold me down," she whispers, rocking beneath me.

I take her wrists in my fingers and pin her to the bed.

"Harder," she begs. Tears cling to her lashes as she squeezes her eyes shut.

"What do you need?"

"You."

"I'm here."

"Don't ever let me go."

"I won't." I flex my hand, then squeeze again. Harder, as requested. I trace the line of her neck with my other hand. "Are you sure you want me to be rough tonight?"

"Yes."

"Why, darling?"

I need to know. The reason doesn't matter. Whatever she wants, I'll give her. But if I know what's driving her here, I can make it even better.

She shakes her head from side to side. "I don't know," she sobs. "I just need you to hurt me. And then hold me."

My heart cracks, and I fall on her. "I'll hold you forever," I growl. "Always. You can come to me and curl up in my lap and ask me—tell me—to do bad things to you, and I will. And then I will always—always—make it right afterward."

"Sometimes I'm so scared that I'm bad to the bone."

"You're not."

"Sometimes I want to be punished." It's the tiniest of whispers. Hotter than anything.

"You need to be shown a lesson?"

She nods jerkily.

I rear up above her and roughly turn her onto her front, baring her ass for me. "What are your words, baby?"

"Red, yellow, green. I'm totally green," she pants. "Spank me, Luke."

I laugh. "Not that easy." I climb off her, leaving her on the bed. She squirms, and I grab her foot. "Stay like that. Or you won't like what I do when I come back."

I step into her closet and go my tiny section of suits in the corner. I need one of my ties. No, two of them.

Back at the bed, she hasn't moved.

"Good girl," I say, running my fingers up her leg, from her ankle to the delectable curve at the bottom of her ass. I raise my hand and bring it down in a sharp, stinging slap.

She cries out.

"Is that green?"

"Yes," she pants.

"Good." I go to her hands and bind them tightly with one of the ties, checking her circulation before I move back down her body—pausing to give her another rough spank—to do the same at her ankles.

Once she's trussed up, I climb back onto the bed and haul her over my lap.

She squeaks at the rough movement.

"Still green?"

"Yes."

"Excellent." I bring my hand down on her ass. "I'm not going to punish you, Taylor."

She cries out.

"Do you know why?" Another smack.

"No."

"Because you aren't bad." Whack, whack. "Say, I know I'm not a bad girl."

She doesn't say it, so I give her three more, alternating back and forth between her jiggling cheeks. Each spanking makes her flesh a little more pink.

It's beautiful.

"Taylor."

"I...I know I'm not a bad girl."

"Good." I grin as I add two more strokes for my own pleasure. "Say thank you, Luke."

"Thank you, Luke."

I trace my fingers lightly over the well-spanked flesh. "Tell me that you love me."

"I love you," she pants.

"Tell me again. Tell me while I hurt you." I grab the tender spot at the top of her thigh, just below her ass, and squeeze my fingers together.

"I. Love—ah. You." She beams at me as her eyes go wide. I release her perfect skin, now marked red where I pinched her. She convulses, and I finally shove my hand between her legs, where I find slippery proof of just how much she likes it when I do that.

Loves it.

"I'm going to untie your feet now," I croon to her as I rub her clit and her swelling pussy lips. "Do you know why?"

She shakes her head as she pants. *No.*

"Because I want to fuck you like this. Trussed up. I've missed having you as my captive sex slave, Taylor."

She groans and buries her face in the blanket.

———

We're both exhausted, and after we fuck, we pass out. But it's like she's unlocked something dirty and depraved in me again, after our stretch of needing to be gentle and careful.

When she wakes up in the middle of the night, I wake up, too.

I watch silently as she pads to the bathroom, pushing the door closed. I roll over and take a condom and a bottle of lube from the bedside table. And then I wait.

When she comes back, I wait until she lies back down, and then I roughly roll on top of her, my hands grabby from the word go. One palm squeezes both of her tits together, the other gropes her hip, trying to get her up on her knees again. That was a fucking hot way to take her earlier.

I want more of that, but primal this time.

Ruthless.

"Mmm," she whispers, rocking back against me. She's insatiable, too. But then, "No..."

It's a mind fuck, and it's hot.

No? Maybe my sweet dirty princess wants to play a game in the middle of the night.

I push myself down on top of her, bringing my mouth to her ear. My voice is extra deep from sleep. Growly. Almost not like me at all. "I don't think you want me to stop, do you?"

She whimpers, but repeats the magic words. "You don't know what I want."

I shove her down onto the bed, my hand big between her shoulder blades. My fingers probe between her thighs.

She's fucking soaked again.

"I know you want me to take this pussy," I snarl.

"My cunt is off-limits," she bites out, twisting beneath me. *Follow my lead. Use it if I use it.*

"Your cunt is *mine*." I pinch her where I spanked her earlier, and she yelps. "You're desperate for it, aren't you? You can't get enough of my big cock. That's why you made me cookies."

"I was just being nice," she whispers.

"You are nice. Such a nice girl. With such a nice pussy. All wet and ready for me." I stroke my cock through her folds, bumping against her clit and then all the way up to her perineum. Touching every bit of her sex without giving her what we both want.

I want her frustrated and worked up. I want her to howl when I finally shove my big, fat cock in her sweet hole.

I want her to beg to be violated by the mean, mean man with the dirty, dirty words.

Me.

I want her to beg me.

"No," she pants. "Stop."

Time to check in again. "You don't want me to stop."

"If you aren't going to stop, then just fuck me already," she hisses.

There's my wildcat. I laugh, full of power and lust for her. "You have to ask nicer than that. Or maybe I'll take you here."

While I stroke her asshole with my thumb, I grab the lube with my other hand and squeeze a bit out onto my middle finger.

"Oh God, oh God," she pants as I stretch her out. First the middle finger, then I add the index. She takes them both faster than I thought.

My knuckles brush her pussy lips and come away soaked.

"Beg me, Taylor. Ask me to fuck your pussy instead of taking your ass."

She moans like a wounded animal and pushes her hips higher in the air.

Fine with me. I slide on protection and add more lube on top of the condom. If she wants me to take her ass in the middle of the night, who the fuck am I to argue?

Even with the stretching, she's tight from the first push. I go slow as molasses, sinking into her inch by inch. Her hands claw at the sheets, her words a depraved song of wonder and mystery.

"Oh, no, yes, God, stop, no, don't stop, Luke, fuck, owwwww, ahhhhh, ohhhh...."

"You're okay," I whisper as I finally sink my hips firmly against her bottom.

She squirms under me. "No I'm not," she pants. "You're mean."

My cock flexes inside her ass.

Fucking right I am.

"And you love it. Your clit must be throbbing right now. I'll let you rub it and get yourself off while I use your sweet bottom. How does that sound?"

She whimpers and shoves her hand in front of her, between her body and the mattress, and she cries out when she touches herself. I feel it from the inside out. The start of her orgasm already, a trembling right along the edge of pleasure and pain.

I move my hips, pulling out halfway, then slowly thrusting back into her heat. She feels amazing. "I'm going to come inside you," I growl. "You make me so fucking hot. I can't help myself."

"Ow," she whispers, her voice floating on bliss. "No."

"Touch yourself," I remind her.

"I am."

"I can feel it. I know how much you like this. Can you feel how hard I am? My balls are aching for you, Taylor. Ready to burst."

Her thighs shake beneath me, her head twisting left and right with abandon as I pick up speed, chasing her now. She's going to come first. She's going to come, and I'm going to feel it and go off like a rocket with her.

I hunch up, a beast on top of her, and fuck her as she howls through the start of it. The first deep clench pushes me over the edge, and it almost hurts how my body tries to turn itself inside out for her.

All for her.

My sweet, beautiful Taylor.

"Love you," I mutter as I roll off her.

"I bet you say that to all your captive sex slaves," she whispers as she climbs on top of me to kiss me.

"Dunno." I fling my shaking arm around her. "You were my first and last and only."

ONE MONTH LATER

"Happy birthday to you," Taylor sings, swaying toward me. "Happy birthday to you. Happy birthday, Detective Vasquez, happy birthday toooooo youuuuuu."

On the last two notes, she sinks to her knees in front of me, holding the cupcake out.

But when I lean in to blow out the candle, she beats me too it. "Blowing is my job tonight," she says with a wink.

I groan and laugh because hot damn, and yessss, thank you.

"Hold this," she says pertly, giving me the cupcake. "But I'll want it back in a second. After I open my present."

"You blew out the candle, and you're opening a present... Whose birthday is it, princess?"

"Yours," she says breathily. "And you'll get more presents later. I have a whole pile of them in my closet."

I can't wait.

But could anything be better than the view I have of her sweet, plump mouth moving against me, sucking like she can't get enough of my swollen, angry cock? Or when she pulls off with a wet slurp to grin at me before licking around my head, her wet, slick tongue hitting all my favorite spots?

Nothing is better than this.

Nothing is better than her eager service, her hot mouth, her sharp, knowing gaze as she watches me watching her.

"Best birthday ever," I growl after I come down her throat in thick, hot spurts. "Kiss me, Princess."

She crawls into my lap and I taste myself on her mouth. Then I tumble her sideways and drop to my knees.

It's my birthday. I'll return the fucking treat if I damn well feel like it.

Once we're both sated with birthday sex, she scampers away and returns with a bag overflowing with presents. Some are big, some are small. As I open each of them, she has a story to go with them all. The book of sports cars she found in a vintage shop. The scarf she wants me to wear when we go to D.C. for Thanksgiving, a holiday Hailey is insisting on hosting for the first time ever. A cleansing of sorts for the Reid sisters.

I fully support.

The last present is a flat envelope, and she doesn't give me a preamble story for it. Just shoves it at me and looks away shyly.

"What is this?" I open the envelope and pull out a letter from Taylor's bank.

It's a pre-authorization for a mortgage.

"I hear that's a thing that regular people do before they buy a house," she says in an adorable rush. "Sodoyouwanttobuya-housewithmemaybe?"

"Say that again slower."

"Come on, Luke! Don't be mean."

I grin. "Slow-er."

"Do you want to buy a house with me, maybe?"

"Ab-so-fucking-lutely. On one condition."

"What's that?"

I crawl on top of her, pinning her down so she can't run away. "You come to meet my family on Sunday night for dinner."

———

My worry about Taylor being overwhelmed was completely misplaced. She loves my sisters, she loves my mom, she loves the noise.

"I love this," she tells me for the tenth time after I drag her downstairs to the basement for a bit of a break from the chaos before we sit down to eat.

"It's a bit overwhelming."

"No, it's amazing. Everyone is laughing and smiling. Do you know how rare that is?"

"Yeah," I murmur. "I do. But thank you for reminding me, because I'd forgotten."

I nuzzle her neck. I thought I wanted to one day find that one special person who would love/hate my family with me.

Taylor just loves them, and that's even better.

"Are you okay?" she asks.

"I'm fine. I just wanted a minute alone with you."

"Mmm." She wiggles against me, then steps back. "Okay, but I promised to help with the salad, so I'm heading back upstairs."

I reach out and grab her wrist. "Did you forget to ask something, princess?"

Her eyes go wide, bright, and then her smile cracks, even wider. Brighter. "Sorry. Uh, can I go to the kitchen and help?"

A heady pulse of power slithers through me. I tug her closer, wanting to breathe in her scent before I let her go. "Of course," I murmur. "But later we'll have to talk about how forgetful you are."

"Okay," she breathes. "I can't wait."

I release her wrist, and she turns, sliding her palm against my thick erection before disappearing.

Fuck.

Yes.

I let her have a head start, then I follow her back upstairs.

I find my mother in the living room, reading a book to two of my nephews. She smiles at me as I join them. Once the story is over, the boys scamper off and she moves over, closer to me.

"So, we finally meet Taylor."

"Yep."

"She's beautiful."

"The most beautiful woman in the world to me."

A thoughtful expression crosses her face. "She's been through a lot."

"Yep."

Ma tilts her head to the side. "Are you going to stick with her through the rest of her journey?"

My mother slays me. She doesn't worry about the impact of Taylor's history on me. No, she's smarter than that. She wants to make sure that I'm going to do what I promise.

"I'm going to stick with her for the rest of my life, Ma."

She beams. "Good boy. Your father would be proud of you."

I exhale roughly, and she squeezes my knee. "Worried about that conversation a bit?"

"Little bit."

"Don't be. We're going to love her just as much as you do."

THREE MONTHS LATER

My hands shake as I open Melinda's email.

Here's the direct link.
It'll go live on the site in the morning.
Thank you for sharing your story with me and trusting me to tell
it right.

As I click on it, my head spins. Like maybe this was a complete mistake. But it's done, and either it will make waves, or it won't.

Either way, I know my own truth. I know I am good, and loved, and safe. For the first time in my life, I have a home, a lover, and best of all, a true friend.

Before I read the article, I go back to my email and forward it to Hailey and Ali. And I grin. That's another truth I know about myself. I lost a trust fund and re-gained a sister. I'm definitely on the right track.

The Art of Self-Forgiveness: Confessions of a Former Party Girl

By Melinda Gray

All names and locations in this article have been changed at the request of Clara, not to protect herself, but to center this story on the things that happened to her, and the the things she did to others.*

** not her real name*

Clara doesn't like the title for this article. She makes a rueful smile when I scribble it across the notebook open between us in a diner well off Broadway. She likes New York City because of the anonymity she has here. She also likes the distance it gives her from her family on the west coast.

She does not like talking about herself, or reporters who get too nosy about her past.

Born into wealth, she knows she's never experienced real hardship. It's the first thing she says to me, to minimize the angle I keep pushing for this article: that she is a survivor of lifelong trauma. That her trauma led her to hurt others.

"I made poor choices. And they were choices. I could have done things differently."

She's talking about an escalation of destructive sexual relationships that ended up imploding much of her parents' social circle. Affairs with older men, violating people's trust. Much of her history is well-known.

"You think that I wouldn't have done any of those

things if I hadn't been abused," she says to me after we order lunch.

That's the angle I pushed for with this piece, absolutely. Clara, like a lot of women in her social circles, was exposed to party lifestyles that would make most parents see red.

Not hers.

At thirteen, Clara spent the weekend with a family friend on his yacht—a floating rape palace off the Florida coast. He was a wealthy billionaire. She was a child.

At fourteen, she seduced a teacher at her private school.

At fifteen, she...

I stop reading there and start skimming. It's too hard to read my mistakes in black and white. At the end, Melinda circles back to our conversations at the diner. It was in West Hollywood, not Manhattan. She inverted almost everything in the article.

But not the blind item hints at Gerome Lively's identity.

Those she kept as precise and pointed as possible.

That was my deal with her in the end. She could write my story so long as we gave it an even chance of launching a national conversation about childhood sexual assault.

Other than Melinda, the only people who know that I am Clara are Luke and my boss. After my second interview for the article, I went to her and explained what I was doing.

LAST is launching a new campaign tomorrow to coincide with the article drop. And I'm ready to go with an anonymous Twitter account to use the hashtags #Iwasonlythirteen and

#rapechangedmeforever and #rapeisnotsex to tell more of my story.

It's scary.

It's unknown.

But it's also freaking healing.

————

THE END (for now, because there's always more with the Horus Group...)

If this is the first book you've read in The Forbidden Bodyguards series, go back and start at the beginning with Cole and Hailey's story, Hate F*@k.

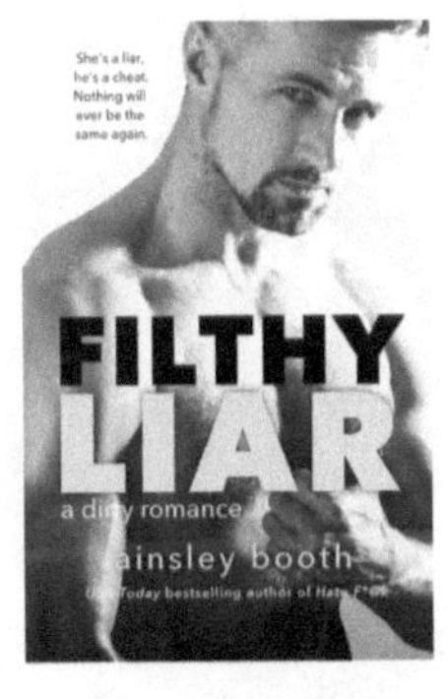

And if you have read all the way along with me and are eager for Jason and Melinda's book...that's coming next year. **FILTHY LIAR** will be the last book in this series.

Also coming in this world, at some point, is **FIRST LADY**, a standalone story first teased at the end of Dirty Love. Don't worry, I haven't forgotten about Ginny and Deacon.

To keep up to date with all of my releases, please join my VIP reader email list at www.ainsleybooth.com. And if you enjoyed Wicked Sin, please leave a review where you bought it!

~ Ainsley

ACKNOWLEDGMENTS

Tasha Harrison, who edited this book in chunks because I'm a hot mess sometimes.

My husband, who told me that every "OMG, this is too over the top" plot idea I angsted over was well-represented in 1980s police procedurals, no worries. I'm so grateful for his encyclopedic knowledge of *Simon & Simon* and *Murder She Wrote*. Also, for giving me the right language to use around how one handles a Glock.

Susan Hayes, who patiently listened to more than one super convoluted back story explanation as I meandered my way toward a "so anyway, what would a cop do in *that* situation?" question.

And finally, every reader who clapped with glee when I told them the next book was Taylor's. Because everyone deserves love.

ABOUT THE AUTHOR

Ainsley Booth is a USA Today bestselling author of more than fifty romances between this pen name and her alter-ego, Zoe York. She lives in London, Ontario, Canada with her family.

facebook.com/ainsleyboothwrites

instagram.com/ainsleyboothwrites

www.ingramcontent.com/pod-product-compliance
Lightning Source LLC
Chambersburg PA
CBHW060903190726
48286CB00002B/355